My Heart's In The Highlands

by
AMY LE FEUVRE

My heart's in the highlands
by Amy Le Feuvre

Copyright © 2024

All Rights reserved.

No part of this publication may be reproduced, stored in a retrieval system, or transmitted in any form or by any means, electronic, mechanical, photocopying or Otherwise, without the written permission of the publisher.
The author/editor asserts the moral right to be identified as the author/editor of this work.

ISBN: 978-93-63050-18-1

Published by

DOUBLE 9 BOOKS

2/13-B, Ansari Road
Daryaganj, New Delhi – 110002
info@double9books.com
www.double9books.com
Tel. 011-40042856

This book is under public domain

ABOUT THE AUTHOR

Amy Le Feuvre was the pen name of Amelia Sophia Le Feuvre, an evangelical Christian author of children's books and short stories who lived in England from 1861 to 1929. She published for various magazines, including The Quiver, and is the author of over 65 books. The topics of Le Feuvre's paintings notably reflected her religious convictions. She also published under the alias Mary Thurston Dodge, despite frequently using her own name. A Strange Courtship, her last book, was released in 1931, two years after her passing. Her first novel, Eric's Good News, was initially published in 1894. Le Feuvre is most known for her 1896 book Teddy's Button, which, like many of her other works, centres on a misbehaving youngster with good intentions that grownups fail to see. Revell in Chicago, Dodd Mead in New York, Religious Tract Society in London, and Hodder & Stoughton in London were some of her publishers. At Exeter, Devonshire, she passed away after 68 productive years.

CONTENTS

BOOK I

CHAPTER I
A DOCTOR'S VERDICT 7

CHAPTER II
ALONE 17

CHAPTER III
MYSIE MACDONALD 30

CHAPTER IV
THE BIRTHDAY GIFT 42

CHAPTER V
FRIENDLY TALKS 51

CHAPTER VI
MISS FALCONER 63

CHAPTER VII
COMPELLED TO THINK 74

CHAPTER VIII
THE LAIRD'S AWAKENING 83

CHAPTER IX
DEPARTURE 91

BOOK II

CHAPTER I
AT THE GREEN COTTAGE 102

CHAPTER II
A NEW FRIEND 112

CHAPTER III
CHASING SHADOWS.. 122

CHAPTER IV
AN OLD FRIEND 131

CHAPTER V
A SATISFACTORY INTERVIEW.. 141

CHAPTER VI
THE LAIRD SPEAKS... 150

CHAPTER VII
AN ACCIDENT.. 160

CHAPTER VIII
AN ALTERED OUTLOOK 171

BOOK III

CHAPTER I
HIS BRIDE.. 181

CHAPTER II
SOME GUESTS... 190

CHAPTER III
HECTOR ROSS... 200

CHAPTER IV
WINTER IN THE GLEN 208

CHAPTER V
ROWENA'S POWER 215

BOOK I

CHAPTER I
A DOCTOR'S VERDICT

"We know
That we have power over ourselves to do
And suffer: What—we know not till we try."
Shelley.

"I DO wish you would be serious!"

"Why on earth should I be?"

Rowena Arbuthnot leant her elbows on the wide windowsill and looked in upon her sister-in-law from the garden, with her mischievous blue-grey eyes which always seemed to twinkle with some hidden joke. Rowena's eyes had been the cause of her continually getting into trouble, from the time she had been a child, when the rector of the parish had requested her not to laugh at him in the pulpit.

She was older now; and had gone through more trouble than most girls of her age. But though her lips were grave, and a trifle sad when in repose, yet her eyes had never lost their gleam of hidden laughter.

Young Mrs. Arbuthnot, sitting in her pretty drawing-room, stitching away at a white frock for her youngest child, felt impatient with Rowena.

"I never shall understand you," she said; "I thought you and Ted were so devoted, that if you had not cared a button about the children or me, you would be disappointed at not coming with us. Our home has been yours for the last four years; and we have always looked upon you as one of the family."

"My dear Geraldine, tears are too expensive a luxury to be wasted in public. Shall I conjure up two for your benefit? I might if I tried hard."

"I hate you when you are facetious!"

"I won't be. Let us talk wisely and soberly. Is it my fault that Ted was cheated in the horse deal, that I mounted a half-broken vixen, and was pitched out of the saddle on the very hardest bit of ground going? Is it my fault that that dear old Niddy-Noddy should insist upon my lying low for a year? I don't want to be an invalid for life. It isn't an attractive prospect. And you wouldn't like a bedridden crock to be attached to you for evermore. Isn't it worthwhile to escape that fate if I can? To forgo my journey to the East with you is, of course, a trial. But what am I, if I can't take my share of disappointments philosophically?"

"Yes, yes, I know you've got an inexhaustible fund of philosophy and patience; but where are you going, what are you going to do? If only Ted had not let the house! But we're so hard up—and—really, Rowena, you ought to be lying down at this moment! What is the good of only following half Dr. North's advice?"

Rowena held up a bunch of dew-sparkling roses.

"My dear, I'm coming in—but I must have these to refresh me." She slipped in over the low window, and went to a couch in the farthest corner of the room. For a moment or two she occupied herself in putting her roses into a bowl of water by the side of the couch; then quietly laid herself down among the cushions with a little sigh—or was it a long-drawn breath of pain?

"Now talk away, Geraldine! I'm chained here till luncheon, and you can say all you have in your mind, but we won't grumble over what cannot be helped."

"Well, have you any idea what is to become of you?"

"Not the slightest. You see Niddy-Noddy only sprang my fate upon me yesterday, and you are the only one who has seen Ted. I was in bed when he returned last night, and he was off to town before I got up this morning."

"He has so many arrangements to make before we sail. And Ted is no good for practical common sense. If you only had money of your own, how easy it would make things!"

It was not often Geraldine Arbuthnot alluded to Rowena's penniless condition; and the girl laughed to hide the hurt of it.

"Yes—and a crippled beggar is worse off than a healthy spry one. I allow I am in an evil case! It's a pity you and Ted set your faces against the job offered me."

"Ted has some pride," said Mrs. Arbuthnot with raised head. "It isn't likely he would let his sister be a paid clerk to that bounder Tom Corbett! And I wanted you badly. Goodness knows what I shall do without you now. You weathered me through my bad time three times over, and I shall never forget it. The chicks will be lost without you—and I was quite counting on you to keep them happy on board ship!"

"Oh, yes, you'll miss me," said Rowena with honest conviction. "What craft can I do on my back, I wonder? Not basket-making! I could make rugs—those Eastern ones—I really think that is an idea! But who would buy them? Would that hurt Ted's pride, if I wrote a round robin—to our friends, asking for their support? How would it run? After this style:"

"'An invalid much in want of the necessities of life, is starting rug-making. Orders received and promptly executed. Designs straight from India and Persia; and colours to blend with purchaser's rooms.'"

"Oh, do be quiet, Rowena. Don't talk such nonsense. Here are the chicks. Nurse, bring them in here."

Mrs. Arbuthnot leant out of the window as she spoke, and a moment after, two little fair-haired boys burst open the door, their baby sister struggling in her nurse's arms to follow them.

"Where's Aunt Rony?"

"Here, Buttons, here; in my little corner!"

Buttons flung himself upon the couch.

"Are you playing a game? Are you in bed?"

For the next few minutes the children's chatter filled the room, but the nurse soon took them off; Buttons and his twin Bertie beseeching their aunt to come up to the nursery and have a game with them after tea.

When they were gone there was silence for some minutes; then Mrs. Arbuthnot folded up her work.

"Well, Rowena, we seem to come to no conclusion. Ted told me to talk it over with you."

"But we have. Ted must lend me a little money—and I'll move into rooms somewhere, and teach myself a craft and pay him back as soon as I can. And then at the end of the year, if I'm cured, I can come out to you if you want me."

"I shall always want you. You do too much for me. I shall never be content to live without you. Well, I must go and write some letters. I'll send Ted to you directly he comes home."

Rowena's bright eyes closed when her sister-in-law left the room. The pain in her back was acute now, and she was glad to rest. Her doctor had told her that there was a slight injury to her spine, and that she must lie on her back for a year, if she wished to be strong again. She had never remembered a day's illness in her life. She rode, she boated, she hunted, and she fished, always in company with her beloved brother. His marriage had not lessened the bond between them, for his wife was devoted to her, and had not a particle of jealousy in her composition. She did encroach on Rowena's good nature, but was conscious of it herself, and told her husband that Rowena was but an unpaid servant in their house.

"She is a companion to me; nurse and governess to the boys; housekeeper and general adviser; and comforter all round. She really deserves double the allowance you give her."

But Ted shook his head.

"She's my sister and chum—I couldn't expect her to take money for her services."

Now he had been summoned to India to join the foreign battalion of his regiment, and Rowena, owing to her unfortunate accident, was to be left behind.

She felt it keenly; she loved the pretty home which lay amongst the Surrey Hills; but would have accompanied her brother cheerfully all over the world. Several times she might have married, but so far, no man had eclipsed Ted's image in her heart. She always compared her lovers with her brother, and always found they lacked his personal attractive qualities.

He came in at five o'clock that June afternoon, and found his way to her almost immediately.

"Rowena, this is bad news."

"Didn't you expect it? I did. I knew from the minute I was carried away from my spill that there would be no India for me."

"But we'll rig you up a bed on board; and in India you can lounge and laze to your heart's content. Old North doesn't know what he is talking about."

"It's no go, my dear boy, you'll be on the move in India yourself, you told me so. I will not be a useless encumbrance to you. No. I'll do the thing in style, and be a bed-lier till I'm cured. I mean to be cured, Ted; and a year will soon slip by. It isn't only Niddy-Noddy who has settled up my fate. That London specialist gave the same verdict."

"But where are you to live?"

"In my skin. Don't ruck up your forehead like a wizened monkey! I've been calculating that I shall require no clothing for a year, and no footgear. I'm very rough on my boots. So my allowance will go for my food. I must get cheap lodgings somewhere. One room will do for me, as I shall always be in bed. Why, lots of old bedridden women in the country villages live on less than you give me for my clothes."

Her brother paced the room restlessly. Then his face lighted up.

"How would you like to go up to that Scotch shooting lodge of mine? Could you stand the quiet and solitariness of it? There's old Granny Mactavish who would wait upon you. And then there would be no rent to pay, and she keeps a cow and some hens, so those would feed you."

Rowena's eyes literally danced in her head.

"And Geraldine says that you are not practical! Ah, here she is. Come along and see how quickly we've settled things. I'm going up to Loch Tarlie. And a cow and some hens are going to nourish and sustain me!"

"Oh, Rowena! Ted, you will never encourage her to go there! She could die and be buried before we should hear of it, or anyone else. Besides, I don't think it would be proper. Isn't she too young to live in the wilds by herself?"

Both Ted and Rowena began to laugh, and Rowena's laughter was so infectious that Geraldine's grave face relaxed.

"Is it a joke?" she asked. "Of course you might like it for the summer, Rowena dear, but think of the winter! How could you live there? And you're a sociable creature and have always been accustomed to see a good many people. Why, it is fifty miles from rail! And there are no shops, or libraries, or theatres, or concerts, or the mildest form of amusement for you!"

Rowena held up her ten fingers.

"And now let us count the advantages:"

"No temptation to attract one off one's couch. A never-ending panorama of colour and light and beautiful scenery before one's eyes. No rent to pay."

"No servants to employ."

"A home of one's own—I have known Loch Tarlie since I was six— milk and butter and chickens all to hand. Ted asserts I want nothing else."

"No newspapers, to make one realize that England is going, or has gone, to the dogs."

"And life-giving, intoxicating moor air to make one feel glad every day of one's life that one is alive!"

"Yes, Geraldine, I am going and will stick it out for the winter there. Old Granny Mactavish is as spry and active as a girl. If she can stand the winter, why shouldn't I? And oh, do you think old Niddy-Noddy would let me transfer my mattress to a boat? Think of my lying on a silver loch watching the trout and salmon leap and flash by! Perhaps with Granny's nephew, Colin, by my side, we could fish between us. Ted, is your mouth watering? And will you write by this evening's post and tell Granny I will have my bed made up in the green drawing-room, with windows down to the floor? I shall feel out-of-doors at once."

"You will want books," said Ted gravely. "I'll order a box from Mudie's to go down with you, and I say, Rowena, there's a first-rate travel book by a chap I knew in the war. He's a humorous sort of fellow, with keen powers of observation. It's about the Frontier up in Afghanistan. You must read it. I was dipping into it to-day at the club, and Murchison, who was reading it, said—"

"Ted, get off books this instant," said Geraldine, "and let us discuss the question of Loch Tarlie. How will Rowena get up there, and who will go with her? And she cannot live alone with old Granny Mactavish. We have always taken our own maids up there and a chauffeur. Rowena must have a nice maid to attend upon her."

"No, thanks—not if I know it! I couldn't stand the whines of a lonely frightened maid. No young person could stand a Loch Tarlie winter. As for me, I am as old as the hills. They say a woman is as old as she feels—and I feel just a thousand and one since my spill!"

"Oh, if you've made up your mind, any objection of mine will be waste of words. I wonder if the Frasers will be there this year?"

"Macdonald has taken possession of Glen Tarlie," said Ted; "but I don't believe he is there much. It's a pity his wife died—she was just Rowena's sort."

"You mean in the way of books," said Geraldine. "Well, I never liked her, she was so indifferent to him; and I think it was sheer wickedness to leave her baby to those Highland folks at the Farm, because she wouldn't be bothered with a child in town."

"I'm not going to see a soul," said Rowena in her cheerful voice; "so don't try to rake out company for me. Ted, write; there's a dear! I'm quite impatient to have it settled up. And as for the journey, Geraldine, I shall have a sleeper, and get on by myself. The guards are always attentive to invalids."

"That you shall not! I shall send Ellen with you. She won't come to India with me, and her home is somewhere in the North."

And so it was settled, and in about three weeks' time Ted with his wife and children were steaming down the Channel on a P. & O. boat, and Rowena was travelling up to Scotland with Geraldine's maid.

Rowena had kept a bright face to the last. But now she lay in her berth with closed eyes, feeling the chubby soft faces of her little nephews pressed against her cheek, seeing the wistful look in her brother's eyes and the tears in his wife's, and wondering if she would ever see them all again. And then she took herself to task in her usual style.

"This won't do at all! You've been shamefully spoilt these last four years—every one wanting you and making much of you. Those fat years have gone and now comes a lean one. Too much fat makes the liver sluggish. And you lived alone for two years with your poor fretful father, when he never wanted you near him, and wouldn't let you go away from him. Now you are going to live by your lone self, with no one to fret you; and if you can't employ yourself and enjoy yourself as well, I'm sorry for you!"

The journey to Scotland was made in driving wind and rain, but though Rowena felt the continual vibration of the train in every joint of her injured spine, she was as cheerful as a cricket, and kept Ellen in constant smiles.

"I never did hear a grown-up person talk such nonsense in all my life," she confided to the friendly guard, who took Rowena under his fatherly protection; "but she'd win a smile out of a cow, she would!"

Half a day's journey from Glasgow brought them to the last stage of their travels. Ellen was to take Rowena to the Lodge and sleep the night there. The little steamer was waiting to take them up the loch. Rowena insisted upon walking on to it, though she was forced to lean heavily on Ellen's arm. The rain had ceased, and the sun now shone out as it only does in the Highlands, illuminating every mountain height, with soft dreamy radiance.

"Ah!" said Rowena, subsiding into a lounge chair upon the deck; "now don't you wish yourself in my shoes, Ellen? And I am not to be torn away from it just when I am taking root, which has always been my fate before—I am going to sink into it and rest in it for three hundred and sixty-five days."

"I'm sure, ma'am, I only hope you will have some amusements to beguile the days," said Ellen.

She was looking round her with apprehensive eyes. The still silent waters of the loch through which they glided with its walls of green on either side, and the blue ranges of mountain that guarded it upon the horizon, seemed to her a type of prison.

Rowena now pointed out a beautiful glen across the loch.

A stack of chimneys rose up behind some trees.

"That's where we're going," she said.

Ellen gave a gentle sigh.

"It seems the end of the world," she said, and Rowena's low mellow laugh rang out.

"You'll be in dear noisy Glasgow again to-morrow, Ellen. Cheer up!"

The steamer put in at the small pier at the foot of the glen. There was a grey-bearded Highlander standing very straight and still upon the pier. Rowena greeted him with a radiant smile. Duncan Cameron had helped her many a time to stalk a stag. He had also been with her when she had caught her first salmon many years ago. He was her brother's head keeper, and had been in his employ for over twenty years.

"Granny was sayin' that you would be wantin' a hand up," he said. "Is it ill ye are, Miss Rowena?"

"I'm an infirm old woman, Duncan—jumped into my dotage in one black day! Why, what is that you've got there?"

"'Tis a cheer, miss—a cheer which the Ker-enel ordered to be brought for ye, an' tis I will be pushin' it up the wee bit brae!"

"Magnificent!" said Rowena, looking at the spick and span invalid's chair with its soft blue cushions: a lump gathering in her throat at this proof of her brother's loving forethought.

Helped into it by Ellen, she relapsed into silence, but she was gazing up the glen with shining eyes. The soft air, the afternoon sun, gilding the raindrops on the pines and birches, the sweet scents of the moistened earth underfoot, all soothed and rested her tired spirit.

Along the winding carriage road they went, under an avenue of ashes and birches; by the side of them a wide trout stream came dashing down from the heights above, finding its way into the Loch. And then they turned the corner, and on a flat plateau of green smooth turf, fringed with pines, lay the house. It was a low, long grey building, with windows opening out upon the lawn, and creeping roses covering an old rustic porch, which led into the hall. Inside the pitch-pine floors were covered with green druggetting. Old Mrs. Mactavish stood curtsying in the doorway. Rowena took both her wrinkled hands in hers affectionately.

"Here I am and here I shall be till you are sick of the sight of me!"

"Ach now, ma'am, with your jokes! Wae's me if ye will be stretched on your back a' the days o' sunshine, but I've done as weel as I know how to mak ye comfortable!"

She led the way into the room which Rowena had chosen for herself.

It was a long, low room with three beautiful windows reaching the whole length of the wall; the loch stretched out below the lawn; and there was a gap in the trees so that the view of the shining water and the wooded heights on the farther side lay open to the eyes. The floor was covered with the same simple green druggetting. Geraldine had good taste, and simplicity reigned all over the house. The walls were painted cream and the furniture was fumed oak, but the couches and chairs were all covered with green and white chintz, and Rowena's couch was drawn up near one of the windows, a table by its side. A bright wood fire was blazing in the low grate. The room looked cheerful; old Granny had even gathered some yellow flags and put them in a china jug upon the mantelpiece. There was a door leading into a similar room behind, originally the smoking-room, and now to be used by Rowena as her bedroom.

Ellen looked round with critical eyes, but even she could not find any faults with the arrangements for the invalid's comfort.

"And there's my granddaughter, Janet, will be up in the morning early," said Granny. "The mistress said she should wait on ye in the morn, and also in the eve."

She introduced a rosy smiling girl to Rowena, and Ellen heaved a sigh of relief.

"I'm glad you'll have somebody to wait on you, ma'am, for that old body seems ready for the grave!"

"Oh, Ellen, for shame! It is the outdoor work she does that makes her so wrinkled. Granny is good for twenty years yet. And you should taste her oatcakes and scones! No one can beat her at cakes!"

Half an hour later Rowena was lying on her couch with the table drawn up by the side of it; and even Ellen could find no fault with the creamy scones and oatcakes, the excellent tea and bowl of rich yellow cream, and home-made butter, which Janet smilingly brought to them.

Rowena went early to bed, and when Ellen left her the next morning she was unwillingly convinced that her charge would be comfortable, but "desperately solitary" she assured herself with a lugubrious shake of her head.

CHAPTER II
ALONE

"When from our better selves we have too long
Been parted by the hurrying world, and droop
Sick of its business, of its pleasures tired—
How gracious, how benign is solitude!"
Wordsworth.

"MY DEAREST GERALDINE,—"

"My thoughts have been with you, of course. At first I felt that my better half had gone with you, and only my feeble carcass left here, but you know my adaptability! In a coster's cart or Rolls-Royce car, a slum garret, or Park Lane mansion, I should be bound to get some fun out of it! And I'm not only getting fun but really steeping myself neck-deep with thrills of delight in my delicious atmosphere and surroundings! And you'll be glad to hear that I am growing into my bed, spreading my roots there, and almost getting to like an invalid's life! Well, what can I tell you? I begin my day with hearing pretty Janet's view of life. She's almost as talkative as her Granny, but has got very modern cravings! I end the day by a crack with Granny, who is anything but modern; and my interim is spent with many pleasant companions. A robin and a gull visit me daily—they bring others of their acquaintance who regard me somewhat indifferently and don't come again. But my robin never misses a day; and my gull walks boldly inside my room and up to my couch, where he expects, of course, some special tit-bits in reward for his friendliness."

"Duncan brings me fish, and talks over the prospects of the shooting. He does not like the man who has taken it."

"'He be ane o' these Englanders who fancies a kilt and a bonnet will turn him into a highlander—an' he be in an awfu' funk lest he miss his shot; an' spends muckle bawbees in endeavourin' to win approval!'"

"It appears he was one of the house-party at the Frasers' last year, and Duncan heard 'accounts' of him!"

"Granny's nephew, Colin, cuts our wood, runs errands, and is a first-rate gardener. The lawn is beautiful: the birds make it their playground. And now I must tell you that yesterday Duncan presented me with the sweetest Highland pup that you have ever seen! His name is Shags, a dog of good pedigree and one that will be a real companion. The collies live out-of-doors—they cannot be enticed into my room. Shags has established himself at once at the foot of my couch, and he understands my talk, and appreciates it. He has a very rough little head, and cocky ears, and bright brown eyes that wink in an understanding manner. His tail is always wagging, and life to him at present is one huge joke. He knows the power of his sharp little teeth, and uses them on everything in his way; but he is learning self-control and discretion, and I make him a fresh ball of rags every day, which he tears to pieces with relish and scatters to the winds. Tell the boys about him. He is quite a personality!"

"Tell Ted I'm steadily getting through the box of books; but I am doing a 'power of meditation' as Duncan says. And when I've nothing to do but dream, I dream with a vengeance. I am fed well, I sleep well, and barring the first two days, I have not had much grinding in my old back."

"Enough of me and my doings! Tell me all about yourselves—how the chicks like India—what they do and say. Have you a nice ayah? What is your house like? Who are your neighbours? Does Ted like his fellow-officers? I expect sheets and sheets from you. Don't you dare to forget the poor isolated prisoner of Loch Tarlie!"

"Oh, Geraldine, why aren't you all here with me! Then we should be happy indeed. Best love and hugs to the darlings."

"Your loving"
"ROWENA."

Rowena had settled down, as she wrote, into a quiet invalid's life. She had severe internal conflicts at first. She wanted so much to be up half the day at least. But a letter from her old fatherly doctor sent her to her couch, and kept her chained there. She was assured it was the only chance for her cure.

The first fortnight was fine. A sense of rest and peace stole into her heart as she gazed over the beautiful landscape out of her window. No two days were alike. The softness of the colouring of the distant hills, the shadows which ceaselessly flitted across them and the loch, and the fresh opening of the spring flowers in the garden, were a continual surprise and interest to her. She got Janet to bring her bowls of pale primroses and daffodils, and her room soon became a bower of sweet-smelling flowers.

Then, suddenly, the weather changed. There was a spell of wet and wind.

Windows had to be shut; the wind howled down the chimneys, and soughed through the trees, and tore some delicate young plants in the flower-beds to pieces, scattering the fragments over the lawn. The loch churned itself into a grey muddy froth, the singing birds fled to their nests and stayed there.

Rowena looked out of her windows, and for three days watched the career of the storm with the greatest concern. It really seemed at times as if everything young and fresh would be swept away.

After a time the wind fell, but the rain continued, and then it began to pall upon her. Would it ever be fine again? Would the hills ever appear out of their thick well of mist? She read till her eyes ached. She worked at her rug till her fingers ached. She meditated till her head ached. She yawned, she fidgeted, and finally she came to the conclusion that she was becoming unutterably bored.

Shags was restless and was unaccustomed to the closed windows. Hitherto he had wandered in and out of his own free will, and he basely deserted Rowena for the kitchen. Depression settled down upon her on the fifth day of storm and rain. After she had had her lunch, she began to wonder how she could get through the winter, if a wet week in June affected her so sorely. Shags' appearance for a time distracted her, but after a little he left her, and lay against the window, his nose close to the glass, showing in every hair on his head how much he disliked the indoor life. Rowena took up a fresh book and tried to forget herself in it; but the rain and wind began to get upon her nerves. Her book did not interest her—she tossed it aside.

"And in India they are revelling in sunshine! Perhaps Ted will be playing polo, or he and Geraldine riding out together. Oh, it's hard lines I shouldn't be with them! I shall forget how to talk, if I am shut up here much longer. I might as well be doing my time in a Dartmoor prison, or at Broadmoor."

Then she started—sounds came to her of a car of some sort coming up the drive. Could it possibly be a visitor? Hardly—on a day like this. She was not long left in doubt. Granny appeared at the door, with signs of agitation.

"If ye please, mem, may we shelter two bodies who be fair drowned in this awfu' rain? I cam' right awa to ask ye—for wi' one o' the family here it is no' to be expected I should do otherwise! 'Tis a mon an' a woman, but they be fair shrouded in their waterproofs and oilskins, an' I've not had a peep at them yet. Ye'll no' need to see them, for the kitchen is good enow for the like o' any traveller be they who they may! An' they do but want a dry an' maybe a cup o' tea! They be quite respectable folk I reckon. I may bid them welcome in your name?"

"Certainly, Granny, and if the lady would like to come in and see me, I shall be delighted, whoever she may be—a Glasgow shop-girl or a duchess! I would welcome anybody on an afternoon like this!"

"Aye, mem, we get mony sich days in our year-r!"

"Of course we do, but I'm not accustomed to them yet; and I've read till my eyes ache."

A few minutes later Granny ushered in a little old lady in a close dove-coloured motor bonnet. Her face was round and soft as a child's.

"How very kind of you to give us such shelter," she began; "and, oh! if I may say it—what a charming room!"

"Now you've won my heart," said Rowena, holding out her hand. "Come and sit down, won't you, and talk to me. I am a prisoner, but I do agree with you that I have nothing to complain of in my prison. How does it happen that you are out on such an awful day?"

"It's my son, Robert; he has only just taken possession of his manse, and I've come to look after him. He had to see a sick man on this side of the loch, and so I wanted to see the country and he has motored me round."

"Is he the minister of Abertarlie? Granny Mactavish told me a new one was coming there."

"Yes, and from our snug little nest we look across at you; but we had no idea that any of the family were here."

"You are not Scotch yourself?"

"I am very Scotch by name—we are one of the Macintoshes, but you are right, I am an Englishwoman by birth."

"And so am I," said Rowena, smiling; "I have Scotch blood in my veins, and when I am in Scotland, I am Scotch. The English are a poor lot, you know! My brother only rents this lodge from General Macdonald. Do you know him?"

"My son has met him, but his house lies empty; he is hardly ever here."

"Won't your son come in and see me? I am one of his parishioners, you know. And we will have tea together presently. It will be my first party. Are your feet dry? Won't you change your shoes?"

Mrs. Macintosh held out two very pretty slender feet.

"I have been in the car the whole time. But as we got nearer your house, the rain came down like a waterspout. I will go and fetch my son. It is very kind of you to offer us such hospitality."

Robert Macintosh very soon appeared, a tall fine-looking young man with rather a stern face; but it softened as Rowena welcomed him with her happy smiling eyes.

It was a very successful little tea-party. Rowena had not seen many Scotch ministers, and those she had met were of a different stamp to Robert Macintosh. He was a gentleman, and his mother was a charming old lady with plenty to say for herself. Rowena explained herself very briefly.

"I am doing a kind of rest cure here—hurt my back out hunting and am obliged to lie on it for a time. My brother is abroad, so we shall have no shooting parties this year. I think he has sub-let the shooting to some fellow-officer of his; but not the house."

"You have books," said the young man, glancing at the low bookcase by the side of the couch.

"Yes, they are delightful company, are they not? Are you a reader? But of course you are? It is your avocation."

"Is it?" smiled Robert. "My mother would say it makes me a very unsociable creature to live with."

"It is irritating when one wants a cheerful gossip with him, to see his shoulders hunched up and his nose glued to a book," said Mrs. Macintosh quickly. "He is one of those readers who get so absorbed, that nothing but a shake and a scream will bring him back to me."

"Ah," said Rowena, "I plead guilty there. It is all right for oneself to be oblivious to all around, but a great bore to one's friends."

Then she and the young minister began talking of some new books; and the old lady sat and listened to them with great content. Janet soon appeared with the tea, and before it was over the rain had stopped, and the loch was shining like silver with the far-away rays of the sun.

When eventually the visitors left, Rowena was her bright cheery self again. But she took herself to task for her changes of mood, when she and Shags were alone together.

"Shags, you show your mistress an example of cheerful equanimity of soul! You are just as ready to wag your tail when the day is sodden and dreary as when the sun shines out; and as it will be my fate to be here through the very darkest, wettest months in the year, I am a poor wisp of a creature to be beaten down by one rainy week in June. It must not and shall not happen again, Shags! My universe does not begin and end with succulent luxury. Oh, Shags, you villain! I know what you're asking me! We'll have the window open, and then you will be free to gambol outside."

She rang the bell. Shags was waiting by the window expectantly, and when Janet opened the glass doors out he bounded. The air was sweet and fresh; the scent of a sweetbrier bush outside made Rowena's pulses beat with joy. She gazed out upon her green lawn. Shags went round it, sniffing at an old-fashioned flower-border. He unearthed a snail, turned it over with his nose in disgust, then made for a pert tom-tit strutting up and down the gravel path. The tom-tit flew away derisively, and Shags next examined with great interest a long tuft of grass. A frog leaped out. It was the first one he had seen, and he backed away from it in fright. Rowena watched him. Then the light on the opposite hills brought a gleam of delight to her eyes. It was so alluring, so exquisite, so varied in its movement and colour!

Granny came in later to inquire how she was getting on.

"Feeding my soul, Granny."

"Your soul wants bonnier feedin' than a' that." Granny was deeply religious. Rowena was not.

"Now you are not to make me discontented! I have a soul that wants beauty, and that will not be satisfied without it."

"I reckon there be mair beauty in the Creator than in His works."

"Granny, how do you like the new minister? Have you heard him preach?"

"Oh, aye—I went to kirk this Sabbath back."

"And does he preach well?"

"He does that, mem. His heart leapeth into his e'en wi' earnestness o' purpose an' persuasion. Eh, if ye cud get across in the wee boatie!"

"I can't, Granny. He will have to come and preach to me. He's a remarkably good-looking boy. I should like to see his heart leaping. Didn't you know he was the minister when you first asked me to give him shelter?"

"Deed an' no, mem, for 'twas in oilskins he were an' his mither was so spry in rinnin' ower to the hoos, that I fair speired she were just a lassie."

"I like them both. I told them to come over again soon."

"'Twill be mair company ye'll be gettin' nex' month," said Grannie comfortingly. "The lodges will be fillin' oop, an' Sir Robert Fraser be openin' his hoos nex' Tuesday!"

"It isn't company I want," said Rowena, smiling; "only the sun. I suppose the Highlands can't have all the good things in this world. There are few parts like it for beauty and romance, but I'm ashamed of my discontent, Granny! And just as I have learnt to be happy on my back, so I shall learn to be happy through the worst of weather. One can adapt oneself to anything! Habit is the main thing. The habit of content shall be mine."

The weather cleared the next day, but it was not settled. One afternoon, about two days later, after a couple of hours lovely sunshine, a sudden squall came on. The clouds were broken and the play of light and shadow on the opposite hills so fascinated Rowena that she took up a telescope which Duncan had brought her, and began studying the horizon.

Suddenly she made an exclamation and rang a bell by her side.

When Granny appeared she said sharply:

"Is Colin near at hand?"

"He has bin killin' a fowl, mem."

"Tell him to get the boat quickly. Do you see some one on the loch in distress? It looks like a small boy. Oh, don't stop to look, Granny! Colin will have younger eyes than yours—call him quickly. It is half-way across here, from the island."

Granny disappeared. Rowena listened impatiently to the voices outside her window. The loch was lashing itself into a fury. The small boat she had discovered with her telescope was now plainly discernible. But it was making no progress, only tossing up and down, a sport of the rough element around it.

It seemed a long time before Colin had started the boat, but Rowena saw it leave the small landing-stage at last and, to her great relief, two men were in it. Duncan had evidently appeared on the scene and offered his services.

Rowena took up her telescope again. She saw a little figure in bonnet and kilt sitting in the boat struggling very ineffectually with the oars.

"How like a boy," she thought, "to venture out on a day like this!" And then she saw from the efforts of the two rescuers what a strong wind and current was against them. Once a wave seemed to dash over the distant boat. Rowena held her breath, and then a call from Duncan—evidently an attempt to hearten up the little rower by telling him help was at hand. Slowly but surely the boats came nearer. At last they touched. Through the telescope Rowena watched the child clambering in from one boat to the other, then saw the men row back to the shore towing the other boat after them. Before they landed, Granny appeared in some excitement.

"It's that weeld bairn o' the laird's, an' near anow was she to her death, to be sure! Shame on Angus for lettin' the bairn tak' a boat this day!"

"What child do you mean? Boys will be boys."

"But she's a girl!"

Rowena looked up surprised.

"Who is it?" she asked.

"'Tis Mysie Macdonald, an' I'll be changin' her things surely! It's just a maircy o' the A'mighty's that the wee bairn is not drooned."

In a few minutes Rowena heard the sound of the men's voices and a clear treble between them. Then suddenly her window, which was half shut, swung open, and a child with sunny brown curls falling over her shoulders, dashed in.

"Granny Mactavish, I've come to tea with you!"

She stopped short at the sight of Rowena on her couch.

She was in a kilt which was wringing wet and dripped on the ground as she moved. But she held herself squarely and proudly, then doffed her bonnet like a boy.

"I didn't know there was anybody here."

"Come and speak to me," said Rowena, with her sunshiny smile. "I am not an old lady, only a prisoner."

The child looked up at her with bright interested eyes. "Who put you in prison?"

"An old man I call Niddy-Noddy."

"Oh, what a lovely name! Tell me about him. What's he like?"

"He speaks like this—"

Rowena drew in her lips till her mouth looked as if she had no teeth—she lowered her brows fiercely, and then nodded her head up and down very wisely.

"This child is wet. Take her clothes off, put her to bed, and a hot basin of bread-and-milk and a good sleep will prevent a chill."

The child's peal of delighted laughter rang through the room.

"Is that what he would say to me? Why, rain and water is nothing important to me! I get drowned nearly, over and over again."

"All the same you are making pools over my carpet. I must suggest that you have your kilt dried and then come and have tea with me. You can tell me then what possessed you to take a boat out on a day like this."

"I'll go to Granny in the kitchen."

She darted out as quickly and lightly as a bird. Rowena was always fond of children, and she felt strangely drawn to this little person. There was something in her small finely-cut face and blazing brown eyes which was very attractive.

"Why," said Rowena to herself, "she must be General Macdonald's neglected child! She speaks very good English. I had no idea she was so big."

It was some little time before Mysie returned, and when she did so she was wrapped round in one of Granny's red flannel petticoats. She seemed quite proud of her attire.

"My kilt is steaming like a kettle! It's filling the kitchen with its smoke! Granny has put it before the fire."

She was dancing round the room as she spoke; then caught sight of Shags, and sitting down on the floor, she took him on her lap and cuddled him.

"He is a bonny thing!" she cried.

"Do you know you might have been drowned this afternoon?" Rowena said gravely. "If I hadn't seen you through my glass and sent the boat out, what would you have done?"

Mysie looked up rather carelessly.

"Nan tells me I have nine lives like a cat. I am thinking Angus would have come after me. He's a Macdonald, you know, and loves Dad. It was really the oars' fault, they weren't able to beat through the waves prop'ly—and then they hurt my hands awful!"

She held up two little blistered palms.

"I took the boat when nobody was looking. I've never rowed all the way across by myself before, but I thought I could, only the wind came down and spoilt it all. Do you know what my name is?"

"Mysie."

"No—Flora Macdonald."

She put much importance into her tone.

"Do you know about the great Flora Macdonald? We belong to her family—and I was called Mysie Flora, but I like my friends to call me Flora. I mean to do something like she did when I grow up. If a prince doesn't come along, I must find somebody else. I'm hoping a prince—a real prince—may be hiding for his life one day, and then I shall go and help him."

Rowena did not laugh. Voice and face of the little speaker were so solemn.

"I hope you will succeed in your efforts," she said.

The little girl will chattered on.

"I live at the farm over there," she said, pointing out of the window. "It's half-way up the mountain. You can't see us, but we see you. Dad's house is nearly always shut up, but it's to be opened soon. He's coming home. The war made him very ill, and now he's coming for a long rest, Nan says. I'm going to try to manage to live with him, if I can. I think I should like to know him."

"You little old-fashioned piece of goods!" ejaculated Rowena. "Would you like to know me, I wonder?" Mysie nodded.

"I mean to. You'll let me come over and talk to you sometimes."

"Not if it means your rowing yourself across the loch."

"Oh, I ride round on Dibbie. He's the pony Angus uses for odd jobs. Do you know Sir Robert Fraser? He had some ponies on the hills and he said if I could catch one I could have it. But I was too frightened to do it. I always thought I might get hold of the water kelpie by mistake. Do you know about him?"

"I'm not sure that I do."

"Loch Tarlie used to be one of his haunts. Long ago when a Baron lived here, his only little boy and some others were playing about the loch, and they suddenly saw a beautiful little pony jumping about with saddle and bridle, and they tried to catch him and get on him; and they caught hold of his bridle and their fingers were glued to it, and they screamed, and the pony dashed for the loch and dragged them in. But the Baron's little boy knew about the water kelpie and he drew out his dirk and cut off his own hand, and the other boys were drowned and his hand with them, but he was saved."

Rowena made her eyes as big as Mysie's were whilst she narrated this horror.

"And is the water kelpie alive now to this day?" she asked.

"Well, I expect he is. When he's very well-known in one loch he goes to another—but I'm not going to let him catch me."

"Tell me some more stories," begged Rowena.

But Janet appeared with the tea, and the little girl turned her attention to the good things spread out before her.

"I like to know a prisoner," she said, munching a piece of cake thoughtfully; "there was a prisoner on a lake in Switzerland. We've got a picture of him. I think his name was Byron. Mr. Ferguson told me about him."

"You mean the prisoner of Chillon. Byron wrote about him. Who is Mr. Ferguson?"

"He's the schoolmaster over at Abertarlie. He teaches me lessons after school hours. Nan won't let me go to school with the other bairns—I'd like to. How long are you going to be in this prison, and is Niddy-Noddy a policeman?"

"I rather wish he was. Then I could run away from him. He's a wise old doctor who has tied me down to my bed, and told me to stay in it for a year! How would you like that? Never to be able to run about out-of-doors, or even change your room."

"It's horrible!" exclaimed Mysie. "Are you really tied to it?"

"By my honour," said Rowena.

"What's that?"

"Well, it's another word for duty. If you make a promise, you must keep it, or you lose your honour. And it's a mark of a true gentleman and lady to keep their honour unsoiled."

"I don't want to be either," said Mysie promptly. "I want to be a boy."

When tea was over Granny came in.

"I've been thinking, mem, it will be Anne Macdonald that will be anxious—an' Colin be drivin' for some corn—the t'other side o' the loch—and Mysie can just ride off wi' him."

Mysie made a grimace in the old woman's face.

"I'm all right here for a wee bit," she said.

But Granny was quite firm, she took her off to get into her kilt, which was dry by this time; and then brought her in to say good-bye to Rowena.

"You must come again soon and see me," Rowena said; "you've brightened up an hour for the poor captive."

Mysie laughed.

"And will you call me Flora?"

"Good-bye, Flora. Take care of yourself. We are going to be friends."

The little girl departed. Granny came in to talk about her when she had gone.

"Who teaches her such good English?" asked Rowena. "I pictured her a little heathen savage, brought up in a crofter's hut."

"Ah, indeed and indeed no! Anne Macdonald was a schoolmistress before she took service with the laird and his lady, a most superior young woman, and she took charge of the bairn from her birth. Ye see Angus have been the laird's gillie all his life for he was his father's gillie before him, an' Angus an' Anne made a match of it, an' then Angus got the sma' farm ower to Barncrassie, an' when the laird's leddy were in toon the bairn mad' her home wi' 'em. An' then Mrs. Macdonald died, an' the bairn have stayed wi' Anne ever since. She've paid a mighty lot o' attention to Mysie's manners and talk, an' in mony ways the little lassie has been bred more carefully than even wi' her own people—for the laird be a dour silent mon, an' when he's doon for a wee bit time has just shut himsel' awa' from all folk, an' come an' gone like a shadow on the wall!"

"And has he never troubled to see his child? What an unnatural father!"

Granny only shook her head hopelessly, and the conversation ended. Rowena began to look forward to seeing her small visitor again.

CHAPTER III
MYSIE MACDONALD

"O blessed vision, happy child,
Thou art so exquisitely wild,
I thought of thee with many fears
Of what might be thy lot in future years."
Wordsworth.

THREE days afterwards, Mysie made her appearance again.

Rowena found her very good company. She was full of Highland folk-lore and superstition; and was a combination of childish trust in the improbable, and old-fashioned sagacity and shrewdness.

"Have you ever seen any fairies?" she asked Rowena.

"I've heard about them," answered Rowena.

"Yes," sighed the child; "but all the nice things happened long ago. People say now that the fairies have gone away; I'm always watching for them. I went to Inverness one day with Nan. We saw two beautiful things there. One was the statue of Flora Macdonald with her dog—only I wish she'd had her kilt on—I believe she used to wear it when she was quite big! And the other was the Tom na hurisch. And when I saw that I said to myself I'd have one for everything that dies."

"What is it?" asked Rowena. "I have never seen Inverness."

"Tom na hurisch is the Fairies' Hill, and they've buried people all over it now. I hope the fairies like it. I think they like people's souls better than their bodies. You know it used to be rather dangerous for people to walk over their hills. They stole their souls out of them. A minister was found one day—at least his body was—and they thought he had had a fit; he wouldn't speak or look or eat, and they took him home; he had been walking round Tom na hurisch—and the fairies kept him out of his body for three days, and then they brought him back. I can't think why he couldn't have remembered what they did with him; he would never talk about it, but he would never go near a Tom na hurisch again—never—all his life long! I wish the fairies would take me one day."

"I would rather not have the experience," Rowena said, laughing. "Who tells you all these stories?"

"Oh, Angus—him and me, we walk over the hills together; and he talks and I listen. Nan laughs at his stories. Nan is an unbeliever! I lie down under the bracken sometimes and watch for the little folk, but I never see them. I thought I did once."

"You will one day! I wonder if you have heard the story of the laird out hunting. He was coming through his glen when he heard the most beautiful pipes playing; and he hid himself behind a tree; and he saw the fairies marching by, and their pipes playing as they went. The pipes shone in the sun, they were silver pipes with glass at the end of them. And the laird suddenly sprang out and threw his bonnet at them, and seized one of the pipes, calling out, 'Mine to yours, and yours to me!' And he wrapped the pipes up in his plaid and took them carefully home, and when he opened them there were some wisps of grass and a puff-ball at the end of them!"

Mysie listened breathlessly.

"Of course they wouldn't have been fairy pipes, if they hadn't been able to change. Fairies always play tricks like that. Did he never get his bonnet back again? I expect the fairies used it to sleep in. It would keep them warm on a wet night. Do tell me some more stories."

So Rowena produced all the fairy stories she could think of, and Mysie drank them in like water.

One day she arrived over in a breathless state of excitement.

"Dad is coming to-morrow. He has been ill since the war, and he's been from one hospital to another; and now he's well again, only he wants to get away from people, and have a rest and quiet. He told Nan so in a letter. She's to get the house ready, and she's not to tell anyone that he's coming."

"And here have you told me!"

"So I have! What a pity! But you're in your prison. I call you the prisoner of Tarlie. You won't tell anybody, will you? It's to be a secret. And I've quite made up my mind to get into his house and see him one day. I shan't mind if he points a pistol at me!"

"At his own child! Is he a pirate king?"

"No—but he's a Macdonald."

Here the child threw her curls back and raised her head almost haughtily. "Angus tells me stories of all that the Macdonalds have said and done. He is one himself, so he kens well. And they never let anyone defy them or get the better of them, and Dad doesn't want to see me. He has said it when Nan has asked him. He would like me swept away!" Here she threw out her small arms tragically. "But I mean to know him. I shall make him speak to me. I ought to be living in his house, not with Nan."

Rowena looked at her with wonder.

"You are growing," she said; "but you are still a baby in years, and your father knows it. Do you want to be sent to school? I suppose by rights you ought to be there now. I can't think how you have escaped the school authorities!"

"But I told you; I learn lessons with the schoolmaster."

"Oh, so you do; I had forgotten. Well, I hope you and your father will have a happy meeting."

With a little wistfulness in her eyes, Mysie went down on her knees beside Rowena's couch. Putting her arms round her neck she whispered:

"Do you think it could happen that he might love me?"

"I think it more than likely," said Rowena, kissing her as she spoke.

And then Mysie sprang up and danced out into the sunshine.

"I have ridden over to tell you, and now I am going back to Nan; for I am going to help her get his house ready."

Rowena lay on her bed looking out on the still blue and trying to recall the Hugh Macdonald she had once seen at her brother's table. It was long ago before he had married, and he was then a thin eager-faced youth, with stern features and a very decided will of his own. He had been abroad for a good many years since then. And his marriage had altered him, people said. She had a dim recollection of a walk round the loch after dinner; but she was quite a young girl at the time. He had not impressed her, except perhaps that he had been too old in his ideas her then.

"If he doesn't own that child, he ought to be ashamed of himself!" she muttered, and then a sudden restless fit took possession of her.

"I am like a mummy. I cannot stay indoors longer. It is breathless to-day. I will write to Noddy and demand release."

She wrote; and by return received 'the usual kind letter from the old doctor, saying that he had written to a local practitioner and had asked him to call and see her and give her his advice. The very next day the doctor appeared. He was a young man and arrived in his car, for he lived about fifteen miles away from her.

Rowena felt impatient as he put her through a regular catechism as to the beginning of the trouble.

"I have been pulled about by all the specialists in town," she said. "I was not going to give up my freedom without a struggle; but they one and all said the same thing—that I must lie on my back for at least a year. I am not rebellious about that; but I can lie on my back out-of-doors as well as indoors, and I am an out-of-door sort of person."

"There is not the slightest reason why you should not do it," the young doctor said decidedly; "didn't you say you had an invalid chair? Let me look at it."

"Mrs. Mactavish will show it to you."

He went out and was some time inspecting it. Then he came in.

"Your chair can be adapted easily to your needs. I know a clever young carpenter, and I'll send him over to tinker it up, and lower the back, till you can lie flat upon it; then you can be out all day."

"I want to vary my life, and sometimes lie out in the boat," said Rowena. "Can you manage that for me?"

"Easily. You must have a flat-bottomed punt and a mattress. Have you anyone who can carry you? We want to prevent the jar to your spine that would be the result of your putting your feet to the ground."

"I have two men who will manage that. Well—you have given me new life! I am very grateful."

Young George Sturt looked at her with a smile.

"I should say you enjoy every moment of your existence," he said, "from your looks."

"My looks are deceptive," Rowena assured him. "I am eaten up at times with an overwhelming envy for every one who can get about on his two legs. And I rage at my fate, and make myself furiously disagreeable to all who come my way."

He laughed, gave her a little sound advice and took his departure. Rowena seized hold of Shags and hugged him.

"Shags, my angel, you and I are going to be Dryads. Wet or fine we will live out-of-doors. My hopes are now fixed upon the carpenter; only I mustn't land poor Ted in too much expense over me. Otherwise I should wire to Glasgow for a flat-bottomed punt immediately. It's a pity we don't possess one."

But when she interviewed Duncan a little later, she was reassured on that point, for he told her he knew a man who owned one and who would be glad to hire it to her for the season.

Mr. Sturt was as good as his word. The carpenter appeared and in a couple of days had done all that was required to her chair. It was a happy moment when she was lifted upon it and wheeled out upon the lawn. The weather was perfect: still and warm with an occasional gentle breeze from the lake.

Rowena lay still, inhaling the sweet air in a state of blissful content. Granny was delighted to see her there; and for three days from nine o'clock in the morning till nine at night, Rowena enjoyed life in her cushioned chair. On the third afternoon about half-past three, just at the drowsiest time in the whole of that summer's day, a stranger walked briskly up the drive and rang at the front door. Rowena was fast asleep; she had neither seen nor heard his approach. She was roused by Granny's gentle voice at her side.

"If you please, mem, 'tis the laird himself—he hav' come over on a question about his shootin' at Tarlie Bottom. He was onawares any of the family were here, so maybe ye'll be answerin' him ye'self. It's wanting to know if it's let, he is."

"Is he here, Granny?" Rowena asked, rousing herself.

"He's waitin' i' the hoose."

"Then ask him to come out here."

In a few moments a tall dark-featured man was standing by Rowena's chair, looking down on her with pity and concern in his eyes.

Rowena held out her hand and smiled in her radiant fashion.

"I am an old crock, but I can talk if I can do nothing else. We do know each other, though it is many years since we met. May I welcome you back? You have been away a long time, have you not?"

"I remember you well," was his prompt reply. "I only saw you once, but your eyes haunted me. I have never seen such joyous ones since; and they are still the same. What has happened to you, may I ask?"

"A spill out riding."

"But you're not alone here? Where's your brother?"

"In India. I am carrying out my doctor's directions. I have no temptations in this quiet spot to evade them. Will you sit down?"

He took the garden chair close to her.

"I am sorry for you," he said with feeling in his tone, "I was a crock for eighteen months in hospital after 1915, so I know what bed is. I never left it for twelve solid months."

"That is my time—a year—and then I hope I shall be cured."

His whole face softened.

"Ah," he said, "when you've suffered yourself, you can feel for others."

"Yes—and I dare say I was in need of a more sympathetic spirit," said Rowena thoughtfully. "I have always laughed too much. I laugh at myself now. You want to know about our shooting. Ted has let it, I am afraid."

They began to talk over estate matters, and then about sport in general. He seemed in no hurry to go; and presently began to revert to his own state of health.

"I am only here to patch myself up," he said. "But they've chucked me out of the army—let me retire as Major-General. I suppose I ought to feel my life is over; but my brain is sound, and it makes me rage at times. What shall I do with myself here? Only vegetate."

"Oh, no; if you are a reader, you won't do that. It's wonderful how much fuller we can store our brains than we do! I cannot fill my empty cells fast enough! Have you any hobbies?"

He shook his head.

"I'm a reader of sorts. I couldn't have lived through my eighteen months without books."

Then Rowena said suddenly: "Have you seen your child?"

His brows contracted.

"No. I've told her nurse I'll see her in a day or two. I've been busy. Children aren't in my line."

"She's a little person of much character," said Rowena slowly. "I don't want to be an interfering meddler, but you'll gain by her acquaintance. I have."

He raised his eyebrows and then smiled.

"I am talking to you like an old friend. If you had been well and jolly, I should have cut and run. I have taken a dislike to my fellow-creatures, especially the sound and healthy ones. And to my disgust I'm nervy—children would get on my nerves. I'll see her when I feel fitter. You consider me an inhuman parent, I can see."

"No, only an ignorant one," said Rowena. "Your little daughter has made some of my worst days very bright."

"Women always worship babies."

"She is companionable, you will find."

His brows did not relax; he leant back in his chair and drew a long breath.

"Her existence brings back some bad times. Her mother hated me, you know. It was the first thing she said to me after the birth of the child. We couldn't pull together, though God knows I tried hard. And poor Evie was forced by her mother to marry me, I heard afterwards. Well, she didn't have a long time with me, poor soul!"

Then he pulled himself up. "I am getting garrulous. I don't generally give way to such personal reminiscences, but I want to explain my want of interest in the child. I was always told she was the picture of her mother."

"But my good man," said Rowena quickly, "bodies may resemble each other, but very seldom souls. And Mysie is—well, I will leave you to find out. This much I will tell you, that she is hungering for your interest and affection. Give her a chance—and yourself too."

He did not reply for a few minutes; then he said rather irrelevantly: "You say you're a reader. Have you enough books to keep you occupied? Because my father bequeathed to me a very fine library. I have been overhauling it and can lend you anything you want."

"Oh, how truly kind!"

With animation Rowena began discussing books, and half an hour slipped by before her visitor attempted to make a move.

He would not stay to tea. As he stood up, he looked down at Rowena with some softness in his grey eyes.

"You don't want to be bucked up," he said, "for you are the essence of cheerfulness. When I have my bad bouts of pain, I think of the thousands of paralysed bedridden young men who have had their health and strength taken from them with one fell swoop in the war, and feel an old crock like myself has no right to grouse. I have done my work, and am wanted by no one!"

"You are wanted by your child!" said Rowena firmly.

He gave a short laugh.

"What a pertinacious woman you are! Are you bored by visitors? May I walk over again, and bring you the books you want?"

"Yes, certainly. I shall be delighted. And then you can give me your impressions of Mysie!"

He departed, but Rowena gave a little sigh as she looked after him and noted the tired bend of his shoulders, and his rather uncertain steps.

"Poor lonely unhappy man!" she murmured. "Why, Shags, you and I must try to bring some zest for living into his soul. I rather fancy Mysie will have a say in that."

Shags cocked one ear and looked wise. He had already had some experience of Mysie. She had certainly contributed towards his pleasure, for she and he invariably had a romp together when she came over.

Two or three days passed. Then one morning Mysie arrived over on her pony. She threw herself upon Rowena in her usual impulsive fashion.

"Haven't you longed to see me! It's been such an exciting time! And I heard Dad say he was coming to see you this afternoon, so I thought I would get over first."

"Now sit up and tell me all about it from the very beginning," demanded Rowena.

"The beginning," said Mysie importantly, "was when Nan came back from the house and said I was to go up and see Dad in the morning. Of course I'd seen him lots of times before that, but I took care that he shouldn't see me. I wanted to find out if I'd like him for a father. I saw him with his gun, he shot two pigeons, and I clapped my hands once. I was behind a tree, and he looked round quickly, but he didn't see me. When Nan wanted to dress me up, I said, No—I would go in my kilt. I hate girls' frocks, and so I ran straight away from her, and walked into the house by myself. And fancy! It was eleven o'clock, and Dad was eating his breakfast!"

"And what did you say?"

"I said, 'Good morning, Dad; may I have some of your bacon?' and I sat down and he laughed, and gave me a big plateful, and told them to bring me a cup of coffee. And then he said:"

"'I don't know whether I'm looking at a boy or a girl,' and then I told him, very earnest, that I had a boy's heart and a girl's body, and then I gave him my present I had brought with me. It was two darling little trout I had caught the day before with Angus. And he was quite pleased and asked me whether I liked fishing, and I told him I liked everything he did, and so we settled up then that we would do things together, and then I told him he'd better let me have a bedroom in his house so that I needn't be running backwards and forwards all day long—and he said yes to that. After that we talked like anything. Why, he's almost as good to talk to as you are!"

"He must be good then!" said Rowena, laughing. "I think he is a delightful father to have, Flora."

"Oh, yes; and we talked about my name—he doesn't like the name of Flora. I said I'd rather be called Macdonald than Mysie, and he thinks he can manage to call me Mac. But he doesn't care to talk all day long, he says, so I've left him. I dare say he'll get used to me after a bit, but he finds me stranger than I do him, you know. For I've always talked to Angus—he's a man, of course, but Dad says he isn't used to children, and doesn't understand them!"

Mysie paused for breath; her eyes glowed as she went on:

"If Dad and I live together and do things together, I shall thank God truly! I've prayed to have a proper father since I was a baby. And after breakfast I went upstairs and told Dad the room I would like to sleep in. Nan says I can't leave her, and Dad doesn't mean it. But he and me mean it very certainly!"

"Ah," said Rowena, "I can see that you're going to have a real good time now. But don't worry a man when he's seedy. Your Dad will have days when he wants to be alone."

Mysie was too full of her own thoughts to take this in.

"I told him there was a prisoner on the loch and that I went to see her, and he seemed to guess at once, and he told Angus he was coming over here this afternoon."

Mysie chattered on: she described her father's appearance with minute details; she said she would like him best in a kilt and hoped he would soon wear it. And she finally departed apologizing for her short visit.

"I feel I don't want to stay away from him too long," she said; "in case he may forget me again."

In the afternoon General Macdonald appeared with his pockets bulging with books. Rowena received him and his books with much pleasure.

"I have seen my child," he said abruptly. "She is bigger and older than I thought. She means to take possession of me. I fancy she ought to be at school, ought she not?"

"Oh, don't worry over school just yet. Get to know her, and get her to know you. What do you think of her?"

He drew up a chair and sat down upon it. Rowena waited for him to speak, and he kept her waiting for three or four minutes, then he said slowly:

"I am a little afraid of her."

"What nonsense!"

"I am afraid of her personality. She does not mean to remain in the background. And when I came down here, a child did not enter into my calculations."

"But I really think she ought to have done so. May I congratulate you upon having such a child?"

He looked at her and smiled.

"I see she has won your heart. A man is handicapped when he has to train a girl child. And she wants training. If she had been a boy, I would have found the task easier."

"Oh, don't take her so heavily," said Rowena. "Let her trot round with you, and do things with you. She'll learn from your talk what is right and wrong."

"Will she? I'm a poor specimen at the best; and I know nothing of women and their ways."

"Bring her up as a boy, then," said Rowena, laughing at his forlorn tone. "She is, as she says, half a boy already. Don't act the heavy father. Of course she will have to be educated later on. But let her have a holiday with you now. Do you know she has prayed that she might have a 'proper father' from the time she was a baby? Don't disappoint her. And when she worries you, send her over to me. Shags and I understand her."

"May I smoke?" the General asked.

Rowena looked at him with laughter in her eyes, as he slowly produced a favourite pipe out of his pocket.

"I suppose," he said reflectively, "you can't mould children as you wish. They resist now, more than they used to do. I should like to mould her after the pattern of my mother. I don't want to have one of these self-assertive modern young women as my daughter, later on."

"I am afraid Mysie has too much character to be shaped into another person's mould. But she is warm-hearted, and if a girl loves, she can be governed through her love."

There was silence between them.

Then Rowena said:

"We might be two old spinster governesses sitting up and discussing the character of our pupils! Look over the loch at the afternoon shadows on the hills. Sweep your small daughter out of your mind for a moment or two—and tell me if that sky doesn't bring delight to your soul?"

General Macdonald gave a short quick sigh, but as he looked across the blue loch, the lines about his lips relaxed.

"Ah," he said, "it's good to get back to it again. There's no place like the Highlands in the world."

"To-morrow," said Rowena blithely, "I am going to extend my horizon. If you see a doubtful-looking craft upon the surface of the loch, it will be me, lying on my back in a flat-bottomed punt. We may fly a scarlet sail. Colin will be with me. But I assure you it will be a red-letter day in my life—therefore the red flag, you see!"

"I congratulate you. But don't put me off my child, for I assure you I hardly slept last night for thinking about her. Knocking about in hospitals, as I have done, I have seen all sorts and conditions of women. I have been bossed by some, and petted by others, and the audacity of some young women filled my soul with awe. Do you think that women—girls, I should say—ought to be trained to earn their own living, so as to be independent of our sex? As I heard some of the nurses declaiming against their dull homes, I gave a thought sometimes to their dull old parents. I shall be one of them when my girl grows up. How can I expect her to stay at home with me, if all the young world is out and away from their homes?"

"By the time Mysie is grown-up the swing of the pendulum will be back the home way again," said Rowena. "I have had great longings for work, you know, and tried to break away from my brother's house more than once. I did leave them for eight months once, but was called back again by my sister-in-law's serious illness. Nothing will keep a girl at home if she wants to leave it, except circumstances. As I say, be a chum and companion to Mysie and she'll never want to leave you, until a possible husband turns up. She is prepared to idealize and worship you. Let her do it, and do, if you want to win her heart quickly, call her 'Flora'!"

General Macdonald laughed.

"Ah, we've fallen out already over that. 'Mysie' was my mother's pet name."

"Then keep it sacred," said Rowena, "and call your small girl by the name she adores and loves!"

They talked on; gradually Rowena got his mind upon other subjects. When he left her, he gripped her hand until she could have cried with the pain of it.

"You have helped me enormously," he said. "I am not going to fight shy of my responsibility as a father any longer."

"Shags," said Rowena, taking hold of a golden brown ear, "am I a hundred years old? Is it always the role of a person on her back to dole out advice to her visitors? Am I, a single woman, to occupy my leisure thoughts in studying a child's character, and the suitable training for her? I am going now to read the most frivolous book I have by me, just to forget the moralities and gravity of life, and to imagine myself a young dog like yourself."

CHAPTER IV
THE BIRTHDAY GIFT

"A glory gilds the sacred page,
Majestic like the sun
It gives a light to every age;
It gives, but borrows none."
Cowper.

ROWENA was moved into her boat the next day. And the sun shone down upon her in real friendliness. Of course Shags accompanied her; and for a couple of hours Colin rowed her over the loch; then, feeling she must not take him longer from his work in the garden, she made him moor the boat to the side of the small landing pier, and there, with her hands dabbling in the cool water, Rowena lay and meditated, and read for another couple of hours. She hardly knew which she liked best, the motion or the stillness.

Granny came out at tea-time and suggested her moving in.

"I could stay here for ever and ever!" exclaimed Rowena. "What is it about the loch that sends such peace and rest into one's soul?"

"It's the still waters," said Granny. She murmured to herself, "'He leadeth me beside the still waters.'"

Rowena never took any notice when the Bible was quoted to her.

"Couldn't I lie here all night?" she said.

"'Deed, an' no, ye will not do that, mem. An' wha would say hoo lang this stillness would be! A storm would come on, and then where would ye be? A helpless leddy, solitary in the nicht!"

"Oh, Granny, what a description! Well, this helpless body must be moved in to bed, I suppose. I can look forward to to-morrow."

But the next day was cold and wet. Rowena by this time was accustomed to the Highland weather. She had a small wood fire made in her green room, and with her books and rug-making spent a very pleasant day. Between four and five the rain ceased and the sun shone out. And soon after five, a motor full of people drove up to the door. It was Lady Fraser, their nearest neighbour. She had brought her daughter and niece over, and two young friends of theirs.

Rowena was not sure whether she liked them pouring in upon her, but she knew it was real friendliness and good nature that brought them.

"We heard of your accident, and your brother told my husband before he went to India that you would be staying here on the quiet for the summer; so we promised him we would look after you, and prevent you from being dull."

Lady Fraser paused at the end of this speech.

"We hoped you might have been able to come over to us, perhaps. We did not know you were a real invalid."

"I am a prisoner for a year," said Rowena cheerfully, "and I am taking fresh views of life. It's astonishing what a different environment does for one. I shall be delighted to see you when you have time to come over, but I cannot return your visits."

"There seem so many invalids now," said Lady Fraser with a sigh. "There is Hugh Macdonald. We heard he had returned home, and wrote asking him to dinner to-morrow, He replied that he was not well enough to go anywhere; but my son George saw him fishing yesterday and he had a child with him. I suppose it is his little girl. I should think she ought to be educated. He has let her run wild since her mother's death. Well, I am truly sorry for you, my dear. I should think it a deadly existence here by yourself. But you say you don't mind."

The girls were full of commiseration. They had always regarded Rowena before as being great fun, and very sporting. She felt that, though they did not put it into words, her invalid life at present formed a gulf between her and their pleasure-loving souls.

"It's so tiresome," said Katie Fraser; "so many of the men are grumpy now like General Macdonald. George is very much the same himself — says tennis and games are boring, and fatigue him. He likes to moon about and go off alone with the keepers."

"My dear," said Lady Fraser, "you forget how ill he has been."

"And the horrors he has gone through," said Rowena slowly. "Forgetfulness is not easy to them all."

"Oh, we will teach them to forget," laughed one of the girls. "They must have a good time now, to make up for all they have lost."

"We're going to get up a pastoral play the end of August," said Lady Fraser; "there will be more people down here then. I do hate the empty time up here, don't you?"

"Well, I'm looking forward to spend the winter here," said Rowena.

They screamed at that statement.

"You can't! Nobody lives here in the winter. You had better be buried at once."

"Why, you will have no neighbours at all! All the houses are shut up!"

"I shall have the minister and his mother; the doctor; Granny Mactavish and her niece, and I can tick off five farms round our loch which will not be shut up! You seem horror-stricken, but I mean to cultivate my neighbours, whoever they may be, if they will be good enough to cultivate me!"

Lady Fraser shook her head at her. "You are joking at our expense! Your eyes betray you!" Her girls were mute, but they looked at Rowena pityingly.

They did not stay very long. She watched them drive off, with a grim smile, and said to Shags:

"We understand now, Shags, how unpleasant perfectly strong healthy people are to the sick. I don't wonder that Hugh Macdonald has taken a dislike to them. I suppose it is their pity which makes me grind my teeth. I always think there's a bit of contempt mixed up with it. Now I am perfectly certain I shan't be troubled with the Frasers much, and how they used to live here last summer! What fun we did have! It is a deadly existence, of course, but content is creeping over me, and I shall not be disturbed."

She returned to her books, but a restless wave passed over her; then she called Granny to the rescue, and a talk with her restored her equanimity of mind.

The next day was windy; she was unable to be in her boat, but she was able to lie out in her chair. And in the afternoon, who should appear but Mysie and her father! They were riding. Mysie's face was glowing with happiness and importance. Her father looked as grave and imperturbable as ever. Mysie in her usual impulsive fashion flung herself upon Rowena.

"Oh, I'm so glad to see you again! And such quantities have happened! Dad doesn't think I'm bad for my age! He really doesn't. I caught a bigger fish than him yesterday morning. We went out in all the rain and did it! And do tell me, were you lying in your boat the day before yesterday? I looked through Dad's glasses and thought I saw you. And may I come by your side in my boat and then I'll tie you up to me and tow you? It will be fun!"

Rowena let her chat on for a few moments undisturbed, then she said:

"Look here, Granny is longing to see you and hear about your doings. Will you go into the kitchen, and ask her to make some of her nice drop scones for tea?"

"Oh, she'll let me help her, I know she will."

Off Mysie darted. Her father looked relieved.

"How are things going?" Rowena asked.

"Rather fast," he said with a flicker of a smile. "We have had one combat of wills already, but I made up my mind beforehand that I would be boss. And she has been more subdued since."

"May I hear about it?"

"It was a question of friction between her and my housekeeper, Mrs. Dalziel. The child marched into her kitchen and helped herself liberally to some of the contents of the store cupboard. Mrs. Dalziel remonstrated, and was told to mind her own business, that Miss Mysie was mistress, and meant to be, or words to that effect. I heard such a shindy that I went out and found them going at each other hammer and tongs, so I called upon the culprit to beg Mrs. Dalziel's pardon at once. This she refused point-blank to do and tossed her head, saying, 'A Macdonald never owns himself in the wrong, Angus told me so.' I told her Angus could go to blazes as far as I cared, but if I told her to do a thing, do it she must, whether she liked it or not. This was a bitter pill to swallow and she held out for two hours. I told her I would allow her half an hour's more grace, and if it wasn't done by that time, her box should be packed and she should be returned to Anne's keeping. She went straight away to Mrs. Dalziel and peace was made. Then she came to me."

"'Have I to beg your pardon too, Dad?'"

"'What for?'"

"'For not doing what you wanted at once.'"

"'No; I don't want words, only deeds,' I said. 'A soldier's daughter must learn prompt obedience from all her superiors.' Then she wanted to know who her superiors were, and she got me into a fog, for it seems Angus and Mrs. Dalziel don't hit it off, and she wanted to know if she was to obey both of them when they 'said the opposite'!"

"'You'll take your orders from me,' I said, giving it up. And I think she's learnt her first lesson."

"How I should like to have seen you together," Rowena said with her happy laugh.

"Now we'll dismiss the child," he said somewhat peremptorily. "Did you enjoy your boat the other day?"

"So much. And I enjoyed this all the better when I came back to it. Change is good for most folk, I suppose. I had a visit from the Frasers yesterday. They were horrified to think I should be meditating spending the winter here."

"They would be. But I wonder if you will do it."

"Yes, I will," Rowena said, a shadow seeming to fall across her bright eyes. "What a lot of thinking I shall do! I have done a good bit already."

He looked up quickly at her.

"Tell me some of your deductions."

"Oh, they are not very original. The mystery of life, and of sadness and gladness. I have begun to have a glimmer of light. There may be some good in our awful experience of the past four or five years. Somehow or other a character without any gravity in its composition has lost its attractiveness to me. The Fraser girls jarred upon me. They do resent and despise those who will not dance to their pleasure. Does it mean that this forced seclusion of mine is making me jump into the solid impassive state of old age?"

He did not answer. Then she asked him somewhat wistfully:

"Have you made any useful deductions during your convalescence?"

He answered her by asking an apparently irrelevant question.

"Did you ever meet Cuff Mackenzie? He was in the Scots Guards, and my regiment lay with his for some considerable time at the Front. Forgive a personal remark, but your eyes remind me of his, except perhaps that there was a graver light in his. A serenity that used to baffle me. He was shot, poor chap, close by my side. I helped carry him into his trench, and he only lived an hour. But he bequeathed me a legacy, and said with his dying breath that it was a key to the present history of the world. He asked me to study it. So I have been doing it. His copious notes on the margins have given me the clue to doing it. And I am intensely interested."

"It's a book? What's the name? Who's the author?"

"Oh, we all possess a copy of it. It's the Bible."

"The Bible!"

Rowena looked amused.

"Do you know, I don't possess a Bible! Granny was quite shocked. She has placed a fat black one on my chest of drawers. I used one at school, but somehow I lost it, and never replaced it. It has never come into my calculations. Of course one hears it in church."

"Mackenzie was very keen on prophecy. He got half the fellows in the Mess hanging on his words one night. He told them that Allenby's victory in the East was a triumphant fact for all Bible students, and proved it. I was there, and since I've owned his well-worn copy, I've been discovering a good deal."

"I thought the Bible was quite out of date in these days," said Rowena. "Even the preachers in London were always putting their knife into it, and trying to prove that most of it was fable."

"Yes, I suppose it's the way of the world. Well, I recommend it to you for study this next winter. You'll find yourself stepping into another world altogether before you've done with it."

"Is that your experience?"

General Macdonald gazed rather dreamily over the loch in front of him, then he turned, and Rowena saw a shining, steadfast light in his dark eyes.

"Yes, I've stepped into another environment," he said; "and it's a very good sort of one, I can tell you."

Rowena was silent.

Then Mysie made her appearance. She was munching a cake, but approached Rowena in a mysterious manner.

"I know something," she said.

"So do I," said Rowena, "many things."

"Ah, but this is an event."

Then in rather a loud whisper she asserted:

"I know when your birthday is. The day after to-morrow. Granny is going to make a special cake for it—she's told me so."

Rowena laughed.

"Granny still treats me as if I were six years old. Will you come to tea with me and taste it, Flora?"

The child clapped her hands, then turned to her father with old-fashioned politeness.

"Could you do without me on Friday do you think, Dad?"

"I fancy I might," said her father gravely.

They did not stay longer. Rowena lay still after they had gone, and mused upon what General Macdonald had told her.

"I knew there was something underneath his tired tones. I don't think I have ever met a religious man before. He will be an interesting study, won't he, Shags? But he will be shocked at my sceptical outlook. I rather wish I could believe in the other fuller life after death. But this world is the main one to me. He has stepped into another environment already, he says. It sounded quite uncanny. And yet—and yet—oh, Shags, I do feel a little more responsible and intelligent than you. I don't quite think you and I will merit the same end! No wonder he has grave views about Mysie's future! I fancy she will lead him a dance before he has done with her. But he and his Bible together won't make me give up his friendship. I enjoy listening to him. He has one of the pleasantest voices I've heard for a long time; and he isn't too sanctified yet! For he had one wicked outburst to his child! Oh, Shags, you and I together must keep him as near our world as we can—I can't afford to lose him. He and I are both crippled crocks, and the mad world doesn't need us. I'll talk to him about the Koran next time and see what he has to say to that!"

On Rowena's birthday Mysie appeared in the full glory of a new kilt—the dress Tartan of the Macdonalds.

"Dad got it in Inverness," she said, showing herself off with pride. "He took me there by train yesterday. We had such a day! But I'm going to wish you a happy birthday, and give you a beautiful present. I bought it for you myself yesterday, all by myself."

She put into Rowena's hands a parcel. Then danced up and down in excitement whilst it was being opened.

"I knewed you were fond of books," Mysie's grammar was not always correct. "So I went into a book shop and asked the man what was the best book in the world for anybody who loved reading. He thought hard and then he got me this—at least it was the same book, but I chose a prettier cover. It's the best book in the world, so you're sure to like it."

Rowena opened the parcel. A beautiful little dark red leather Bible lay inside.

She looked up at Mysie with a mixture of curiosity and pleasure in her eyes.

"My dear little Flora What can I say? It's beautiful! I suppose your Dad had a hand in choosing it?"

"He didn't know nothing about it, till I'd brought it home. It was the shopman who showed it to me."

"It's a wonderful gift and a remarkable coincidence," said Rowena thoughtfully.

"I suppose it's what they read in church," said Mysie. "Dad said it was a present fit for a queen. I couldn't have done better, he said. And one day he's going to give me one. Have you got one of any kind? I hope you haven't, but I know Granny Mactavish has. But it isn't red leather like this, is it?"

Rowena put her arm round her and kissed her.

"Thank you a thousand times, Flora darling! I will keep this till I die."

"And what did you call it, not a Bible, but an unmarkable concordance, didn't you?"

"That's near enough," laughed Rowena.

Then they had tea, and Granny's birthday cake was much appreciated. Mysie, of course, was full of the subject of birthdays.

"When is God's birthday?" she asked suddenly. "Does the Bible tell you? I know Jesus' birthday is Christmas Day. I should like to know God's birthday, if He lets people know. He must be very, very, very old."

Rowena was never shocked by Mysie's questions.

"God Almighty has no birthday, for He was never born. There never was a time when He did not exist. But don't puzzle your head over that mystery. Let us talk of other things."

"Dad's birthday is in November," said Mysie after a moment's pause. "Mine is in November too. Isn't that funny? Mine is on the 10th. His is on the 20th. Will you be here on our birthdays? Do you think you could come to tea with us? You could come across the loch in your fiat boat. That would be fun, wouldn't it? And we'd have a birthday cake as good as Granny's."

"We must wait and see. I dare say I shall be here, but the fairies may have wafted you off somewhere before November. Perhaps to school."

"Ah," said Mysie, shaking her head, "Dad talks about school, but the fairies and I may manage something better. I'll go round one of their hills; if you go nine times the wrong way, at sunset, I think, you'll find a door leading you inside. And if I once go inside I shan't come back for years and years!"

"That would be a pity. I shouldn't do anything that would make you into a prisoner."

"Would I be a prisoner? Well then, I should find a way to escape. That would be most exciting."

"I would rather try school."

"Would you? But I couldn't live away from the Highlands, I should die. The great Flora didn't go to school. She had governesses. I know all about her."

"Oh, yes, she did go to school. I have a life of her here," said Rowena.

"Then Angus told me wrong. Perhaps I will go to school then—only I must come back for all the holidays."

Mysie sat and talked, then she had a romp with Shags, and departed about seven o'clock.

"I have to be back by eight, Dad said so. He's a very particular man. Angus says it's because he's a soldier."

Rowena lay thinking after Mysie had left her. The advent of the red Bible had not altogether pleased her.

"I suppose, Shags, it means that I shall have to read it, but as to studying it, I shouldn't have the faintest notion how to set about it. I think I'll wait till I see the General again. He may be able to give me a tip about it. Is it a case of thought telepathy between father and child, I wonder?"

CHAPTER V
FRIENDLY TALKS

"Faith alone is the master-key
To the strait gate and narrow road,
The others but skeleton pick-locks be,
And you never shall pick the locks of God."
Walter Smith.

ROWENA did not see her friends for ten days, for a week of storm and rain set in, and she managed to catch a cold which settled on her chest, and forced her to remain indoors and be nursed by Granny. She was solaced by a budget of Indian letters, and she straightway replied to her brother:

"DEAR OLD TED,—"

"It was good to see your fist again. I am as hoarse as a raven, and Granny has got full possession of me. You know what a dragon she is. I suppose the knowledge of her superior power keeps her from feeling the pellets of abusive epithets with which I pelt her! Shags, my devoted one, lies at the bottom of my bed, ready for the least spark of fun that can be got out of his mistress. He and I, of course, hold long conversations together. I don't know which speaks most intelligently—his stumpy tail, his two wicked little ears, or his sparkling brown eyes. I sometimes wish humans had that eighth sense, a tail! It would give one away too much, I expect! I often wonder whether it is entirely under Shags' control or whether it gives an independent wag of its own on occasions. If so, it must be rather unpleasant to poor Shags."

"Well, I must try to write sober sense if I can. I congratulate you on your polo match. I sometimes get a strong yearning to leave my prison, and get some movement into my slow torpid existence. No—I am not torpid. I feel my brain is keener than ever. You will laugh at a literary effort of mine. I was reading a minister's account of his village, historically, botanically, geologically, and legendarily. So I've started a book on our loch and neighbourhood, and I can't tell you what an interest it is. I have routed out some of your old books here, and I've sent to Mudie's for a few more, and I hope to borrow some from Hugh Macdonald, who has become quite friendly. I can see he thinks me harmless, so has accepted my friendship accordingly. I am also getting hold of a lot of old folk-lore from Donald, who, though grimly sceptical of certain traditions, holds others fast and firm. The Frasers are here, and have paid me one visit. I don't think they will trouble me much. Granny told me this morning that the pretty cottage at the top of our glen has just been taken by a single lady, a Miss Falconer. She is a connection of the Grants, Granny says. I don't know where she gets her information from! Our garden here is a dream. Colin is a good hard-working boy. Picture our herbaceous border a riot of pink and white and blue colour. The phloxes are luxuriant, so are the delphiniums. And our roses go on and on, blooming for ever! I lie here and enjoy nature, and I'm learning an awful lot about the birds and insects. Hugh Macdonald has quite adopted his child, and amuses me by his high ideas of training and education. She is too independent for him. He said to me the other day: 'But she's a girl—why is she so assertive, and so strong-willed and fearless?' I reminded him that our sex is that way inclined nowadays, and he must make the best of it. But he didn't see it. I think she wakes him up and keeps him lively. Anne has given up the charge of her rather unwillingly, but still keeps a motherly eye on her, and there is jealousy between her and his housekeeper."

"This won't interest you. Oh, Ted, do you, from the depths of your heart, believe that I am going to be a sound member of humanity again? I am beginning to doubt it. My spinal cord has gone to smithereens! I can't sit up for five minutes without feeling it, and it makes me rant and roar against fate in general."

"This is the lament of Brer Tarrypin 'Loungin' round an' sufferin'.' If you were to walk in at this moment, you would grin broadly, and tell me that I know how to do myself! For I'm in my green room with a cheerful wood fire. Bowls of flowers are everywhere, and an appetizing lunch of beef-tea and crisp toast has just appeared and I've written myself into a smiling humour again. My fits of depression don't last long. I'm as happy as I can be away from you all. Good-bye—a thousand kisses to the bunch of you."

"ROWENA."

As Rowena was finishing this letter, Granny came into the room.

"'Tis the minister and his mither called to speir for ye. I telled them ye were just lyin' by, and wud na' be seein' folk for a wee bit."

"Oh, I should like to see Mrs. Macintosh. I promise not to talk more than I do to you, Granny. Don't be a dragon. Bring her in."

Granny shook her head doubtfully; but presently ushered in the visitor, raising a warning finger at her as she did so.

"Ye'll no mak' me young leddy force her speech. She micht bring on inflammation o' the lungs an' throat, for she's sair vexed wi' hoarseness just noo."

"My dear, I am sorry for you," said Mrs. Macintosh, taking the seat Granny had placed for her. "I have been long in coming, but I have been laid up for six weeks with a severe bout of my enemy, rheumatic-gout, and am only just able to get about again."

"Bodies are troublesome items," said Rowena; "but I'm quite convalescent again. Granny makes the worst of me, for she dreads my going out-of-doors before I'm perfectly well. Tell me all the news of the neighbourhood, and I'll lie and listen. I quite understand how bedridden folk are entranced to hear that there has been a quarrel between Mr. and Mrs. Black, and that Mr. White's cat has stolen Mrs. Green's cream, and that Billy Smith saw John Wood and Mary Tibbs walking out together! Tell me all and everything that has happened to the outside world since I left it."

Mrs. Macintosh laughed.

"It is so easy to gossip," she said; "and I'll do it with a right good will. Of course the first bit of news is that the Macdonald child is living with her father. They have been to the kirk every Sabbath, and very well behaved the little lassie is. But she stopped Robert last Sabbath when she saw him come out of the kirk."

"'Do be a wee bit shorter next Sunday, will you,' she said with her mischievous eyes gleaming with fun. 'I get pins and needles in my legs, and Dad requires that I should keep still. He says a fidgety neighbour is worse than a fidgety horse.'"

"We are wondering what her father will do with her in the way of learning. Robert called on him the other day, and was very pleased with his visit. It seems the laird is keenly interested in prophecy, and Robert's soul is full of it. They talked for three or four hours."

"They would," said Rowena, laughing.

"And I suppose you have heard of the new arrival?" Mrs. Macintosh went on. "It is a Miss Falconer at Glen Cottage. I went over to see her and she has been once or twice to us. She is very friendly. A sweet-looking young woman. It seems that she is very clever. Has been to Girton and is a B.A., and for some time taught in one of the big English High Schools. Then she had a bad illness and has never been very strong since. She came in to a little money, and determined to get a cottage somewhere up here. Her mother was a Grant, she is well connected. She loves the quiet and seclusion here, but longs to be busy. I was talking about the Macdonald child and she begged me to ask the laird if she could teach his little daughter. She said she would prefer to walk over to the house every day and give her as many hours' tuition as he thought necessary, for in that way she would get air and exercise. So I broached the subject to the laird, and he is going to think it over. It does seem the very thing for the child, does it not? Robert is hoping the laird means to settle down here. It will be so good for the place and the people."

"I always feel I'm back in the feudal times when I'm over here," said Rowena. "You are all so devoted to your chief. I think I should like to know Miss Falconer. I wonder if she would waive ceremony and come and see me?"

"I am sure she would be delighted to do so. May I tell her?" Mrs. Macintosh continued to give her all the local news, then when she declared she had got to the end of it, she said:

"And now I am going to ask you a favour. We have a little sale of work every year for parish needs. Will you do one of your beautiful rugs for it?"

Rowena pursed up her mouth.

"I never, on principle, do any work for bazaars."

"May I ask what the principle is?"

Rowena laughed.

"You've driven me into a corner—on the principle of selfishness I always refuse—because in town there's a never-ending stream of charity bazaars, and if you work for one, you must work for all."

"And you think if you work for us, you will be worried by other people?"

"I suppose I must say 'yes' to you; but I really was going to stop my rug-making. I'm doing something so much more interesting. I'm writing a book."

"You are writing? How delightful!"

"I'm making a history of Abertarlie and its glen and loch."

Mrs. Macintosh forgot her sale of work and became quite enthusiastic.

"Robert could help you; he has legends and folk-lore at his finger ends. Oh, my dear, may I tell him? He will be so interested and pleased."

"Tell him to give me information about the kirk and all the ministers there. Wasn't there a certain Hamish McGregor who drew his sword in the pulpit, hearing a fray going on outside, shouting, 'My text is, "In the name of the Lord I will destroy them." Brethren, we will carry this precept into practice immediately,' and down the kirk he flew, the whole congregation after him, and the next moment he and they were fighting for all they were worth with the rival clan?"

"Oh, yes, I have heard that story. May I bring Robert in to see you? He may have reference books he could lend you."

"Bring him in, but don't tell Granny. After all it is a minister's business to visit his sick parishioners."

So Robert came in, and he and Rowena talked about Abertarlie with great zest and interest.

Mrs. Macintosh left them together and went out to see Granny in the kitchen. Just before Robert left, his eyes fell on Rowena's little red Bible which was lying on her table. He looked quite pleased and put his hand gently upon it.

"I'm so glad you read this," he said.

"But I don't. I never have. That absurd child Mysie gave it to me for a birthday present. I always consider it so out of date. Isn't it audacity on my part to speak so to a minister?"

The young man shook his head at her with a smile.

"It's the fashion of the world to talk so," he said; "but these are days in which this out of date Book surprises all who study it, by its accurate prophecy. Its truth and inspiration are being proved up to the hilt. Do you know, I put down all the unrest and godlessness of our country to the neglect of the Word of Life, and the Lamp to our feet!"

"Ah, yes; I knew you would speak so; but then it is your profession to place it highly. You see I have studied other religious textbooks. The Koran—the writings of Confucius and of Socrates, and Mrs. Eddy's book of Christian Science. The Bible is only one of many."

"I deny that."

The young minister spoke hotly.

"Those other works may appeal to the intellect, to the head, but the Bible is the only book that reaches the heart, and wins the love of its readers for the Author of it. The books you mention lay down moral laws, but they don't give you the secret for keeping them; they don't bring peace and happiness to an aching restless soul."

"I think Christian Science does," said Rowena slowly.

"Self-hypnotism," said Robert curtly. "Ignoring facts does not efface them. And I have seen the breakdown of their faith stagger and distress poor souls to the extent of making them unbelievers of everybody and everything!"

"You are severe. We won't have an argument. I like you much better when you are talking about fairies' mounds and folk-lore!"

Robert smiled and said no more.

When he and his mother had gone, Rowena put out her hand for her red Book.

"Well, I must make a beginning. I'll read the New Testament through. I don't expect I shall find anything fresh in it. I'll take a chapter a day. Shags, I don't like young ministers. They are so dogmatic. I wonder if the laird will talk in the same strain. I shall test him when he comes next time."

General Macdonald came over to see her the first day she was out again on her couch beneath the shady trees on the lawn. He expressed his regret at her bad cold, and settled down to smoke and talk like an old friend.

"I really think I've fixed up Mysie's education," he said. "A most charming young woman has arrived in these parts, a full-fledged and certificated teacher. She's not obliged to teach, but she loves it, and she's started coming over to give the child lessons every day from nine to one. Have you made her acquaintance yet?"

"No. I've heard about her. She makes a favourable impression upon everybody. I am quite anxious to see her. You do seem lucky. Is she fond of children?"

"I should think so. She's fond of teaching—the two go together. She has great ideas about education. I could hardly follow her, after a certain time. But her heart and soul are in it."

"And how does Mysie like her?"

"I have not asked. She's too critical—that child. She began at once to say she didn't like people who smiled when they said nasty things. I shut her up. Told her that governesses were not to be criticized. That they were to be respected and obeyed. And then what do you think she said?"

"Something to the point, I expect."

"'When I grow up, I shall trample obedience to the ground, and do all the things I'm told not to do now.' What do you think of that for a child of nine?"

"Oh, she means nothing. It's a fit of petulance. I used to talk like that when I was young."

"You are very comforting," he said with a grave smile. "I would like Mysie to grow up like you."

"Oh, never!" cried Rowena. "You don't mean it. I hope she'll do something more with her life than I have with mine. I have never done so much introspecting in all my days as I have since I've been on my back. I've been too busy and one just lives without questioning the whys and wherefores of life. But I'm beginning to see I haven't much to show for my years of life, so far."

"How do you regard life?" asked General Macdonald.

"Not as seriously as you do," said Rowena promptly; then laying her hand on her red Bible, she added, "nor half as seriously as this Book would have us do. I am a frivolous, careless person by nature."

"How are you getting on with the study of it?"

"What? My Bible? Oh, I haven't begun to study it. I am reading it. Well, I haven't answered your question. I think I regard life as a journey in which we are bound to help our fellow-travellers by the way, and keep a cheery heart. That's my creed. At least it was, but now I'm beginning to think I might have contributed towards bettering the bad conditions that exist."

"And the end of the journey?"

Rowena shrugged her shoulders.

"An unknowledgeable finish, I am afraid. You know I don't regard the Bible as you do. It is one of many religious textbooks."

"Yes, that was my belief; but Cuff Mackenzie knocked that on the head. His life was a living vital force—inspired by what he got out of the Bible. And he was one of the best chaps going. I have now proved what he did: that it solves all life's puzzles, and brings one into touch with a glorious new world, and a certain hope, and a mighty Power."

"Anything more?"

General Macdonald turned steady, glowing eyes upon her.

"It makes one acquainted with the Saviour of the World." Rowena was absolutely silent for some moments, then she said:

"I wonder if I shall get out of it what you do?"

"I dare say you will get more."

"You see," she said somewhat wistfully, "it is only since I have had so much time alone that I have begun to think. But I don't feel, even now, that I am dissatisfied or want more than I can get. I mean I don't need the Bible as a prop or guide."

"Perhaps you have never had a flash of light showing you our cause of existence."

"I haven't. I think the only thing I was born for was to be kind to Ted."

General Macdonald was silent. Then Rowena suddenly turned the subject, and told him of her attempt at literature. He was interested at once.

"I'll lend you our clan book. As this is our part of the world, there's a lot of local information in it. I congratulate you on the idea. When one is on one's back, writing is an immense resource. It is even better than reading for taking away from oneself."

"Have you done anything in that way yourself?"

"Yes, I have done a few articles for magazines—chiefly military subjects. I believe I have a book on the lochs of this part. Would you care for it as a reference?"

"I should be charmed. I envy you your library! Being shut up for the greater part of the year, this house does not own many books."

General Macdonald looked at her thoughtfully.

Rowena was always good to look at. Her face was extraordinarily alive with interest and emotion. One of her friends said that her soul seemed to be leaping forth from her body. Now, as she lay back among her cushions, there was a magnificent energy and force in every feature of her face.

She drew a long breath.

"Oh, it's good to be learning new things," she said. "This small attempt of mine has taught me so much of this dear place! By the by, do you know our new young minister? He is very interested in all local history, and has the superstitious soul of the Highlander in spite of his religion."

"I have met him and like him. I lent him an old book of mine the other day, written by one of those early divines, and its quaint phraseology pleased me. I copied a bit out for you. Tell me how you like it?"

General Macdonald produced a notebook out of his pocket and read the following:

"I walk the world now with the World's Creator."

"He opens many doors for me. One door I fain would have open, but He opens it not. I know He will do it on the Great Surprise day, and till then I wait patiently and serenely, being assured verily that were I to have all doors unlocked now, I should lose that goodly champion Hope."

"This one closed door has many crowds about it. Some tamper with the lock and endeavour to spy through the keyhole. They do not endeavour long, but depart with high head and pouting lips; saying that because of their inability to see through to the other side, there remaineth no other side at all."

"And others sit down and weave imaginary conceits about it which they pass on proudly to the unimaginative ones."

"And I, with my hand in the Almighty one, have learned and am
still learning daily how to love the Unseen Presence which leads
and surrounds me."

"I know His keys will be used as He sees fit."

"And one day that last door shall be opened to me."

"Till then I am content to smile and trust and wait."

"I like it," said Rowena emphatically. "It is sound philosophy. I have no patience with those who have cravings for the moon. Nor do I wish just yet to attain all my desires. Hope is a goodly companion. I suppose this experience is yours. You told me a new world had opened out to you and taken possession of you."

"It's my aim to make it mine," General Macdonald said slowly. Then he gave a short laugh. "Meanwhile I think great thoughts, and lose my temper at the least provocation! I nearly swore at the child this morning! Her continual motion gets on my nerves. Thank goodness Miss Falconer will keep her quiet for half every day now. She's an ideal companion when one wants to lounge or laze, but not when one wants to read and attend to business matters. And in the early morning I'm testy and crusty—always have been."

"I do like you when you're human," said Rowena, laughing. "Why is it that absolutely perfect people never appeal to one? I suppose one likes to be surprised. The dead monotony of the virtuous good ..."

He put out his hand as if to stop her.

"Don't!" he said. "There's no chance of monotony with the best people in the world! They ought always to be rising higher."

Rowena gave a little groan.

"I hope you won't try to rise to a higher plane than your present one. You are quite far-away from me as it is."

He shook his head.

"Have you heard of the Hermit of Abertarlie? You ought to bring him into your book."

"No, do tell me."

"He made himself a hut at the bottom of the glen. If you look opposite you'll see a very old oak down by the edge of the loch."

"I know it well. There are not many trees that I do not know. I lie here and look-out at them all day long. Was his hut over there?"

"It is said so. Of course he was a very devout man, and every morning and evening he knelt down at the water's edge and said his prayers. But, the tale goes, the water fairies used to rise up and mock at him, and having been a keen fisherman before he turned hermit, he found the rising trout and salmon too much for his peace of mind. They mixed up too much with his prayers."

"'I have made a mistake,' he said. 'I am too close to the earth, too low down—too far from heaven.' So he moved his hut to the top of the glen, just in the thicket where Miss Falconer's cottage now stands. But the high road over the moor passed too close to him. He was annoyed by the drovers driving their cattle to market. He heard their bad language. 'Too close to wickedness,' he sighed. He finally climbed a very thick beech tree, and up there made another home for himself."

"'The birds will not disturb me,' he assured himself; 'they live too near heaven.'"

"But a storm came one night and, the legend goes, not only swept him out of his tree, but swept him from the top of the glen to the bottom, and when he woke to consciousness, it was to find himself with a broken back lying by the edge of the loch once again."

"'Ah!' he breathed, just as he was dying, 'I am afraid I have been mistaken. Close to the earth I was born; close to the earth I die. Close to the earth I was meant to live. I tried to change my atmosphere too soon. It was before my Maker's time!'"

"What a good moral!" said Rowena delightedly. "I shall certainly put that legend in my book."

Macdonald got up to go. She looked up at him with her laughing eyes.

"'Close to the earth you are meant to live,'" she quoted. "The Frasers consider you a hermit already. And I am glad that you have such an unsaintly little daughter! She will keep you in your right atmosphere."

He smiled gravely as he walked away. And Rowena's eyes softened as she looked after him.

"I hope he won't become too saintly to enjoy a talk with a sinner like myself," she murmured.

CHAPTER VI
MISS FALCONER

"Who gives himself airs of importance exhibiteth the credentials of impotence."
Lavater.

AUGUST came, and gradually the neighbourhood began to grow lively with visitors and tourists. Once or twice Rowena had visits from the Frasers. And then one day Miss Falconer came. Rowena had written to her and asked her to come to tea. Mysie had had a good deal to tell Rowena about her new governess.

"You won't mind anything I say, will you? I beseech you to let me talk anyhow! When I'm with Dad I don't. He says I must respect and obey Miss Falconer."

"So you must, you little imp! But you can tell me anything you like."

"Then can you really like a person you respect and obey?"

"Rather. You can't like people unless you do respect them. You respect your Dad. I hope you respect me.'

"And I hope you respect me," put in Mysie eagerly. "Do you?"

"Yes, I do," Rowena said promptly. "I respect your feelings, and wouldn't hurt them for the world."

"Then," said Mysie with big earnest eyes; "that's just what's the matter with Miss Falconer, she's always hurting me inside. She smiles, and she never loses her temper; but she says things that shows me she's mocking me. And I can bear it all except her laughing at fairies and all the stories Angus tells me. Dad says she's not a true Highlander, but she says she's related to them. And she laughs at Flora—she calls her a misguided, 'motional female; and Prince Charlie, she actually calls him a rascal, and says he lived to be a bad old man!"

"She's not a Jacobite," said Rowena. "Lots of good people didn't like Prince Charlie. They were staunch and loyal to their own king."

She found it rather difficult to comfort Mysie. And when Miss Falconer came to see her, she resolved she would say something to her about her little pupil's romantic tendencies. She found her an extremely pleasant and clever young woman. Her fair golden hair, delicate pointed pale face, and large dark eyes gave her a very refined and youthful look. But her conversation was stimulating and Rowena quite enjoyed her little talk with her on the current topics of the day.

"My friends tell me I am burying myself alive here," said Miss Falconer; "but all through my busiest times I looked forward to a country cottage as a far-away ideal to be realized. And when I came into a little money and had a breakdown I thankfully came off here. My cousin, Lady Grant, told me about it. They will be coming here in September. I suppose you know them?"

"The Grants of Dalghetty? Yes."

"I have wanted to see you so much. I heard that you, like myself, are driven by your health into forced seclusion. Does the quiet really rest you, or does it after a time irritate and bore you?"

"It doesn't irritate me," said Rowena. "But I dare say in my case the contrast is not so marked. I have not been like you, one of the world's workers."

"But during the war surely you did something?"

"Nothing but look after my sister-in-law and her children."

Miss Falconer's face expressed surprise and disapproval.

"I was working at fever heat those four years. I could not give up my teaching. I was at a High School in Hampstead, but in my off hours I did canteen work. And, in addition, I was coaching Ambulance classes. I longed to go abroad. But I could not be spared. That was a real grief to me. When I first came here, I felt exhausted with life; then, after a good bit of rest, I began to long to communicate myself to somebody. Do you know that craving? I have so much that I feel I must give out—share with my fellow-creatures. I tried to befriend the parish schoolmaster. What an antiquated, conservative bit of humanity he is! and so slow in his drawling speech that I have not the patience to listen to him! It was through him that I heard of little Mysie Macdonald. I hope he does not bear me a grudge for taking her away from him, but really, what kind of education do you think he could give her? I dare say he may do very well for the Highland children, but Mysie is too quick and clever to be placed in their groove."

"Then you find her clever?"

"On the surface, very—but she is sadly wanting in stability of thought and in solid perseverance."

"She's rather small for that."

"My dear Miss Arbuthnot, a child's never too small to be trained in good habits."

"She's a fascinating monkey. A very pleasant companion I find her. I love her mystical and romantic beliefs in all our Highland folk-lore. Whatever you do, don't take that from her."

"Oh, all that comes from her being brought up by these Highland servants. If I were not so intensely fond of teaching, I should be rather downhearted sometimes. For, my dear Miss Arbuthnot, it is hard to get some children to learn, but it is a thousand times more difficult to get them to unlearn. And that is the bed-rock with Mysie. I must shatter some of her ignorant prejudices before I can start to build."

"Don't shatter her faith. It's such a precious quality."

"Would you have a clever child believe in witches, and incantation, and barbaric superstitions?"

"Yes, I would," said Rowena with a little laugh, "till they can replace them with other things. A child ought to have strong faith when she is young. You'll turn her into a critical unhuman little prig if you make her sceptical of all the beautiful childish imaginary folk-lore we have here."

"And what about religion?"

"Oh, her father will teach her that. He has enough himself and to spare."

"A growing girl has such an infinite amount to learn," said Miss Falconer; "the growth of her threefold nature demands it. Mysie is past the age for pretty fancies. I want to teach her the worth of her body, soul and spirit. Her body and her soul, or intellect, I feel I am well able to cope with, but as regards her religion I want to have a talk with her father about that. I keep an open mind myself. I have had Roman Catholic pupils, Anglican and Nonconformist. I have had one or two Mohammedan pupils, and my rule is to train them absolutely in their parents' creed and faith."

Rowena felt this delicate young woman was rather astonishing her.

"Can you teach what you do not believe yourself?" she inquired.

"Assuredly. I have always had the power of throwing my whole soul into the subject which I am studying. My head grips it and holds it, though my heart remains untouched."

"Mere mechanical motion," murmured Rowena; "well, machinery accomplishes wonders nowadays. But you cannot inspire them with enthusiasm if you do not feel it yourself."

"Enthusiasm is not good in religion," said Miss Falconer calmly. "It leads to fanaticism, which is unhealthy."

"And are you enthusiastic about nothing?" asked Rowena.

Miss Falconer's eyes glowed.

"Ah, you ask me a great question. I want to train the girlhood of England to know their value. In these times it is more than necessary. Our sex has made great strides in all that they have put their hands to. They are the most valuable asset of the nation. Is there a single position of power or influence which woman is now not competent to fill?"

"The biggest position of power and influence for a woman is the home," said Rowena very quietly.

Miss Falconer looked at her, and once as often before Rowena's eyes misled her.

"You are laughing at me. Thank goodness we have enlarged our borders, and broken the chains of subservient, degrading service under the male."

"And now we'll have tea," said Rowena, turning to welcome Janet with the tea tray. "Whatever the modern woman has learnt, she has not yet broken away from the thrall of the tea-cup."

She refused to be drawn into serious discussion again, but showed her most ridiculous and frivolous side for the rest of Miss Falconer's visit, and when she had gone she said to her dear dog:

"Shags, my dear, you took a good sniff at her, what is your honest opinion of her? I am afraid she is somewhat of a firebrand. I hardly like to think of darling warm-hearted little Mysie being brought into conformance with her will and teaching. I wonder if the laird has any idea of the character of his governess? I would enjoy hearing them have a religious talk together! Well, my dear young woman, you have a strong belief in yourself and your own power. But personally I would like you to fall head over ears in love with a man who would box your ears when you dared contradict him! You are very, very young in your self-assertiveness, and you make me feel very, very old when I am talking to you!"

It was some time before Rowena saw General Macdonald. He went up to London on business and was away ten days. Mysie seemed settling down with her governess, but the day before her father returned, she came flying over to Rowena.

"I am so excited I can't keep still. I do hope Dad won't forget to come home to-morrow. I want to ask you something. It's very solemn and sober—so you're not to laugh, and you're to shut your eyes and listen—just like people do in a long sermon."

"All right. Go ahead."

Rowena was always ready to oblige her little friend. She shut her eyes obediently.

"I am ready," she said, "and my ears are stretched as wide as they can be, quite impatient to hear."

"You know Miss Falconer talks and talks and talks to me, and she thinks it wrong of me to be always wishing I'm a boy. She says girls are the best people that God has made. And she says I must be proud I'm a woman, for women are going to rule the world. I asked her if that meant that they need not obey anybody—and she said yes. Full freedom and liberty was a woman's, now. So I asked her why I need obey grown-up people now—and she said it was necessary—and I asked her how long—and she said I would know when I grew up. So I said that when I was twenty need I obey Dad? And she said when I was twenty-one, I was of age, and could live my own life like a man, and then she asked me what I was going to do, that I ought to make up my mind to earn my own living, and be free of everybody. I rather like that; and I've made up my mind to be a traveller and discover new places. I shall travel in an airship—and just think if I could find my way to one of the stars! And Dad won't be able to say 'No' to me when I'm grown-up."

"I rather think he will," said Rowena gravely. "Of course Miss Falconer hasn't got a Dad to look after and to love; but your Dad will want you with him, I am sure. And by the time you will have lived with him a few more years, you will love him so much that you won't want to leave him."

"Perhaps he would like to come with me in my airship, but I should have to be captain. Miss Falconer says all men are worn out, and women are getting fresher and stronger every day. Dad is rather tired, you know; he says he is worn out. But I shan't be, and when I grow big I shall be stronger than him in every way. Isn't that splendid to think of?"

Rowena felt a blank dismay settle upon her as she listened to the child. She wondered how her father would like this style of teaching. Mysie was full of the superiority of the female sex and could talk of nothing else. It was quite a new idea to her, and she had seized hold of it with the greatest avidity. And Rowena felt it was impossible to contradict her governess's statements, for fear of upsetting her authority.

"Well," she said, "what do you really want to ask me?"

Mysie pursed her lips into a round ball.

"I want you to ask Dad to give me a dear little flying machine for my birthday. I really shan't care for anything else now. Miss Falconer told me girls can fly just as well as men. They can do everything better, she says. And I want to learn as soon and as fast as I can."

"That is a very big ask," said Rowena. "I think Dad would say you must grow up first, and by the time you have grown-up, Flora, the air machine will have grown less dangerous, and more easy to manage in every way."

"Ah, but I don't like easy things, and Miss Falconer says men have always given the easiest softest jobs to women, and they won't take them now."

"But you are not a woman, only a little girl. Look at Shags, he has been thumping his tail on the ground for ever so long to attract your attention. He hates these grave grown-up talks. And so do I. We won't grow up, Flora, just yet. I like to pretend I'm just your age. And I'm going to ask you to come out on the loch with me now. I said I would go this afternoon. And I'm going to pretend we have been shipwrecked, and are on a raft searching for land."

In a moment Mysie's knitted brow had cleared. She clapped her hands joyfully.

"Hurra! And I'll row you—and you'll be dying for water, and we daren't drink the sea all round us. And then I'll be desp'rate and drink a lot and go mad in the boat! Oh, it will be fun! Come on! Shall I call Granny's Colin to take you out?"

Rowena was almost sorry she had proposed such a game, but she trusted to her authority and to Colin's stolid good sense to be able to curb Mysie's high spirits when in the boat.

They had a very enjoyable time on the loch that afternoon. And Rowena had the satisfaction of seeing that for the time the problem of the woman in the world no longer troubled the curly head of her little friend. When Mysie finally left her, she said:

"Oh, I wish Miss Falconer would make up games and play with me; but she goes away directly lessons are over. She thinks everything but lessons is waste of time. I'm glad I only have her half a day!"

A few days later General Macdonald came over.

He looked more cheerful than usual, and began to tell Rowena of some new books he had read in town, and which he thought might interest her. He always took the greatest interest in what she was doing, and rarely mentioned his own affairs till other topics of conversation were finished.

"I suppose Mysie's in the seventh heaven of delight at having you back again?" Rowena said presently.

He smiled.

"I have her in my dressing-room every morning when she is dressed, to read me ten verses out of the Bible. I don't keep her long. She was reading about the centurion and our Lord. We had a talk about 'under authority' and what it means. She had some wild idea in her head that men and women when full grown were not under any authority, that no law need touch them. I fancy I made her understand a little more about that matter than she has ever done yet."

"You think she is getting on with Miss Falconer?"

"Excellently. I had a most interesting talk with Miss Falconer yesterday. It was raining, so she stayed to lunch; and whilst we were having coffee in the library afterwards, she spoke to me about the child's religious training. She seemed to grasp my ideas at once. I should say she was a sincere Christian woman, and I'm thankful to think the child's training is in her hands."

Rowena was dumb.

"She's a most interesting talker," he went on; "she quite held me spellbound. And young though she is, she seems to have had tremendous experience of life. She told me a little of her family history. I'm so glad you know her. She seems a lonely little soul, and has met with little sympathy through her life."

"I have only seen her once. She is a great talker, so I learnt a lot about her different views. She was absolutely frank with me. Very broad-minded, I should say. She has dipped into many creeds."

"Perhaps you did not get into such deep waters as we did. She agreed with my views entirely, and means conscientiously to train the child's spiritual part as well as her intellectual."

Rowena began to feel bored. She turned the conversation into other channels.

"It is none of my business," she assured herself when the visit was over. "And I'm not religious myself. She seems so adaptable that I dare say she will train Mysie in a mechanical way as he wishes her to be trained. He must discover for himself whether she is training her rightly. She is not my child, and I shan't bother my head about her."

But it was one thing to say, another to act, and Rowena's mind was much exercised over Mysie's education. She thought about it day and night.

"Mysie will come to loggerheads with her father sooner or later and then there will be disaster. Miss Falconer is sowing seeds of rebellion against authority in that small mind. I wonder how it will end? Surely the child herself will repeat some of her governess's speeches to her father."

But that was just what Mysie did not seem to do. She threw her small self into the affairs of the moment. When lessons were over, her fishing or boating or riding with her father were of paramount importance; lessons and Miss Falconer were forgotten. Only the enjoyment of the moment remained.

Gradually Rowena became aware that Miss Falconer was impressing the father, as well as the child. Her strong personality could not but be felt in the laird's house. And yet, to the General, she seemed a type of all that was feminine and sweet. One day they all came over to tea with Rowena. Jeannie Falconer was at her very best. Bright and sympathetic, not self-assertive, rather appealing to the General for his opinion upon subjects, and by her interested silence making him believe that she was an appreciative listener. Mysie was unusually quiet. Rowena thought that she seemed a little afraid of her governess. Once, when General Macdonald took Miss Falconer round the garden, Mysie crept very close to Rowena's couch.

"We don't see each other often now," she said wistfully. "Miss Falconer tells Dad I oughtn't to go about the country alone. And if he doesn't come over, I can't. Dad is very nice to go about with, but he doesn't quite understand like you do. Why do you understand so well?"

"Understand what, you whipper-snapper?"

"Oh, how I feel sometimes."

"I remember how I used to feel when I was as little as you," said Rowena rather gravely. "I was a wild bit of a girl myself. But you're a happy child to have such a father."

"I do worship him!" Mysie said fervently. "But I can't talk to him about lessons as I do you. He says I'm a happy child to have such a good governess. But Miss Falconer isn't always good to me."

She held out one small hand to Rowena, palm upwards.

"See that red mark; she hits me with the ruler when I make awful mistakes. And she makes me cry when she laughs at Prince Charlie—she likes me to cry, I know she does."

"Oh, Flora darling, I'm sure she cannot."

"But she does. I don't talk to her now, for I won't be laughed at!"

There was a vindictive tone in her voice that made Rowena draw her close to her. And then Mysie, always so self-controlled, surprised Rowena by beginning to sob.

Clasping her round the neck she cried:

"Oh, get Dad to send me to school. I'd like it better than Miss Falconer. She's too heavy upon me. I feel I can't rise up. I think, do you know, that she stamps upon my soul inside. She always seems to know what I'm thinking, and then she mocks me!"

No more could be said, for Mysie's father returned. She and her governess walked home first, General Macdonald was going on to a farm. When they had gone Rowena suddenly resolved to speak.

"General Macdonald, do you think that Mysie is happy with Miss Falconer?"

"Certainly I do. Do you doubt it?"

"The child seems to have lost her joyous spirits. From Miss Falconer's talk to me, I should think her more fitted for older girls than a child of Mysie's age and sensibilities. She doesn't understand imaginative children. She seems to me, if I may criticize, an admirable machine, capable of managing and controlling girls en masse, but having no love for individuals."

"You astonish me! She seems so very sympathetic. Of course Mysie was let run wild too long. I think she has improved wonderfully with Miss Falconer: much quieter and more tractable."

"Oh, I love originality," said Rowena with a snap in her tone. "I don't like a child modelled according to pattern. Win Mysie's confidence. Let her pour out her soul to you, for I assure you she won't pour it out to Miss Falconer. And it is bad for a child to be secretive and reserved."

"I am very sorry you do not like Miss Falconer," said General Macdonald somewhat stiffly. "I can tell from your tone that you do not. She has my full confidence and regard."

"She only felt strong arms lift her."
My Heart's in the Highlands

She only felt strong arms lift her.

And Rowena threw prudence to the winds.

"I don't trust her. I think she adapts herself to anybody, and does not let you know her real opinions, which are not what you think them to be. I wouldn't let her have the handling of a little niece of mine for all the world!"

"My dear Miss Arbuthnot!" General Macdonald was gazing at her perturbedly. "Don't you think you may be mistaken in your estimate of her? I have had more opportunity than you of judging. You have only seen her once or twice. They say women never understand each other. And yet she speaks so warmly of you. Thinks you are so patient under affliction. She told me she is torn by pity when she looks at you!"

Rowena gave a little snort, then began to laugh.

"I dare say I seem a brute! I will shut up. But I love Mysie, she's a darling, and I hate seeing her spirits broken. Get her to talk to you about her lessons. Ask her what Miss Falconer talks to her about. You know half an hour of her lessons every day consists in a monologue of Miss Falconer upon topical subjects and the present state of the world. Afterwards Mysie has to write out as much as she can remember of it. Get her to show you some of her papers. You will judge then whether Miss Falconer is suitable for a little child of nine. And do forgive my interference, and be friends with me still."

Rowena held out her hand, and spoke in her most winning tone.

General Macdonald took it as he rose to leave her.

"You have given me food for thought," he said; "but I think and hope you are mistaken."

He went, and Rowena turned to Shags.

"Oh, aren't men great simple blundering darlings? How easily they can be taken in! We certainly are their superiors in diplomacy and deceit! Shags, I have become a mischief-maker, and I am not a bit sorry for what I have done!"

CHAPTER VII
COMPELLED TO THINK

"Unlike Philosophy, the Gospel has an ideal Life to offer."
Jowett.

IT was some time before Rowena saw either Mysie or her father again. Mrs. Macintosh came over to see her one afternoon, and began speaking about them.

"I am glad to think that Miss Falconer has been such a success," she said; "and really people begin to think that she may one day change her role from governess to mother. Forgive this gossip. But the laird seems greatly taken with her, and for myself I would like to see him married to some good woman. Every house wants a mistress, especially where there are children. Robert and I went to lunch one day last week; the laird is becoming a bit more sociable, neighbours tell us; but Miss Falconer was there and did the honours of the table very prettily. I wish you and she were a little nearer to one another. I suppose you do not see much of her?"

"No, she is otherwise engaged," said Rowena.

"She and Robert found plenty to say. Robert loves an argument, and he does not see eye to eye with her on woman suffrage. The laird seemed quite surprised to hear her views, but I thought it was quite touching the apologetic way in which she kept turning to him."

"'I know this will shock you,' she kept saying, 'but these are the views I was taught at college.'"

"'Then Mysie shall never go to college,' said the laird, in that stern tone of his. And Miss Falconer smiled up at him."

"'Ah well,' she said, 'as we grow older we see the error of our ways. I am not so keen as I was on these questions. The war has altered many things.' I was glad to hear her speak so. And the laird seemed to watch every word and movement of hers. I should like to hear that they are engaged."

"You are a regular matchmaker," laughed Rowena. "I do not think General Macdonald a marrying man. He told me once that matrimony was always a risk, and a little of it went a long way."

"A very unchivalrous speech to make to a lady," said Mrs. Macintosh in a tone of disapproval.

Rowena laughed gaily.

"He is not a man who makes pretty speeches," she said. When her visitor went, she subsided into grave thought. Shags tried to attract her attention, and failed. At last she roused herself.

"My dear young woman," she apostrophized herself; "at your time of life, you ought to expect anything and everything. They say any woman can marry a man if she sets her heart and will upon it. And if it will mean giving up some of her misguided but cherished principles it will be a very good thing for the fair falcon! As long as her talons are clipped and she is not allowed to hurt my little Mysie, I don't care. Men must take care of themselves. But Hugh Macdonald is just the man to blunder into another unsatisfactory marriage!"

She said these words aloud, but her eyes had lost their sparkle, and when Granny came to help her into the house she said:

"You look tired out, mem. Are you feeling your back again?"

"I am feeling rotten," said Rowena with a short laugh; "but don't for pity's sake take any notice of me. Life is a very crooked stick, and it's quite impossible to bend it the way one wants to. So the only thing is to smile at it, and adjust oneself to the crookedness."

A few days afterwards, Rowena went out in her punt. It was a still grey day, rather sultry and oppressive, and she longed to feel the coolness of the water round her Colin took her out a good way upon the loch, and for a wonder a boat came up to him with Angus in it, and a stranger. Rowena guessed at once it must be the man to whom her brother had let the fishing and shooting. Her first instinct was to let them pass her without a word or sign of recognition; but Angus prevented that.

"An' hoo are ye this day, mem?" he said, pulling in his oars and beaming upon her with his fatherly smile. "'Tis Mr. Crawford I will be takin' to Abertarlie."

Rowena acknowledged the introduction by a bow.

"You have taken my brother's shooting," she said in her clear pleasant voice. "I hope you are enjoying it. You must excuse my getting up. I am quite an invalid at present. I heard the guns going yesterday. Did you have good sport?"

"Splendid!" was the quick enthusiastic reply. "I had thought of calling upon you, Miss Arbuthnot, as I hear you have a wonderful book on the deer forests about here, and I wondered if I might ask for the loan of it. Did we not meet some years ago at Cowes?"

"Yes, at the regatta," said Rowena. "I thought I had seen you before. You were with the Radcliffe-Murrays. Of course you may have the book; I will send it over to you. Are you staying at 'The Antlers' in Abertarlie?"

"Yes, they do one first-rate! I have two cousins with me and a nephew. Don't trouble to send. I am often past your way, and I will call in for it, if I may."

"I will look it out and have it ready for you."

"May I say how sorry I am for your accident? It was out hunting, was it not? I heard about it."

"Yes, it's rotten luck, but thank goodness I'm only temporarily laid up. I have to be a year on my back. I mustn't keep you. Good-bye."

"There be a storm on the way," said Angus a little anxiously; "you'd best get back, mem."

"All right, Angus. We can't afford to run risks with this craft." She laughed as she spoke. Angus plied his oars in one direction, and Colin in another, but before they came to the shore the storm burst upon them. Rowena watched the waves lash round her with serenity, but Colin got agitated, and seemed to lose his nerve.

"Och, mem, whatever will happen?" he ejaculated.

"I feel like a trussed pig!" said Rowena. "But if you really can't manage, I can, at a pinch, sit up and take an oar. I must! I don't want to be drowned."

She had hardly said the words before a hurricane of wind swept down upon them, and the next moment the punt was engulfed in the waves, and Rowena and Colin were in the water. With wonderful presence of mind Rowena threw out her arms and floated on her back. Colin, completely losing his head, made for the punt instead of for Rowena.

But help was at hand! A boat shot out from the Arbuthnot's landing-stage and pulled rapidly towards them. In a very few minutes Rowena was rescued. She was hardly conscious as to how she got into the boat, for the waves had washed over her more than once, and she was in a very exhausted state. She only felt strong arms lift her, and a voice she seemed to know said:

"Thank God I'm in time!"

The next thing that she knew was finding herself in her own bed, and Granny bending over her.

"Eh, mem, the Lord be praised! Ye are safe an' soun'! An' noo it's just this wee drappie o' whusky ye'll be takin'."

Rowena meekly obeyed, then looked up with her irresistible smile.

"Oh, Granny, I'm not dead yet! I shall live to continue to plague you, but it was a near shave. Who came out to us?"

"Why, sure it was the laird! Him an' me saw ye caught, and never shall I forget the sight of your boat in the ragin' wind and waves! The laird, he set his teeth and wi'out a wor-r-rd tore at the boat an' was after ye! An' when he put ye oot o' his ar-rms, he said, 'Mrs. Mactavish, she must live—there are not mony like her.' He helped me get ye to bed an' rubbed and chafed ye, an' noo he's awa' to get the doctor—an is pretty well soaked to his skin. That Colin be a puir creater! Niver will ye be gain' oot wi' him agen, mem—niver! He cam' back wi' his heid fair mazed—an' all he cud cry was, 'Wae's me—the young leddy be drowned and 'twill be I which have doon it!'"

Rowena smiled but could not speak.

Presently she made the effort.

"The laird must have his clothes dried. See to him, Granny!"

"Deid an' I will, if so be he gives me a chance!"

It was not very long before the doctor arrived, but Rowena hearing that General Macdonald had returned with him, sent him out a message of thanks and begged him to let Granny attend to him. Then she saw the doctor.

"Don't examine my poor back to-night. I don't believe I am any the worse. The salt water may have strengthened it. I did not strain it in any way."

And it was marvellous that she was not seriously the worse for her accident. She kept to her bed for three or four days, then was moved out to her couch, but the doctor forbade any more loch expeditions.

"The weather is too treacherous, be content to lie by the side of it; the open-air is good for you, but don't attempt the punt again."

"Oh," groaned Rowena, "instead of widening my borders, I have to narrow them!"

She felt very low and depressed for a day, then recovered her spirits. General Macdonald, coming to inquire for her, found her outside on the terrace, looking rather white, but with her usual bright smile.

"Well," he said, "I thought it was all up with you the other day, and now I hear you are none the worse for your spill."

"Not a bit worse," said Rowena, "but I have been thinking rather hard. What a bit of luck you came this way! I don't believe Colin would have ever towed me to shore. He's a good swimmer, but his one idea was to get hold of the punt and then come for me. And I don't think I should have lasted out long enough."

"I don't believe in luck," said the General gravely. "I had no intention of coming over to see you that afternoon. I was reading in my study and I came across a bit that I liked in one of my old books, and suddenly thought I would like to share it with you. But when I got out into the hall Mysie begged me to take her upon the moors. I very nearly did; but a strong persistent sense of wanting to get to you made me send her away disconsolate, and I came off post haste. I had only just arrived when the squall came on, and we saw your punt capsize from the terrace here. Don't you think I was sent to you?"

"By whom? By my guardian angel, I suppose, if I have one. If you had not come and I had gone down, I wonder where I should be to-day?"

There was a silence, then Rowena looked straight at him with shining eyes.

"Well, honestly, I didn't feel quite ready to leave this world. I thought it out as I floated on the water, and I think I prayed the first fervent prayer in my life. I wanted to be spared. I wanted it desperately. I suppose the love of life is hard to kill, because I am leading a very useless existence at present, and there's no particular reason for me to be spared, when so many others are taken."

"Your prayer was answered."

"Yes, and I am digging into my Bible furiously; I have read it for an hour at a time. I want to discover the secret that the early Christians had, and which enabled them to go through fire and water unmoved. The Epistles are interesting me. I told you what a heathen I was, didn't I? What a high ideal we are supposed to have of our purpose in this world. It staggers me; I don't like feeling small, but there's no doubt the Bible does that."

"Infinitesimally small," said General Macdonald. "But you've read the paradox: 'When I am weak then I am strong.'"

"I don't understand half I read."

She looked at him with a mixture of shame and amusement.

"I wish you would preach me a dear little sermon, General Macdonald. I know you could do it quite as well as our young minister. I never get to church."

"No; I could never preach," said General Macdonald seriously; "but I think I can tell you the secret of the early Christians' faith and endurance. They 'endured as seeing Him Who is invisible,' we are told. Our Master's last words were: 'Lo, I am with you alway, even unto the end of the world.'"

"I think," said Rowena very slowly with downcast eyes, "the result of my Bible study is that I want to have Him with me."

General Macdonald looked at her with a sudden brightness in his eyes. He murmured to himself, but just loud enough for her to hear: "'But one thing is needful—she hath chosen that good part which shall not be taken away from her.'"

There was silence again.

Suddenly Rowena brushed her hand lightly across her eyes, but not before the General had seen some glittering drops on the ends of her long lashes.

"And now we'll leave this uninteresting subject of myself," she said abruptly. "Tell me about Mysie."

"What shall I tell you? She is making good progress with her lessons, I hope. Do you remember your words about Miss Falconer? I am thankful to find that you are mistaken in your estimate of her. She has a very high ideal of woman's position in the world, and is trying to train Mysie accordingly. I want her to grow up an honourable, pure, and devout woman, and I believe Miss Falconer will be influential in making her this. I gathered that you did not care about Miss Falconer, but if you would have a serious and confidential talk with her about the deep things of life, you would find her a real help to you, I am sure. She is going away for a fortnight or three weeks to her relations, the Grants. When she comes back I hope you will try to see something of her."

Rowena looked at him now with a mocking light in her eyes. Her soft serious mood was over.

"Miss Falconer and I are antipathetic," she said. "If she and I were on a desert island, I would live on the farthest edge of the island away from her. But I am glad you are pleased with her. Only if she spoils my dear Mysie, I shall never forgive her, nor you for not discovering it."

"I wish you would explain yourself."

"I hardly ever see Mysie now," said Rowena irrelevantly. "Will you, as it is holiday time, let her come over and spend a day with me?"

"She will be delighted. I will send her to-morrow, for I have to go down to Glasgow on business, and it may keep me away a night."

"Then let her sleep here. Granny will look after her, and of course you may trust me not to say a word of criticism on the subject of her governess."

So it was settled. Just before he took his leave, as he was shaking hands with her, he said:

"We could ill have spared you." Then he added with a whimsical smile: "It's odd at my time of life to be blessed with two women friends like yourself and Miss Falconer. Since my poor wife's death I have kept away from women, but having a girl child to bring up does make me value the advice and counsel of your sex."

"Please don't apologize for knowing me," said Rowena gaily. "I value your friendship whether for the sake of the child or not."

And when he was gone she caught up Shags and laughed till she shook.

"You dear, ridiculous man! I hope we shan't turn you into an old woman between us. You look quite careworn when you talk about your child! I think I shall advise some shooting and golf for a change."

Mysie appeared the next day in high spirits at the thought of a day and a night away from home.

"You haven't forgotten me?" Rowena asked, as the little arms went round her neck and hugged her.

"I couldn't never forget you. You're my best friend, but Miss Falconer simply won't let me come and see you. She throws excuses in the way, and she told me I bored you, and that it wasn't fair to worry you so. Do I bore you? Do I worry you? Now I know I don't. Your eyes tell me I don't! I don't like Miss Falconer's eyes—they never laugh, only look round the corner at you. But she's gone away, and I'm pretending that she's not in the world at all, and never coming back."

"We won't mention her. And now, little Flora, how shall we map out the day? I'm unfortunately forbidden to go on the loch again, isn't that a trial?"

"Oh, it's ripping anyhow with you! I love to talk and play with Shags. And there will be the meals. I love meals away from home, they're so lovely. And oh! I do love and adore you when you call me Flora!"

Another hug followed, then in more sober tones Mysie said:

"Dad came back and told me how nearly drownded you were! I told him if you went dead, I would never smile again. I couldn't! My heart would be broken right in two. And when your eyes twinkle and smile at me as they are doing now, it gives me a lump of joy in my chest. Do you know the feeling?"

"I know you're a darling little bundle of emotion and Highland sensitiveness!" said Rowena. "And as I'm very much alive, we won't talk of that disaster of mine any more. Tell me all you've been doing since we last met."

Mysie began at once.

"We won't talk of the lessons—or of Miss Falconer. I'm rather afraid of her, you know; Angus says she's wanting in soul. What does that mean? She says Angus is an ignorant fool. I'll tell you about the other day. I got in a scrape—it was the day Miss Falconer left. I went riding up the moor with Angus and then I got away from him—and then I saw far-away two darling deer—and I tied my pony up and I crept up to them like Angus does—only he calls it stalking. And I didn't know there were other people creeping about, until I saw a man with a gun. And then I knew he meant to shoot them, and my blood boiled up, and I clapped my hands and screamed, and the deer scampered away, but the man came out of the bushes with his gillie, and they both swore at me. They were frightfully angry, and the man said if I didn't make tracks for home he'd lay a stick across my back. And fancy, he called me a boy! I stood still and just told him who I was. It made him rather surprised. I told Dad about it, and he said it was a wicked thing of me to do, but I said it was wicked to shoot the poor deer—I love them all. I had a little tame deer once before its horns grew."

So Mysie chatted on, and Rowena lay and listened. Then she read her some of her legends and folk-lore which she was collecting for her book. Once started on that subject, Mysie's tongue went faster than ever. The day was a complete success. But when Mysie was on her way to bed, she said:

"I wish—I wish you were my governess! Don't you think you could be, when you get up from your back and walk again? I am sure you know quite as much as Miss Falconer does, and a good deal more. Don't be angry, like Dad, if I tell you quite privately, that I hate and detest and abhor her! I went down to the tom na hurisch and besought the fairies to come and take her one night. There's a little rowan tree outside her window, and I'm afraid that keeps her safe. Angus won't hear of it being cut down, as he says it will bring us bad luck—I want bad luck to be brought to Miss Falconer!"

"Oh, hush! Now I really am shocked, and must protest!" said Rowena. "Never wish ill-luck to come to anyone, even to your worst foe. It isn't generous or right. And this is holiday time: we are not going to think about lessons or about Miss Falconer."

Mysie shook her curls a little defiantly.

"Dad doesn't know what I know, or else he wouldn't like her so much."

"Good night, little Flora; pleasant dreams!"

And Mysie said no more, but went obediently to bed.

CHAPTER VIII
THE LAIRD'S AWAKENING

"Yet to be loved makes not to love again;
Not at my years, however it hold in youth."
Tennyson.

MYSIE stayed with Rowena till the afternoon of the following day, and very unwillingly departed. She had hardly gone before another visitor was announced, and this was Mr. Crawford whom Rowena had met on the loch with Angus. He was full of her accident, and told her they had hardly got to the shore themselves before the storm burst upon them.

"Upon my honour, I'd half a mind to row back and look for your remains," he said. "We felt convinced you would be upset, and then we saw a small boat go to your rescue. Donald was beside himself till he heard you were none the worse for your immersion. It was risky being upon the loch a day like that."

"Yes, that pleasure is over," said Rowena regretfully. "I shall no longer be able to enjoy my punt, for it is now a forbidden pastime. If General Macdonald had not happened to be at hand, it would have been all up with me."

"Oh, he's the laird of Abertarlie, isn't he? I was dining at the Grants' yesterday evening, and he was under discussion. A Miss Falconer amused us very much. It seems she is teaching a small girl of his—more as a pastime than anything else. She's one of these modern women—you should have heard her take him off! He has those old-fashioned mid-Victorian ideas of women, and wants his small daughter patterned after their style. Miss Falconer is the wrong sort of person to do that. She's an awfully good sort. Have you met her?"

"Yes," said Rowena; "but I have not seen much of her."

"How do you get through your time? You must be bored stiff, aren't you?"

"No," said Rowena, smiling at him. "I lie here and watch the eternal patience of the hills, and get a little of the spirit of Nature to solace me. Look over the loch now, did you ever see such a play of light and shade? I have a never-ending panorama passing before my eyes. I am Highland to my heart's core. You don't know the magic of our lochs and glens. In your eyes they are only places where you can fish and shoot; to us they are something more."

"I believe that," said Mr. Crawford sincerely. "There's a look in the eyes of the Highland folk that is peculiar to their part of the country. They gaze at their burns and their braes—like a lad gazes at his first love!"

Rowena nodded. "And then there's such history behind them all. You see our moors lying peacefully under the summer sunshine; we see them alive, and bristling with conflicts and battles—the glens trodden by refugees fleeing from death, the caves sheltering heroes, the lochs full of legends and romance. We feel the atmosphere of the past impregnating that of the present, and we love every blade of grass that grows! To you the moors hold deer and grouse; beyond that you do not go!"

"We are just matter-of-fact butchers!" said Mr. Crawford with a laugh. "Now will you, in spite of my inferiority to a Highlander, bestow upon me that book on your deer forests? You promised me the loan of it."

"It is here waiting for you," said Rowena, putting out her hand upon a small parcel which lay on her book table by her side, "but I should say you get little time for reading now."

"That's a fact—but I like a smoke and read after dinner."

They chatted away in very friendly fashion, and when Mr. Crawford departed he determined he would come again very soon, for all men liked Rowena, and not even her invalidism could make her uninteresting to them.

General Macdonald made his appearance very soon again.

"I am being drawn into society now against my will," he said; "the Grants insist upon my going to dine with them next week. Lady Grant met me out to-day and won't take a refusal. She and Miss Falconer came in and had some tea. I don't often entertain visitors, but they are an exception. My small girl did not show up. She seems to disapprove of Miss Falconer visiting her in the holidays, and though I sent her a message to make her appearance, I saw her flying across the lawn, and she has not come back when I left. I must punish her for disobedience. I am not going to have my orders set aside. But punishments are not in my line. Give me advice."

"Oh, don't ask me," said Rowena; "you will think me too indulgent. I should give Mysie a good scolding and tell her whether she liked a thing or not, do it she must, if you wish her to. A talk is sometimes more efficacious than a punishment. Children are reasonable creatures. When I was small, punishments were too common! We hardly took any notice of them—Ted and I!"

"Yes," said General Macdonald slowly; "but I find she often worsts me in a talk. She is apt to be argumentative, and then I lose my temper. I've a hot one, as I dare say you know; and I'm not accustomed to deal with children."

"I want to read you a lovely legend about your house," said Rowena, trying to turn the subject. "I got it out of a book Mr. Macintosh gave me."

The General's brow cleared. He and Rowena were soon absorbed in their local history. It was about six o'clock, and a slight mist was sweeping down from the moor. Rowena was in her green room, as the air was damp and cold. Suddenly they heard a pony gallop along the drive outside, and the next moment Mysie dashed open the door in a state of wild excitement: She looked greatly taken aback at the sight of her father, but in her impulsive fashion threw herself upon Rowena.

"I've come to you to tell you! I had to! I won't believe it, and you must stop it, my darling prisoner, oh, you'll know how to!"

"What is the matter?" asked Rowena, laughing, yet regarding the child with some sympathy. "Have you heard any more guns shooting your beloved stags?"

"Oh, it's a hundred times worse!"

"I wonder where you have been, since I summoned you to tea?" said General Macdonald rather severely.

Mysie stood up, twisting her small hands together in agony. "I knewed you would be angry," she said; "but I just felt I couldn't be smiling at Miss Falconer. I was tired out of her. And she always says she hates grown-ups and children mixed together. Oh, Dad, don't be angry but if it's true, I shall run away from you. I shall go back to Nan, and if she won't have me, I shall hunt for a water kelpie and let him drown me, or I shall go round and round the fairies' hill till they take me in."

"Tell us what the trouble is."

Rowena had drawn the hot excited child to her, and was holding one of her little hands in hers. Then Mysie burst into a passion of tears.

"Dad is going to marry Miss Falconer. They all say so. She's coming to live with us for ever! And—b-b-b-be my stepmother! Oh, stop it, stop it, won't you? Miss Falconer says women can always manage men; do try to manage Dad and make him not do it. I can't live in the house with Miss Falconer for my stepmother. I told you how I hate her! I do! I do! She tries to make me cry, so that she can laugh at me."

Rowena looked across at General Macdonald rather helplessly. But if Mysie was excited, he became more so. Rising impatiently from his chair, with a warm flush in his thin brown cheeks and blazing eyes, he thundered forth:

"Stop this foolish nonsense at once, child! Who has been putting such a preposterous idea into your head?"

"They've all been saying it. Mrs. Dalziel and Angus, and even Nan; and Miss Falconer is always saying what she would do if she was mistress! I can't bear to think of it!"

"How did you come here?" he asked hotly.

"On the pony. Dad, don't be angry with me. I'm sorry I disobeyed you. It was Elsie who was doing my hair; she said of course I was to go down and see my new mamma, and I wouldn't believe her, and then I went to Mrs. Dalziel in the kitchen, and she said that folks were saying so, and I rushed away to Nan and Angus, and they've been saying it too; and then I went away into the woods and I was miser-rubble; and then I thought I'd come to my darling prisoner, and she might prevent you doing it!"

"Now look here! You go straight back on your pony and tell Mrs. Dalziel that if I hear she is circulating such mischievous gossip and lies, she will leave my service at once. I have no intention of marrying. And then go off to Angus and tell him and his wife the same. Off with you at once!"

A thunder-cloud was on his brow, but Mysie stopped sobbing, and then she flung herself on her father and wound her small arms round him.

"I'll be good, I'll be good—if you never give me a mother! Oh, I'm so very, very glad you aren't going to marry her."

Her father turned sharply away from her.

When she had disappeared, he paced the room in angry silence. Rowena waited. Like Mysie, the relief of realizing her fears were groundless, brought strange content to her soul. At last she spoke.

"Well, we seem to have had a storm over nothing."

"It's not a trivial matter to me," said the General sharply. "It's unspeakably annoying. I, who have kept away from women ever since my poor wife's death until I came here, and to find that I can't be friendly with my child's governess without this confounded gossip starting! It's outrageous! Marry a girl like that! A girl who is young enough to be my daughter!"

"Perhaps you praised her to others as much as you did to me," said Rowena demurely. "You should be more cautious. I am sorry for the annoyance it has caused you, but no harm has been done. Mysie will forget it."

"I shall send the child to school and shut up the house."

"And run away? Don't do that! Ignore such gossip—but I do advise you to change your governess."

"I shall never have another. I am more annoyed than I can say. I have a great mind to send Mrs. Dalziel straight away. She ought to be thoroughly ashamed of herself. An elderly respectable woman like her, to chatter of me and my governess to my child! It's abominable—iniquitous!"

Rowena waited till he had calmed down.

Presently he turned to her with a rueful face.

"And now you see how I lose my temper! What am I to do? Am I not to show any kindly feeling for any woman that comes across my path without having it said that I mean to marry her?"

Rowena began to laugh. She could not help it.

"I beg your pardon. I know it is no laughing matter to you; I do sometimes realize that men are the sheep, and women the wolves. And it is rather awkward being asked to counsel you. Because you know that I have an aversion to Miss Falconer, so that my views must be prejudiced. Of course, my advice is to decline any further educational help from her. She does not consider herself your governess, but a friend who loves teaching so much that she is taking Mysie in hand out of sheer kindness of heart. I hope you will dine with the Grants next week; then you will see Miss Falconer from another point of view."

"Lady Grant told me I ought to be very grateful to her," General Macdonald said more quietly. "I suppose I have acted like a fool. However, no more governesses for me; Mysie shall go to a boarding school at once."

Then he stopped in his restless pacing up and down the room. Looking at Rowena with a fierce frown he said:

"May I ask if you have heard these ridiculous reports? It would have been only kind if you had warned me."

"Oh, nobody likes to repeat gossip. I am not a mischief-maker," said Rowena a little impatiently. "I did hear something after Miss Falconer had presided over a luncheon-party at your house; but people always like to make up matches. Romance appeals to all of us. Take it lightly."

"No one can say I have said or done anything to warrant such talk," the General said huffily. "Well, I shan't be good company for you to-day, so I had better go. I'll shut up the house and go abroad. Why, the next thing will be that they will gossip over my coming to see you!"

"Oh, I think I am safe, as an invalid," said Rowena, looking at him with her laughing eyes.

General Macdonald met her glance, and smiled in spite of himself. Then he held out his hand.

"Good-bye for the present."

"And don't go and pack up and flee from gossip," said Rowena; "for you get that everywhere. It's best to have a thick skin and ignore it. My love to Mysie, and don't vent your anger upon her."

"You do think me a brute!"

"No, only a helpless man."

Rowena was left with the last word. Shags immediately received her confidence when the General was gone.

"The fair falcon is beaten, Shags! And I'm enough of a heathen still to rejoice in her discomfiture. I hate humbug and insincerity. Thank goodness Mysie will escape out of her clutches. What a storm in a tea-cup! But I shall miss his visits if he goes. He wants a wife to laugh at him and rub off his angles—to give him a little petting, and make him realize that he is a very human man, and not a cast-iron statue to be worshipped, but never to be approached at close quarters! I wish he had a little more humour! I wonder if he would be boring if one lived with him!"

She was rather surprised in two days' time to get a letter from General Macdonald, the first that she had ever received.

"DEAR MISS ARBUTHNOT,—"

"I thought you would like to know how things are going with us. I quite accidentally met Miss Falconer out the other day. She had called at the house for a book of hers, and we met as she was returning to the Grants. I suppose I ought to be glad the matter has been taken out of my hands. She began to talk about Mysie at once, then said that her people wanted her to give up teaching—that Lady Grant did not like her living alone, and was trying to persuade her to leave the cottage and come and stay with them for a long visit. I told her I quite agreed with Lady Grant, and that I could easily make other plans for Mysie. It seemed so easy—the whole thing—that I was surprised when she seemed so disconcerted; said she was afraid I was not satisfied with her. I told her I thought she had done wonders with Mysie, and so she has in the way of teaching her manners and self-control. We parted friends, I hope. I told her I should be sending Mysie to school."

"Mysie herself is a radiant piece of goods at present. I suppose she looks forward to a long holiday, but she does not seem to have liked Miss Falconer. I cannot fathom the reason of her dislike. I am having an old pal of mine to stay for a fortnight's shooting. May I bring him over to see you one day?"

"Yours,"
"HUGH MACDONALD."

A few days after this Rowena was rather surprised to get a visit from Miss Falconer. She arrived in the Grants' car.

"I took the opportunity of coming to see you," Miss Falconer explained, "as Lady Grant wanted to call upon the Macintoshes at Abertarlie. It will be a good-bye visit. I am leaving this part. I only meant to stay in my cottage for the summer, and of course I never meant to take up my job of teaching beyond that time, though the dear general seemed to think that I was a fixture here. I flatter myself that even in these couple of months I have made an impression upon his wild little tomboy. She has brains. It is a pity they are not going to be developed in the right way."

"You don't think that school will develop them?"

"Not a private school—but don't let us talk of education. I am off it. Do you know Mr. Crawford? He has taken your brother's shooting. We have seen a great deal of each other lately. He is always at the Grants'. I don't know why I tell you this, but you're a sympathetic person. Yesterday we came to the conclusion that we liked each other, and I am engaged."

"My congratulations," said Rowena warmly. "I always felt that marriage was more your vocation than teaching. I know him, and should think he's a very good sort."

"Why do you think marriage my vocation?"

"Because you were so bent on persuading me that you were superior to its attractions," said Rowena, laughing, "and those sort of natures are the first to succumb."

Miss Falconer did not look very pleased.

"We are agreed on the equalities of the sexes," she said. "He is not narrow and old-fashioned and prejudiced, like that dear friend of yours, Mysie's father. Of all dull, commonplace, uninteresting men, he takes the cake, as they say! I'm thankful to have severed all connection with him."

"He is simple-minded," said Rowena quietly, "and easily taken in. He does not understand diplomacy."

The glance that Jeannie Falconer flashed towards her was not friendly.

"Oh," she said, "how I pity you! This Highland life would kill me. I have had only a few months of it, but it has sapped all the energy out of me already. I have told Herbert that London must be our permanent home, and he quite agrees. I am thankful that he is English to the core."

She did not stay much longer. Rowena was amused by her visit, but her heart felt as light as a feather. Never till now had she realized how thoroughly she had believed in the gossip of the neighbourhood.

CHAPTER IX
DEPARTURE

"But none shall more regretful leave
These waters and these hills than I,
Or distant fonder dream how eve
Or dawn is painting wave and sky."
Whittier.

NOTHING would deter General Macdonald from placing Mysie at school. He came over to Rowena with a most cheerful face, and introduced his friend, a Colonel Cavanagh, to her. He was an Irishman, and Rowena could see at once that his cheery personality had already done the laird good.

"Cavanagh knows of a first-rate school in Edinburgh, where his own daughters are, and I have written to the lady, and she says she can take Mysie at once. The term will be just beginning."

"Then it is all arranged?" queried Rowena. "I hope you have asked her to be lenient to the poor little wild bird when first she is caged?"

"Oh," said Colonel Cavanagh, with a hearty laugh; "Miss Gordon has had experience with wild birds. My girls were as wild as hawks when first she took them; but she has a way with her, and they're quite devoted to her now."

"That sounds nice! Mysie can be led easier than driven."

"Miss Arbuthnot has seen me do the heavy father so often that she speaks from experience," said the General.

"No," said Rowena, "you have got Mysie's affection. Nothing matters when that is won."

Then General Macdonald told her he was going over to Ireland with his friend for a visit.

"And we'll send him back ten years younger," said the cheery Colonel. "He wants to laugh more and think less. We're not given to deep thinking in Ireland."

They did not stay long. As they walked away from the house, Colonel Cavanagh said:

"I'd soon lose my heart to that woman. Why, hasn't she bucked you up, old chap? The very look of her does one good. It's amazing how a woman on her back can get so much fun out of life."

"I'm very fond of Miss Arbuthnot," said General Macdonald, in his simple way. "We have been good chums since I came back, and my small daughter adores her."

Colonel Cavanagh looked at his friend with a spark of amusement in his eye.

"Ah, well, she's not dangerous, down on her back. If she were up and about, it would be a different matter."

General Macdonald said nothing. He would not be drawn. Mysie came over to wish Rowena good-bye; and there were some tears shed.

"Of course, I'm not a baby," she said valiantly; "and Dad says I shall be home for Christmas, and he'll be here too, but I feel as if I'm going to be a prisoner now. And if it gets beyond bearing, I shall run away. I know I shall, and then what will happen?"

"You will be caught and sent back again. I wouldn't do that if I were you. Only cowards run away from disagreeables. A Flora Macdonald never would!"

Mysie tossed her curls back and snorted like a thoroughbred horse.

"Of course I couldn't be a coward. Didn't you say Flora Macdonald went to school in Edinburgh?"

"Yes, I believe so, but I don't know where."

"How wonderful if it was my school she went to!" Rowena laughed.

"I imagine it was," she said.

And Mysie's wonderful eyes grew dreamy and soft, as she thought of her heroine.

She went off fairly happy; but Rowena felt, when both father and child had gone, as if she were bereft of all her friends. If it had not been for Mrs. Macintosh and her son, these autumn months would have been very lonely. The lodges and shooting boxes were soon vacated, and the country round became deserted; wet and storms set in. But Rowena's spirits were never down for long. She was deep in her Highland book, and her bright wood fire and cosy comfort all round her prevented her from feeling the inclemency of the weather. She wrote continually to her brother, and her Indian letters were the delight of her heart. Occasionally the young doctor arrived over to see her. Shags was her constant companion, and Granny was always ready to come in for a "crack."

Snow fell towards the end of November, and Rowena lay looking out at the fairy-like scene with keen enjoyment.

Mrs. Macintosh paid her a visit before it went. She arrived over in a sledge.

"You brave intrepid woman," said Rowena, when she saw her. "How can you venture out in such weather?"

"I am very hardy. It is a real treat to have a talk with you, so don't pity me. I only wish we were nearer you. It is an unnatural life for you to live. You are so young to be so much alone."

"But I feel very matured and old," said Rowena, "especially since my dear Mysie has left me. A child keeps one young."

"Do you have good accounts of her?"

"We write to each other once a fortnight; I believe she is getting on, but a child never expresses her feelings as we should."

"Her father has shut up his house for the winter?"

"I fancy he will come back for Mysie's holidays."

"I was so thankful that my match did not come off! I heard several things afterwards about Miss Falconer that surprised me very much. But I am sure she was in love with him."

Rowena laughed; and Mrs. Macintosh said hurriedly:

"I know you think me an old gossip! But in the wilds here we can't help taking an interest in our neighbours. And I would like to see the laird married again; he is not an old man, and he wants some one to brighten him up, and make him younger!"

"I think he's having a good time over in Ireland," said Rowena. "Perhaps he'll bring back an Irish bride. He is in a house full of young people. Colonel Cavanagh has an old-fashioned family, five daughters and three boys, and three of his daughters have finished schooling and are at home."

"I wish I had a daughter," said Mrs. Macintosh somewhat wistfully. "Robert is a good son to me, but his heart and soul are with his parishioners and his books; and I'm human enough to want a little, idle, frivolous talk sometimes. I have not the 'stability' of the Scotch nature."

"Don't try to get it," said Rowena. "You and I must leaven these Scotch folk with a little seasonable froth."

"Don't think I don't admire goodness," said Mrs. Macintosh hastily. "I do from the bottom of my heart. But a good person need not be dull."

"No," said Rowena, in a more thoughtful tone; then she said abruptly: "I am having fresh aspirations this winter. I wonder if you will see any difference in me by the time the spring is here. I am very slowly going through a transformation. My outlook on life is altering, I am seeing everything from a different standpoint. Pardon my egotism, but tell me, what is your experience? Is life here an enigma to you, or have you the key to it?"

Mrs. Macintosh's whole face softened at once.

"I think I found the key long ago," she said. "Nothing is a puzzle, nothing is a mystery, if you have enough love and trust."

"Ah," said Rowena, with a long-drawn breath, "and that is what I am slowly discovering."

Mrs. Macintosh laid her hand very gently on the little red leather book that was never very far-away from Rowena's couch.

"You are learning out of this," she said.

Rowena nodded brightly.

"It is a new book to me. I have never really studied it in my life before, and it's simply wonderful. It does what the other religious writings never do—it leads you straight to a Person Who becomes more real than anyone else in the world!"

Then there was silence between them which Rowena broke.

"So you see," she said gaily, "I can't be lonely or desolate; it is quite impossible. I have so much lost time to make up, so much to learn and discover."

She did not often open her heart to anyone, and Mrs. Macintosh was touched by it.

After this little talk, she and Rowena drew closer together. And Mrs. Macintosh tried to come over and see her as often as she could.

Rowena had one or two letters from General Macdonald. Then, as December was drawing towards a close, she had one which much distressed her.

> "I have just been wired for. Mysie is dangerously ill of pneumonia. I leave to-morrow. Pray for her. Yours.
> HUGH MACDONALD."

Rowena found it hard to lie patiently under this blow. Mysie, with her laughing eyes and active spirits to be stretched on a bed of suffering! It brought an ache to her heart as she thought of her. She longed to rise up from her bed and go off to her. Granny was loud in denunciation of Edinburgh schools.

"The wee lassie hasna the constitootion for that freezin' toon. I aye was once awa' there, an' niver shall I forget et. I cudna keep body and sperrit together. 'Tis the Highlands for soft sweet air, an' winds that blaw aisy, not wi' knives piercin' into your bones!"

Rowena could only write her sympathy and possess her soul in patience. She got a wire one day, when Mysie's life was in danger, and then another to say she was pulling through. Christmas found Mysie still very ill, and her father in an Edinburgh hotel, learning day by day how much he loved his child.

And then when Mysie was quite convalescent, her father wrote that he was bringing her home.

Rowena wrote promptly:

> "Will you let Granny and me have her here, to pet her and nurse her back to health again? She is not too fond of that worthy housekeeper of yours, and I should love to have her."

By return of post she heard from the General:

> "I can't say how good I think it of you! There is no one I would have her with more willingly. I have business in town, and did not want to return just yet. I will bring her down myself the first day the doctor says she can travel."

And so one day, a very frail white little Mysie arrived, but her eyes were blazing with delight and rapture.

When Rowena's arms were round her, she looked up into her face with passionate devotion.

"I've never had anyone to talk to like you! And I've been just sick with wanting you and the glen and the loch!"

"Keep a bit of your heart for your old father," said General Macdonald.

His face looked worn and weary, but Rowena saw that he had improved in health and spirits. His step was brisker, he held himself more alertly.

Mysie looked up at him affectionately.

"Dad has been so kind," she informed Rowena; "he used to play halma with me in bed, and told me stories, almost as good as yours."

When she had been packed off to bed, her father began to talk about her.

"She has not the constitution for a town life, and the doctors advised me to let her go easily for the next year. The schoolmistress said she was, if anything, too eager and quick over her lessons; but her appetite failed, and she had constant headaches; and then, in this last spell of extreme cold, she did not seem to have the strength to withstand it. I don't want to lose her. Do advise me. What shall I do? Not try another governess?"

Rowena laughed.

"Let me have her. We shall be company for each other, and then you roam the world as you will. I don't believe you will settle down here."

"I want to do something with my life," said the General earnestly. "I'm not keen about politics, I'm afraid; but I've been offered a post by a friend of Cavanagh's. It has to do with the welfare of the deserving unemployed, and they want me to be secretary. It will entail a few months in town, and a good deal of travelling round, but I shall feel I am working again. At the same time, I am not going to live entirely apart from my child, and I have my duties as a landlord here. So the spring will see me opening the house again. I will gladly leave Mysie with you till then."

The matter was settled, and he departed.

Rowena and Mysie were supremely content. The child's rapture at being in the Highlands again was extremely touching.

"I hate towns and houses and people—they make me giddy. When I smelt the air coming in the train from the hills, I nearly cried. I told Dad I couldn't never live away from the Highlands, and he said he didn't think I could, and he wouldn't ask me to. Isn't he a darling! And the girls thought a kilt shocking! But you'll let me wear mine again, won't you? Oh, dearest prisoner, how happy you and me will be! Will Shags be jealous, do you think? He's looking at me out of the corners of his eyes, something like Miss Falconer did. And oh I do just look at the darling loch. Isn't it perfectly sweet with the sun on it? There's nothing for the sun to shine on in Edinburgh. When it did come out, it must have been rather disgusted only to have the streets and houses to shine on, instead of the loch and hills and moor. I kissed the earth when we got out at the station. The only thing I really enjoyed at school was learning poetry. I learnt a lovely piece, but when I had to say it, I cried instead, and Miss Gordon wasn't cross, she said she understood, but I wouldn't not have learnt it for anything. It began:

> "'The Highlands, the Highlands, oh, gin I were there,
> Though the mountains and moorlands be rugged and bare;
> Tho' cold be the climate and scanty the fare, Oh, my dearly loved Highlands, oh, gin I were there.'"

"And it ends:

> "'The Highlands, the Highlands, my once happy home
> Through thy glens and thy straths my delight was to roam;
> Though on a bright shore, where all nature is fair, My heart's in the Highlands, oh, gin I were there!'"

"I think it was rather cruel to make you learn that," said Rowena; "but we won't think of the time you were away, little Flora; we'll only think of the good time we're going to have now. Do you know, I'm counting the months to my freedom? Only three more months and then I'll be staggering to my feet. I shall have to learn to walk again, shan't I?"

"And you'll lean on my arm," said Mysie with shining eyes; "and then in a few days you'll be riding and rowing and fishing with me. Oh, it will be glorious!"

Time slipped away very pleasantly. Mysie fast regained her health and strength; and then Rowena suggested a couple of hours at lessons every morning. She was delighted with Mysie's quick intelligence, and Mysie was very naïve in her comments upon Rowena's knowledge.

"Why, you know heaps and heaps more than I do! You're as clever as Miss Falconer, and yet you never show off like she did!"

And then spring came, a late spring in the Highlands, but a marvellously beautiful one.

Rowena had her couch moved out-of-doors for an hour in the sunshine sometimes, and she lay and gazed at the soft shadows chasing each other across the distant hills and loch, and watched the green buds bursting into blossom, and the pale primroses in the banks.

"I may never see another spring here," she said rather sadly once to Mysie. "I feel I'm a bit of the soil, but I shall have to depart when my legs are given back to me."

Mysie was loud in her laments.

"Don't try to get well! We can't spare you. Nobody wants you in India half so bad as Dad and I want you here."

But Rowena shook her head, and very soon her brother Ted received a letter from her which rejoiced his heart.

"DEAR OLD TED,—"

"My year is over! I can hardly believe it, and actually old Niddy-Noddy took it into his wise old head to take his holiday in Scotland this spring. Of course he came on to see me, and much against my will he brought some other old wiseacre from Edinburgh—a chum of his—and they examined me and poked me about, and were highly pleased with the result of my year's rest. I am at present like a baby trying to walk! I am to go slowly, but they say my unused muscles will harden in time, and my back is really cured. What a wonderful thing it is to have a body which will go! I never valued mine properly before, and I assure you I'm going to be very careful and cautious with such a precious possession now. My first walk was taken two days ago. Mysie and Granny nearly cried with the excitement of it. And I staggered and rolled like a drunken tar. But I'm walking more respectably now—only the fatigue of it! I ask myself am I a Rip Van Winkle, and have I spent a hundred years instead of one upon my bed?"

"Well, this is enough about my body."

"Now about plans. You and Geraldine are very impatient to have me. It is rather pleasant to feel I am wanted so much, and of course the thought of being with you so soon makes me want to dance a jig! This is May. Shall I come out the end of August? Will it be in the middle of the monsoon? But that will be a matter of indifference to me. I must tell you frankly that I shall say good-bye to the Highlands with real concern. My heart has been stolen by its soft air and elusive colours, and the dear simple Gaelic people, not to speak of the charming personality of Mysie Macdonald. And Granny and I have grown into each other's ways, so that it will be hard to snap ourselves asunder."

"I have written to the laird. He's in a predicament about his child, feeling that school has been a failure, and yet governesses are worse. I wish I knew a dear old motherly body who would teach and love the little darling with the same breath. How are your chicks? Grown out of knowledge, I expect. I can't believe that I shall be with you before very long now. Good-bye. My love and kisses to the batch of you. And tell Geraldine that I will stop in town and be fitted up with frocks before I sail, so as not to disgrace her. Your last cheque was far too generous."

"Ever your"
"ROWENA."

General Macdonald arrived over one afternoon. He had returned from town unexpectedly, and had told no one of his coming. Mysie was out when he came. Rowena received him in her green room. The couch was absent. At first he looked quite dazed when he saw a radiant vision crossing the room to meet him. Rowena looked so very much alive, as if every pulse in her body were beating with intense vitality.

"Don't you recognize me?" she said with her mellow laugh.

"Hardly. I did not realize you would be so tall. It is a resurrection. May I say how glad I am!"

His eyes met hers with smiling admiration, then when they were seated his brows contracted.

"Is it true that you're leaving this part for good?"

"I am going to join my brother and family in India."

"But do they want you?"

"How can you be so uncomplimentary! Of course they do!"

He drew a breath.

"I was hoping, for the child's sake — for our sakes — that you would be here a little longer. What am I to do with her? Can you advise me?"

"What do you think about the Macintoshes? Mrs. Macintosh is such a nice woman. She might be inclined to take her, and later on perhaps she would be strong enough to go back to school."

"I can't afford to lose her, but I like Mrs. Macintosh, and if her son would give her an hour or two of lessons every day, it would be the very thing. What a wonderful woman you are for lightening my burdens! I will go to them on my way home and see if they would be willing to do it. I think I shall be away on and off all the summer. There will be no inducement to come down here with you gone."

He stopped and looked at her as Rowena had never seen him look before. She was conscious of the quickened beating of her heart.

Then he compressed his lips.

Rowena said lightly:

"You must be more sociable this coming summer. For your little daughter's sake, you must be; and you will find it better for yourself to mix more with your fellow-creatures. I have come to the conclusion that my enforced seclusion has had its purposes, but it would not be good for me to continue it. A solitary life tends to selfishness; don't you think so?"

"Not in your case," he said warmly; "I have never met with such sympathy and understanding in my life before!" Then abruptly he rose to his feet. "I will go to the Macintoshes now. You will hear from me, if I do not come over to-morrow."

He took his departure. Rowena shook her head when he had gone.

"My dear," she soliloquized to herself, "you're not a young romantic girl! Remember your age and experience. You have had many men friends. Don't expect this particular man to mean anything more than mere platonic friendship. A very good and useful thing in its way!"

The next day came, and the next, but no letter from the laird.

Then at the end of the week Mrs. Macintosh came over and told Rowena that she had promised to give Mysie a home for the summer. And Rowena heard that the laird had gone off suddenly to town. She still waited for his letter, but it did not come, and the next thing was a wire from her brother, asking her to sail at once in the Lesbia, a P. & O. steamer going in a fortnight's time. Mysie went off to Mrs. Macintosh. She felt the parting from Rowena keenly, but, child-like, intended to enjoy her life at the manse.

Rowena hastily packed up her things and went up to town. She knew General Macdonald's address there, and one day had talk with him through the telephone.

It was strangely unsatisfactory.

Rowena told him she was going sooner than she had thought, and had left Mysie comfortably settled in the manse. His replies were cold and grave. He wished her a safe journey, and thanked her for all she had done for his little girl.

At the end of the interview, he said:

"I understood your silence, so have not troubled you with any more correspondence."

Rowena was about to inquire what he meant, but they were cut off, and she did not see or hear from him again.

Later she puzzled over his words, then strove to put them from her.

"My Highland life and Highland friends will be only a memory now," she assured herself. "That chapter is closed. I am in another atmosphere altogether."

And she sailed for India with a smiling face and an aching heart.

BOOK II

CHAPTER I
AT THE GREEN COTTAGE

"All are not taken! There are left behind
Living Beloved's tender looks to bring,
And make the daylight still a happy thing,
And tender voices to make soft the wind."
E. Browning.

"ROWENA, I hope you mean to be kind to him. Remember he has taken all the trouble to travel down from Yorkshire to see us."

"But we did not invite him."

"Well, on board ship I gave him a kind of general invitation, seeing how smitten he was with you."

Rowena's brows contracted. She was silent.

Mrs. Arbuthnot looked at her a little anxiously.

"You know how desolate I and the chicks would be without you. Don't think for a moment that I want to lose you, but I do want you not to miss the happiness of married life, and dear Ted often used to say to me how he hoped you would marry. We thought when your letters were so full of Hugh Macdonald's child, that you would marry him; personally I never found him attractive. He had no sense of humour. And Ted said he couldn't see you tied up with him somehow." A heavy sigh followed, then impulsively Mrs. Arbuthnot turned to her sister-in-law.

"Oh, Rowena, I can't get accustomed to being without Ted! I can't believe he is silent for ever! I think it is cruel taking men so suddenly away; one day in full enjoyment of health and mental powers, the next struck down, and buried before one realizes they are dead! I wish—I wish we had never gone to India, I wish he had never taken that trip into the cholera-infected region! Nothing will ever comfort me! Men and women ought not to die till they lose their individuality. It is cruel, unreasonable. I never shall understand the reason for it."

"Poor Geraldine! It is difficult for you, but let me pass on a sentence a very nice woman gave me long ago. I have never forgotten it: 'Nothing is a puzzle, nothing is a mystery, if you have enough love and trust.'"

"Love and trust in whom?"

"In the One Who holds our lives in His keeping. Ted is not going to be silent for ever. I never felt so certain as I do now that he has stepped into the Kingdom of Heaven. Just before he went on that trip I had such a nice talk with him."

"Oh, I know, I know! He used to tell me that he believed in what you believed, because of your life. And you aren't a long-faced mute, I will say that for you. You comfort me when you talk so, but I'm a worldling. Don't let us talk of our sorrow, let us return to Major Cunliffe. Don't you like him? Oh, I wish you would, for your own sake! He is an old friend of Ted's, and has such a lovely old house in Yorkshire! We stayed there once when his mother was alive."

"He's a nice man," said Rowena slowly; "but I don't think he will ever be anything more than that to me."

"Don't you ever mean to marry?"

Rowena laughed.

"Nobody axed me, sir," she said.

"Now that's a fib. You had three out in India who were your devoted admirers."

"I feel like a kitchen-maid when you talk so," said Rowena.

She was sitting over the fire with her sister-in-law in a small house in a Surrey village. They had not long returned from India. Colonel Arbuthnot had been carried off by an epidemic of cholera about five months after Rowena had joined them out there. As soon as she was able, his widow returned to England, and Rowena accompanied her. An old friend of Colonel Arbuthnot's, Sir Henry Hazelwood, had offered her a pretty cottage in the village of which he was squire; for young Mrs. Arbuthnot had found it necessary to economize as much as possible. Her husband before his death was finding himself in difficulties, and had arranged to give up his Scotch lodge, much to his sister's regret. They had now just settled in the cottage, and the young widow was striving to take up life again for the sake of her little ones.

Rowena, of course, was the mainstay in the house. Her cheery personality kept them all going, and she was ready to turn her hand to anything, from painting a gate to repairing a lock; she had just started poultry, and they were thinking of having a little rough pony and trap, for the market town was a good three miles away.

It was a cold afternoon in March. Outside it was cheerless and grey. Inside, though simplicity reigned throughout the cottage, the little drawing-room was a picture of cheery comfort. Mrs. Arbuthnot was seated on a comfortable Chesterfield couch by the fire, her sewing in her hand.

Rowena was in a lounge chair opposite her, knitting away at a boy's sock.

"I suppose I must feel snubbed," said Mrs. Arbuthnot with rather a sad little smile. "I will drop the subject. And I am sure, as I said before, it would be my own loss if you left me. Aren't you afraid we shall find this place most painfully dull?"

"No," said Rowena brightly; "why should we? It's a lovely part of the world. Think of the woods and meadows for your pale-faced children. How many picnics we shall have this summer! And Sir Henry and his wife are always wanting us to join their social gatherings. Of course, you don't feel inclined to do so yet, but you will by and by. Ted would not like you to shut yourself up. And I think we're very lucky in our parson. I like him extremely. I have a great admiration for his eldest daughter, mothering the parish as she does, in addition to mothering her small brothers."

"Oh, Mr. Waring is all right enough! He's a gentleman and a scholar, and you and he have a good deal in common. I suppose India spoils one, and nothing will ever be the same to me without Ted—I hate a house without a man! It is like a cart without the horse, a train without an engine."

"Well, now turn your attention upon Major Cunliffe. I see him walking up the path."

A moment after, a tall handsome man was shaking hands with them both. But it was easy to see which of the women was the object of his visit.

Rowena leant back in her chair with easy friendliness. Not a blush on her cheek, or quiver of her eyelash, told that she was in the least impressed by his personality.

"We heard you were coming to the Hall," she said, looking at him with the usual twinkle in her eyes; "but we did not expect to see you quite so soon. You only arrived yesterday evening, did you not? Sir Henry called here just before he drove to the station to meet you."

"My inclination was to come round immediately after breakfast," Major Cunliffe replied promptly; "but Lady Hazelwood insisted upon inspecting her pet rock-garden, and she kept me there the greater part of the morning. I do not like people with hobbies. They ride them so hard."

"I think if a woman has no children it's a good thing to have a hobby," said Mrs. Arbuthnot, "especially in the country. The Hazelwoods are hardly ever in town. He's a born farmer. Don't you remember how he used to yarn in India about his shorthorns and pigs?"

"By Jove, yes. And we called him 'Mangels' in the mess. What a ripping little house you have here. How are the youngsters?"

"You remind me of my duties," said Mrs. Arbuthnot. "I promised to go up to them to-day when nursery tea was on. I shan't be long."

She slipped quietly out of the room.

Instinctively Major Cunliffe drew his chair a little nearer Rowena.

She looked up at him with her frank smile.

"Geraldine's hobby is her children, and they have comforted her a lot."

"Poor Mrs. Arbuthnot, she must be feeling rotten. But she's awfully sensible—she knew I wanted to see you alone, so she's bolted. Now, please don't put on that careless bored expression. I mean to have it out with you, and now is my chance. You kept me from speaking on board ship—circumstances always seemed to favour you. I shan't forget that ass of a Captain in a hurry, but you must listen now. I beseech you to be kind. You know I just adore you, and can't live without you."

"I don't know anything of the sort," Rowena replied very calmly and sweetly. "I know you were a most kind friend to us on board, and I always had a liking for you, because you were so fond of—my poor brother." Her voice faltered. He broke in quickly:

"Yes—I felt you had a liking for me—one can tell it—and now I want something more. Don't say you can't give it to me."

She looked at him gravely, and shook her head.

"I'm afraid it is no use, Major Cunliffe. I hate to give pain. You can never say I have encouraged you. I honestly think I shall never marry."

"It will be a sinful shame if you don't," said the Major hotly; "and I'm positive you and I would pull together A 1. Do just think of it—I'll wait a bit longer if you like. Why on earth should you be so detached? I suppose I'm not up to your level."

"Oh, please, please don't make me out such a brute."

There was real feeling in Rowena's voice. She went on a little unsteadily:

"I tried to make you see on board that I could never be anything but a friend. I was afraid of this. You would make anyone a good husband, Major Cunliffe; you are so unselfish, so tender as far as women and children are concerned. But I will be frank with you. My heart is not mine to give away. We women are foolish creatures; and I am the most foolish of my sex—I can say no more."

"You love some one else."

He murmured the words, but blank dismay was in his eyes—Rowena was absolutely, silent, then she put out her hand.

"Shake hands, and bear me no ill will. I shall live and die a single woman. Of that I feel sure, but life is full of interest to single women, and we do value friendship. May I think that I can still have yours, even if our paths in life lie apart. I wish I could give you the answer you want, but I cannot."

Major Cunliffe looked at her in a dazed sort of way. Then he wheeled round towards the window, and stood looking out with his back to her trying to bear his disappointment courageously.

Rowena sat with clasped hands and dejected mien. She was very tender-hearted, and could not bear to give pain. In a few minutes he turned to her.

"Well—you seem sure of your own mind. I will say no more. It's no good prolonging our interview. Say good-bye to Mrs. Arbuthnot. I feel I can't face her—and if ever you do happen to think differently, I hope you'll let me know."

He wrung her hand, and stumbled out of the room. Rowena watched him striding down the little path to the gate with tears in her eyes.

"I hope we shall not be meeting any more of them here," she murmured to herself. "And now I shall have to smooth down Geraldine's ruffled feathers." That was soon done. Mrs. Arbuthnot was too truly fond of her sister-in-law to wish her to marry a man she did not care for; but she was disappointed, and it needed all Rowena's brightness to bring smiles to her face again.

Fortunately another visitor called that afternoon.

Mrs. Arbuthnot loved society, and for the time she forgot Major Cunliffe's dismissal.

This visitor was a wealthy widow who lived alone in a big house about three miles off.

Her husband belonged to the county, and had died many years previously.

Mrs. Burke was very popular with her neighbours, but the Hazelwoods had told Rowena that she was a little too rapid and go ahead for them.

"She is never quiet; the life she leads would wear me out in a month," gentle Lady Hazelwood said. "She has a house in Park Lane, and is hospitality itself, and very kindhearted. Young people adore her, for she gives them such a good time. Even in this quiet place, she keeps the ball of gaiety rolling. She has plenty of money, and spends it on amusements for herself and her guests."

Mrs. Burke was a handsome woman about fifty. As Rowena watched her talking to her sister-in-law, she felt a sudden liking for her.

"Oh, you mustn't be dull or unhappy," she was saying; "you will have nice neighbours, and I always have house-parties during the summer. There will be plenty going on soon. Come over and see me before my visitors arrive, if you like. I am alone now, and it would be a charity to take pity on me. The only time I get the blues is when I have nobody to talk to."

"Have you a dog?" asked Rowena. "I had a winter of solitude up in the Highlands and found my little 'Shags' a great comfort when I wanted to deliver my soul!"

Mrs. Burke turned quickly to her.

"I never make friends with my dogs. I have no time. It takes me all my time to live. I tried companions, but oh! how they bored me! They were either a mild echo of myself, or tried to manage me. Will you waive ceremony and come to lunch with me next Wednesday? Do—I have quite a good cook, and she does hate wasting her dainties on me. I never know or care what I eat when I'm alone."

Mrs. Arbuthnot accepted the invitation, but when the day came, her little girl was not well, and she would not leave her. She insisted upon Rowena going, and begged her to enjoy herself.

"There is so little going on here, that I am quite glad of a sociable neighbour, and I shall look forward to your account of her when you return. You always see the amusing side of everybody!"

Rowena walked off. She thought nothing of the three miles, and enjoyed every step of her way. She found that Mrs. Burke was not alone; two girls, by name Violet and Diana Dunstan, were lunching with her, and the talk was chiefly on hunting, and the last meet which was taking place the following week. The girls went off directly after lunch, but Mrs. Burke pressed Rowena to stay, and took her into a very cosy little morning-room.

"I'm very fond of Vi and Di, as they are called, but one soon gets to the end of them, and I haven't got to the beginning of you yet."

"I shan't take much knowing," said Rowena easily. "I am pretty well what I look. An ordinary sort of every-day person."

"You are neither one nor the other," replied Mrs. Burke promptly. "Now I have powers of observation, and you're a reader; that I know from the way you scanned my bookshelves when you came in here."

"Well, yes, I am. My truant eyes betrayed me."

"You'll find nothing but novels, and books of travel and adventure," said Mrs. Burke. "I cannot understand poetry, and history is most unsatisfactory. Theology and all the other ologies are too stiff and dry. I have no time for thinking. Like the Americans, I like to make things hum. And people interest me more than anything else in the world. Would you like to hear about your neighbours?"

"Very much," was Rowena's response.

"Well, to begin with, Vi and Di, they live with their brother, who only came into his property two years ago. It came to him through an uncle. They lived up in the north, and are thorough sportswomen—up to any larks, and make the hair of old-fashioned folk about here stand on end at their pranks. Their brother Bob is a good sort, but a little rough. You know the Hazelwoods, they're a model squire and wife, and are nothing if not correct. Eight miles distant are the Easterbrooks: he's a new-made peer, and everything about them is new—their house, their garments, their furniture, and their manners. There are two old Miss Humbers of whom I'm rather fond, they pretend they are old-fashioned and out of date, but they love to be shocked, and I and my friends do it pretty often. They have one of the loveliest gardens in the country, and of course their gardener is an autocratic tyrant. Then there is a bachelor establishment about four miles off. Two brothers, both been in the army and retired one a general, the other a colonel. They live together; one hunts and shoots, the other gardens, and has a pet aviary. Their name is Sheringham. The parsons and doctors never interest me in the least, nor do their families, and most of my friends come down to me from town. I may as well tell you that I was a parson's daughter myself and lived in the Cotswolds before I married. I know too much about parsons and their kind to have much to do with them now."

She compressed her lips rather bitterly, then laughed. "My motto is 'keep the world rolling with smiles'; nobody can say I do otherwise. But, oh dear, I have times when I long for a secretary or companion to take some of my duties from me. Just look here!" She opened a bureau, which seemed almost bursting with letters and papers. "That's a week's correspondence, and I haven't touched it yet. I sometimes want to burn the contents of my postbag before I look it through. I get such thousands of begging letters, and my friends are always worrying me with their wants!"

"That is one of the penalties of wealth," said Rowena. "You can't escape its responsibilities."

"Don't you hate that word responsibility? I try to be as irresponsible as I can. And if you're clever, you can always shift your burdens on to other's shoulders. Now I've talked about myself enough. Tell me what your line is. You're neither a prude, nor a rollicker."

"I don't think I have ever set to work to dissect myself," said Rowena, amused. "I'm interested at present in my sister-in-law and her family, and in making two shillings go as far as five. We have never been used to economy before, at least she has not, and it takes a bit of doing. And just now I'm on the look-out for a rough pony and trap in which we can jog about the lanes, and enjoy the country."

"I know the very thing for you. A farmer wants to sell one: his wife used to drive about in it, for she was lame, and now she is dead, poor thing!"

In discussing a possible bargain, personal topics were dropped. Rowena returned home well pleased with her neighbour, but she said to her sister-in-law:

"She's a jolly easy-going soul, and kindness and good nature personified, but she's hiding away from something in spite of all her careless abandon of talk: I should like to know her better."

In a short time Mrs. Arbuthnot had contentedly settled down to their quiet life. Rowena got her trap and pony, and trundled about the sweet-smelling lanes with the children inside it.

Before long they were on pleasant terms of intimacy with their neighbours, but to Rowena Mrs. Burke was the most interesting personality of them all.

She was always entertaining; and as the summer drew on, private theatricals, tennis parties, and picnics followed each other in quick succession. Her friends from town were not always liked by the county. She had a good many Bohemians, and stray geniuses, who contributed towards the general gaiety with their freakish talent.

Once she arrived at the Green Cottage early in the morning, and besought Rowena to return with her at once.

"I want you to take the place of a girl whose father has just died. So tiresome of him to choose this week to do it in! She's simply unique in running my musical programme for the village concert coming off; she keeps every one in good temper, and plays all the accompaniments. I know you'll do that all right, and I'm sure you'll help to keep the peace. My dear Italian Countess is nearly tearing out the eyes of my best tenor because he said she sang sharp in the duet they have together. To sing sharp is a more deadly crime than to sing flat, I find. Come along just as you are, we must have a rehearsal this morning, for we're all going off to the sea in cars this afternoon, and you know it is only fifteen miles away?"

Rowena went off obligingly. She returned about three in the afternoon, tired, but very interested.

"Oh, Geraldine, she reminds me of those men with a happy family in a cage! Her elements of humanity do not harmonize. Aristocrats and violent radicals, oldish women who have been beauties, and young intolerant girls who laugh at them. I admire her wonderful adaptability, and good temper in dealing with them all. But I wouldn't have such guests in a house of mine for all the wealth in the world! And yet she hasn't a wrinkle on her face, and her energy in 'rolling the ball,' as she expresses it, is superhuman!"

"She's a very tiring old woman," said Mrs. Arbuthnot; "she ought to be content with a quiet life at her age."

Rowena laughed.

"She does not consider she is a day older than she feels, and that is about twenty-three, I should say! But I hope she is not going to come upon me to make up all her guests' deficiencies. I like the simple life, and a little of hers goes a long way!"

"Sometimes," said Mrs. Arbuthnot slowly, "I think that year of solitude in the Highlands was bad for you, Rowena. You ought to love gadding round at your age."

"My age, madam, is past that of giddy youth!" And then Rowena quitted the room, singing as she went:

> "I have a smiling face, she said
> I have a gist for all I meet,
> I have a garland for my head,
> And all its flowers are sweet—"

CHAPTER II
A NEW FRIEND

"Is not making others happy the best happiness?"
Amiel.

"MY dear Geraldine, what is the matter? Your face is a yard long. Have you had bad news?"

Mrs. Arbuthnot looked up from her letters and sighed.

She and Rowena were at breakfast. It was a lovely morning in June. The windows were open, a sweet brier bush outside was scenting the room with its fragrance.

"Madge is going to be married almost immediately."

"Three cheers for Madge! If I had a sister, and a sister who has been engaged for five years, I should be overjoyed at the event."

"Oh, I am glad for her sake, of course; but I have had four sheets from her showing me how impossible it is for mother to live alone, and imploring me to take the children and make Whitecroft my home."

"A most sensible arrangement. It is a roomy old house, and nearer town than this is. You will be very happy there, my dear!"

"I like a house of my own. I have always had it."

"Yes, but your mother is a dear, gentle, old lady. Madge always ran the house, and you can do the same."

Geraldine sighed again.

"I hate changes, and Madge is going to be married in a fortnight and going straight out to the Cape with Frank, and she wants me to pack up my things and go to mother the end of this month."

"Sir Arthur will let you off the rent of this, and nowadays he will have no trouble in getting another tenant. I would take it on myself if I had enough money."

"But you will be with us, of course."

Mrs. Arbuthnot raised a startled face to her sister-in-law.

Rowena swung herself up on the low window-ledge, and sat there with her hands in her pockets, and her feet swinging to and fro. She whistled softly to herself, but did not speak for a minute, and Mrs. Arbuthnot repeated her words:

"You will come with us? I am not going to part with you."

"My dear Geraldine, leave me out of the question. Your first thought is your mother, and being what she is, and having no other children to look after her, I consider it is your bounden duty to go to her. Make up your mind to it. Whitecroft is a sweet home, and it is your mother's own, and too big for her to live in alone. That point is quite clear, and now when is the wedding, and what are you going to wear?"

The question of clothes brought a smile to Mrs. Arbuthnot's lips. She began to see sunshine again; and after she was thoroughly reconciled to her duty which lay before her, Rowena left her to write her letters, and went off out of the house and along the lanes with swift light steps.

Once she knitted her brows, and murmured:

"It's a game of see-saw. Geraldine will go up, as far as comfort in her surroundings go, and I shall go down. What a darling Ted was to leave me enough to stave off starvation! But it won't give me a home. And I must have a roof over my head. And to think that only a few weeks ago I scoffed in my heart at Mrs. Burke's offer. The bread of dependence is not palatable, but it must be munched and eaten by you, my dear Rowena, and the sooner you settle it the better."

The three miles to Minley Court seemed of no account to Rowena. She was a good walker, and was too deep in thought to notice any details by the way. She found Mrs. Burke in her morning-room, and it was a propitious moment for her request. The impatient lady was seated at her writing-desk; letters and papers were fluttering all round her, and as she turned to greet Rowena, she swept a packet of papers upon the carpet with her elbow.

"Thank goodness, somebody has arrived to distract me from this chaos! Come out upon the terrace, and I will enjoy a cigarette if you will not join me. I have the car coming round in half an hour, I am going to the Fletchers. May I take you with me? They're charming people, and you ought to know them. He's a retired admiral, and she's a daughter of Lord Gallway."

"I'm afraid I must return home quickly. I have come on business this time, and will get to it at once. Do you remember you were good enough to ask me the other day if I would be your companion-secretary, and I told you how impossible it was for me to leave my sister-in-law and her children? Well, circumstances are changed. She is giving up her house and going to live with her mother in Berkshire, and I am not going with her. I couldn't: a mixed household is a mistake, so I am on my own, and able to do what I like. If your offer still holds good, I would like to accept it."

"You will? My dear girl, that's the best bit of news I have had for a long time! I shall be enchanted to have you. I feel inclined to plant you at my desk now, and start you at that infernal—well, we'll say unpleasant—mass of letters and bills. It's an accumulation of a couple of months. I never can overtake it. Why is the art of begging, and dunning, and boring, made so easy to all of us? When will you come to me? To-morrow?"

"Indeed no, but in another week or two."

"I suppose I shall have to wait your time. Now we must settle your salary. Will two hundred pounds suffice? Remember, it will be an arduous post, for I drive every one about me they say. My days are overfull, and I shall expect you to be at my beck and call for a good many hours I am afraid."

Rowena laughed.

"Your salary is munificent, and I am not afraid of work. I shall get a little quiet time to myself in and out. Thank you very much. Then it is settled. I should love to tidy up your papers to-day, but I must be getting back. Will you expect me this day fortnight?"

"You're too good for the post," said Mrs. Burke, putting her hand on her shoulder affectionately. "I shall pretend you're a sort of daughter, but daughters nowadays wouldn't do their mother's dirty work, would they? Oh, I'm delighted to have you. There's something so restful and dependable in your face, and you do enjoy a joke! I hate these stuffy solid folk who open their eyes widely, and think one a lunatic if one indulges in a bit of fun. Good-bye, if you must go, and I'll give you the second best spare room; it's sunny, and bright, like yourself."

Rowena marched home feeling she had burnt her boats, and wondering why she had such pride of heart as to mentally squirm at the thought of her future.

"An empty purse and high head don't harmonize," she said to herself. "I must consider that I'm benefiting one of my fellow-creatures by becoming one of her dependants, and I shall have a chance of getting beneath her outer crust. There's something I don't understand in her composition. She's too sensible to be so frivolous."

When Mrs. Arbuthnot was informed of Rowena's plans, she was very perturbed and vexed.

"I have a great mind to refuse to go to mother. What shall I do without you? It's cruel of you! You're like a bit of Ted left to me—and the house is big enough for you, and mother would be charmed to have you."

"It can't be done," said Rowena firmly. "Ask me to pay you a visit sometimes."

"Oh, if Mrs. Burke gets you into her clutches, she will never let you go! I wish you had never met her. She's like an octopus for drawing all the best into her nets. I cannot see her attractiveness. To me she's thorough bad style, and you'll lead a most rackety life, and will never be able to call a moment your own!"

Rowena could not comfort her. Happily, there was so much to do and arrange that it took away her thoughts from their parting. She arranged to go to her mother before the wedding, and the little house was dismantled and bare within the prescribed fortnight. Rowena was the last to leave it, and when she eventually drove off to Minley Court in the car sent for her with her luggage packed up behind, she felt as if this second rooting up of her life was a very black and gloomy performance. But she arrived at her new home with a cheerful countenance. She found Di and Vi Dunstan with Mrs. Burke.

"We feel so deadly when the hunting is off," said Vi. "Mrs. Burke is our only cheer. We are trying to concoct a few new games for her next garden-party. Come and help us with your wit!"

"You're going to have diggings here, aren't you?" questioned Di. "Good for you. I'd like the job myself."

"Miss Arbuthnot's job is not going to be an easy one," said Mrs. Burke with her jolly laugh. "She's going to supply all my deficiencies, and run me and my household in a more orthodox fashion."

"Oh, dash orthodoxy!" cried Vi. "How I loathe the word, as bad as conventionality and propriety, and all the rest of the prudisms and prisms!"

Rowena had to sit down then and there and discuss seriously whether a game of hare and hounds, in which the hare was to trail the contents of scent sachets or scent bottles behind him, could take place in the grounds of Minley Court.

"We'll have six hares, all men, and ladies must be the hounds, and one might use pepper as his scent, and another onions; and another might scatter rose-leaves behind him—nothing like variety! It will be topping!"

It was difficult for Rowena to show much interest in their childishness, but Mrs. Burke took pity on her. "Come on up to your room, and we'll leave you in peace till tea comes. Vi and Di are quite equal to organizing their own schemes."

So Rowena followed Mrs. Burke up the old staircase along a very broad corridor, until they came to the room prepared for her.

It was, as Mrs. Burke had told her, one of the brightest rooms in the house, and looked, in its dainty dimity coverings, very cool and sweet.

Rowena glanced at the comfortable chairs and couch, and at the charming writing-table in one window.

"My dear Mrs. Burke," she said gaily, "how can I thank you for indulging me so? I hope this luxury will not unfit me for my duties."

"Duty is never mentioned in my house," said Mrs. Burke, putting her hands on both her shoulders and suddenly stooping and giving her a quick warm kiss on her cheek. "We slip along as we like, and pick up what fragments of necessary work we can, just to prevent the house tumbling to pieces. You'll work, and I'll continue to play, but I shan't work you hard, and I warn you that you must suffer gladly continual interruption. To-day you are to be my guest; to-morrow you can tackle my correspondence."

"Thank you, then I'll take this hour before tea to settle my belongings, and congratulate myself upon such a role!"

Mrs. Burke left her. When she joined her young friends again, she said:

"I'm in luck's way at last. I can't think why she has not married!"

"There's time yet," said Di laconically; "there's a reaction set in, now there are no more embryo heroes to be wed. There aren't many sound able men just now, plenty of boys, but they'll keep."

"You always go for a fresh pal like hot bricks!" said Vi. "She isn't a bad sort, this Miss Arbuthnot, but she's hardly one of us. I see something more solid in her face than her first appearance would warrant. Her eyes make you think she's out for larks, but there's a twist to her lips that shows she's a quizzer!"

"I like her," Mrs. Burke asserted stoutly, "and you'll like her too when you know her better."

Rowena was relieved when she came down to tea to find that the Miss Dunstans had taken their departure. She and Mrs. Burke were alone, and they had tea under the rose pergola at the end of the terrace.

"There's one thing I want to ask you," said Rowena presently; "and that is if I may have Sunday to myself? I don't care how hard I work in the week, but I should like to feel free on Sunday."

Mrs. Burke looked at her rather curiously.

"Oh, well," she said, after a minute's silence, "I shan't want you to do any secretarial work on Sunday, but socially it's a day that hangs a bit heavy, and I may want your help with my guests. I have a good many week-end parties, you know."

"Yes. I don't want to sound disobliging, but I still want that day for myself."

"I wish you would explain. Do you want to go right away, or is it a question of principles? Are you a Sabbatarian? Nothing so out of date, I am sure. I go to church occasionally, when it's not too hot, and when I'm not too tired. Very often I keep to my bed till lunch. If my guests bore me I invariably do so."

"I like a quiet Sunday," said Rowena, looking at her with her frank smile. "I suppose I have always been indulged in that way. In India my brother and his wife always went down to the Club, but I retired to my room for the afternoon; they never minded. And of course I shall go to church, I always have done so."

"Oh, you can go to church all day long if you want to," Mrs. Burke said with impatience in her tone; "only don't dictate to me as to how I should keep the Sabbath. I had enough of that when I was young!"

Rowena looked at her sympathetically.

"I expect you were driven with too tight a curb, weren't you? Isn't it a pity when children are made by force of circumstances to hate what should have been their joy?"

"I don't think you will find children look upon church-going as a joy," said Mrs. Burke, with bitterness in her tone. "In one case I have a vivid remembrance of sitting up in church with aching head and back, and with a positive loathing for the unutterably weary prayers, and lengthy sermon. My father was a parson, and when I grew older I had to be at early service at 7.30, Sunday school at ten, service again at eleven, school at three. Evening service at 6.30, and sometimes a choir practice afterwards. I would come into supper after our day of devotion was over, sick in body and soul of it all!"

"If your heart wasn't in it, it must have been torture, I've always had a lax bringing up as regards church, but somehow from a child I enjoyed it. About eighteen months ago I had an accident in the hunting field, and was laid up on my back for a year. I went to my brother's house in the Highlands, and used to hear the church bells across the loch as I lay on my couch and longed that I could go. After a year's privation from church-going, I went out to India, and there we only got a service about once a month when we were in the hills—at other times a church parade lasting about half an hour. Now since we have been back in England I'm thoroughly enjoying my church. I learnt a lot of things when I was lying on my back, and it is a matter of principle with me to have a quiet day on Sunday; I hope you don't like me the less for it."

"I didn't think you were that sort," Mrs. Burke said. Her tone was almost sulky.

"Have we made a mistake? Shall I throw it up, and go away with my sister?"

"Good heavens, no! You shall have your Sundays, but don't let me feel you're carping at us if we can't live up to your level."

"My dear Mrs. Burke, if you saw into my mind you would know that it's the last thing I would do. I'm such a stumbling sort of creature myself, that I feel at the very lowest level of all. One day, when I'm more at home with you, perhaps you'll let me tell you of a bit of my Highland experience. Till then believe me, that I shall never be your critic. I have come here to give you my help, and I honestly will try to do my best in your service."

Mrs. Burke's face cleared.

"All serene then! And now we'll talk of other things. Do you know the Fortescue Bakers? I hear they have just taken a farm house near here. They've bought it, and mean to turn it into a lovely little house. He is an artist you know, and bound to make everything beautiful that lies across his path."

Rowena listened to the local gossip, and pleased Mrs. Burke by her interest and sympathy.

For a wonder Mrs. Burke was alone. She was expecting visitors the next day. After dinner they strolled through the beautifully kept grounds, and Mrs. Burke told Rowena the details of her past life.

"I was, as I told you this afternoon, a parson's daughter, and my father was of the strict evangelical school. We were supposed to live apart from all worldly gaieties. Never allowed to dance, or go to a play, or enjoy ourselves with any young people who did so. And strange to say I was content and even happy in those days. I was the youngest. Two of my sisters married neighbouring curates. One is now a missionary with her husband in China; the other is in Liverpool. I have lost touch with her; we did correspond before my husband's death, but she and her husband thoroughly disapprove of me. My third sister was the one who kept everything going at home, but a bad time came. Our mother, who was always delicate, went down with 'the Flu.' It raged round us. One of my brothers had it with the complication of double pneumonia, and both he and my mother died. Then my sister got it and went into a decline. She was overworked and could not battle with it. I was just seventeen then, so had to take command and run the house and parish. There was never a question of recreation or rest for a parson's daughter. We were wretchedly poor, and the struggle to keep up appearances was awful. My remaining brother was at college, and we fought hard to keep him there. I often wish he had earned his bread in a humbler sort of way, for three years afterwards he died in London—a question of underfeeding and overwork—the same as my poor sister. I can tell you the record of those years sent the iron into my soul. There is no tragedy so great as some of these parsons' lives! Well, to make a long story short, my father died when I was twenty-three, and I was left penniless and homeless."

"My sister in Liverpool said I must come to her till I got some sort of employment. Now romance steps in. In spite of my training, and discipline and poverty, I was a bright pretty girl then. I thoroughly believed in my father's steadfast creed that all things worked together for good to those who love God, and that belief served to keep my head above water. Whilst the contents of the Parsonage were being sold, our Squire's wife, Lady Mary Crosby, took pity on me, and insisted that I should come up to the Hall till things were settled. It was there I met my husband. He was Lady Mary's nephew and young and handsome: there were no other girls for him to take notice of, and we fell headlong in love with each other. Lady Mary treated it as a boy and girl flirtation; she never gave Alfred credit for anything serious. When I eventually went to my sister, I considered myself engaged to him. She was horrified. Everyone at the Hall had always been considered 'worldly'; and she tried to show me how impossible and wicked such a union would be. But they say a worm will turn at last. I had had enough of the hard penurious life of the godly. I was young, and felt the blood rising and beating in my veins. Before me was a life of pleasure and luxury. I looked at my sister with her thin cheeks and prematurely wrinkled face, I noted her children, seven in number, were all growing up, and requiring food and clothing which could not be given them. I saw her husband too weak in body to be strong in soul. His preaching was a failure: He was a dispirited disappointed man; an irritable husband and father, a gloomy narrow-minded parson. Oh, I know you think me hard, but looking back, I don't wonder that my youth rebelled against such a fate as my sister's! I felt secure of Alfred's affection, and determined to stick to him. To make a long story short, we wrote to each other and in spite of much opposition from both his family and mine, we finally married, and I have not regretted doing so!"

There was something almost defiant in Mrs. Burke's tone. Rowena was deeply interested.

"How well I seem to see it all!" she said. "But did you discard religion as an old glove when you married?"

"I did. I was nothing, if not sincere in those days. I knew my husband was out to enjoy life, and I meant to enjoy it with him. It had to be one thing or the other with me. I felt that a certain part of me had always been starved, my sister assuring me that it was the worst part of me. But I meant to have my fill of what the world could give me. I threw my ultra-fastidious conscience to the winds. I determined to live as the greater part of the young world lives, for pleasure and amusement, and I have done so ever since. My motto is to have a good time and to help everyone else to have the same."

"And when your husband died?"

"Ah, don't remind me of the black blots in my life! I have had two. I lost our darling little only child at two years old, and then my husband, after only five years of happy married life. He was killed out hunting. But these times come to us all. I forget them or try to do so."

Rowena remembered that only two years previously she had been living the same life as Mrs. Burke; and felt that she could not judge her.

There was a little silence, then Mrs. Burke said with an effort:

"They say every one has a skeleton in the cupboard. Do you know what mine is? It's a certain verse from the Bible that haunts me, and turns up at times to disturb my tranquillity. You see I know my Bible well. We were too much nourished on it ever to forget it, and the verse was a favourite one of my father's; he used to preach on it:

"'Cast not away therefore your confidence which hath great recompense of reward!'"

"That comes up at intervals. Of course I have cast my confidence away. I have none in God or Heaven or in any of the unseen things which good people say we ought to have even down here. I have made my choice and must abide by it. There now! To no living being have I ever confessed so much before. What is it about you that makes me talk so?"

"I don't know," said Rowena with her sunshiny smile, "but I know now why you have attracted me. I felt there was something beautiful deep down out of reach."

"Beautiful! Deep down! What do you mean? Haven't I just shown you, as parsons would say, the depravity of the human heart?"

Rowena did not speak for a moment; she was looking away dreamily as if into space. They were pacing up and down an old box-bordered walk, and now for a moment paused at the end of it. The sun was sinking slowly behind a belt of pines silhouetted against the line of the blue distant hills.

"I remember about a year ago," said Rowena slowly, "talking to my brother's Scotch gardener about a certain part of the shrubbery where things grew in the most wonderful thriving way. He said that long ago that bit of ground had been a vegetable plot, and had been well worked. Later on a summer-house had been built upon it, then it had fallen into ruins and the shrubbery planted. He said that deep down under the rubbish cleared away of the summer-house, there was real good soil, and it was making itself felt in spite of the time that had elapsed since it had been worked."

"Now what on earth are you doing? Giving me a parable to read. There's no good soil left in my soul, let me tell you! Come along in, and don't for goodness' sake set my skeleton walking! He is shut up and locked away as a rule."

Rowena said no more.

When "good night" was being said, Mrs. Burke remarked with her jolly laugh:

"One day I shall demand an account of your depths, and you will have to give it to me. But I warn you in my house, you will have to frivol whether you like it or not."

CHAPTER III
CHASING SHADOWS

"Heart buried in the rubbish of the world—
The world—that gulf of Souls—immortal Souls."
Young.

IT was a strange life into which Rowena had slipped. Anyone else who held the same views that she did would have found it impossible. But Rowena had always a wonderful adaptability to her circumstances. And she had a supreme faith and hope in the best of people, which is often hidden from those who only look on the surface. Those in her company were strangely conscious of this. They knew that if she did not agree with them, she would not harshly judge them, and that she always believed in the best of them, not the worst. Vi and Di in their reckless youth were inclined to look upon her with hostility at first. Before long she was in their full confidence. Vi confided in her continual and varied love affairs, Di, confessed her many debts and her subterfuges for escaping payment. They turned to her when Mrs. Burke did not please them. More than once she had to act as peacemaker, for she soon discovered that there were certain days and occasions when Mrs. Burke's spirits collapsed, and she was irritable and captious with all around her.

Rowena tackled her sheaves of unanswered letters, and all her business with indomitable patience. As a rule she never left the library from breakfast to luncheon. In the afternoons she was at Mrs. Burke's disposal, and that lady had generally need of her, but her Sundays were her own. Rowena appeared at meal times, but often in the afternoons would take some biscuits in her pocket, and her small tea kettle, and would go out into the woods with her books, have her tea there, and not come in till evening service. She rarely missed the morning and evening services in the little country church. In the morning, she took a class at the Sunday School. Her Sundays refreshed and strengthened her for the week. Minley Court had not a restful atmosphere.

There was a continual stream of visitors, and perpetual entertainments for them.

There were a certain number of steady Bridge players, but Mrs. Burke herself would not play much.

"I hate sitting still," she said. "I like to be on the move."

There were moonlight picnics on the river, and at the sea; there were tournaments of croquet, tennis, bowls, and archery, and any other game that was in vogue. There were impromptu plays and charades, and any amount of childish games and romps in which the elders took part quite as enthusiastically as the younger ones. Rowena played accompaniments, organized the games, looked after the comfort of all, and was her easy humorous self amongst a set of people whom she might have condemned and despised. She was soon a general favourite. One poor lady's maid departed suddenly owing to the death of her mother. Rowena met the tearful lady in the corridor bewailing her fate, and went straight into her room, and helped her dress for dinner, even dressing her hair. It was little acts like this that made her popular, and somehow or other Rowena got many an opportunity, which she was eager to seize, of a word upon the human world, and upon the high destiny of each soul that is born.

She never preached; she simply dropped a seed here, and a seed there; and prayed that it might be nurtured and brought to fruitfulness. And as she never spoke of these things in public, the guests were willing to talk to her in the privacy of their bedrooms, or when taking a solitary walk with her. They told her frankly of their troubles and difficulties, and she told them frankly of an infallible remedy for all.

One girl who was thinking of taking up the stage as a profession said to Rowena after they had had a long serious talk together in her bedroom one evening: "You know I've never heard of these things. I've never come across good people. They always keep away from us, and I get my ideas of religion through the Churches which I hardly ever attend. And it never entered my head that I, as an individual unit, shall be held responsible for my influence and life. I don't like the idea at all; but somehow you have made me believe in it. It's most upsetting."

She left after a week's visit, but persisted in starting a correspondence with Rowena, and some time later, told her she was giving up the idea of the stage, as she did not think it would be satisfying.

One day Mrs. Burke and Rowena were driving out when they met the rector and his daughter Maude. He wanted to speak to Mrs. Burke about some parochial matter, and whilst he was speaking to her, Rowena and

Maude chatted together. The girl was devoted to Rowena, and carried on a very animated conversation with her. Mrs. Burke glanced at her in surprise, and suddenly turned to her and asked her to come to tennis the following afternoon.

After a little hesitation on the part of her father the invitation was accepted, and they drove on.

"Why that girl is quite pretty," Mrs. Burke said. "I thought she was a little stiff prig. I have only seen her in church, and hurrying in and out of the cottages. I wonder if I should be allowed to give her a good time? Remembering my own poverty-stricken youth, I always pity these parsons' daughters."

"Maude is a very happy girl," said Rowena; "and you can't look upon her father as a tyrant. He gives her all the pleasures he can."

Mrs. Burke nodded her head knowingly:

"We'll see. I shall cultivate her acquaintance."

"Don't bewitch her," Rowena said, laughing: "don't try to make her discontented with her lot."

"Leave me alone, and don't spoil sport."

Rowena had reason to fear Mrs. Burke's influence. She had a way with her of captivating all young girls, and Maude fell an easy prey to her. When she went home from the tennis party, she told her father that Mrs. Burke had been adorable to her, and wanted her to come to dine the following Saturday, when she would have a house-party. "Do let me go, Dad. You like Miss Arbuthnot and she will be there."

"No, my child, not on Saturday. I know the style of Mrs. Burke's week-end parties, and don't want a daughter of mine mixed up in them."

"Oh, I shall be so disappointed. You might let me this once."

The Rector was immovable, and for the first time his bright little daughter left his study with a cloud upon her face, and a feeling of resentment in her heart against her father's will.

Rowena watched with anxiety Mrs. Burke's efforts to capture the girl's affection. She saw how much she loved her popularity, and how she tried to attract the young. Always fearless, Rowena spoke to her one day about it: "Do you really think you will put fresh happiness into Maude's life by making her discontented with her home, and giving her a taste for things out of her sphere?"

"I love to see the young thoughtless. They ought to be."

"It's the crackling of the thorns under the pot," said Rowena. "I often wonder how you can keep it up; you are worthy of higher things!"

"Stuff! Don't lecture me! My life is my own. If I fritter it away, I have only myself to blame."

She continued to waylay Maude. She sent her presents, she took her drives, and the girl's head was becoming turned. Then Rowena determined to interfere. She met Maude in the village one day, on her way to visit a sick woman at a distant farm, and she volunteered to accompany her.

Maude was delighted, but her conversation was entirely upon Minley Court. She asked Rowena who the next guests were going to be, what entertainments were going to be given to them, and said in her enthusiastic way:

"I do think Mrs. Burke so delightful, she's so unselfish, always trying to make people happy! I don't know why Dad does not like her. I suppose it is because she comes to church so seldom. I envy you living with her, the whole house is so jolly, every one seems so happy!"

"My dear child, if you were to ask my opinion, I should say the atmosphere at the Rectory was far happier. Clowns laugh, you know, with breaking hearts. Laughter and noise are no true test of happiness. Don't barter away your substance for a shadow, Maude. Minley Court is a place of shadows and unrealities of paint and camouflage, and Mrs. Burke, for all her jolly gaiety, would give a good deal I believe to have your father's outlook instead of her own. You see I am taking you into my confidence when I talk like this. I am very fond of Mrs. Burke and I'm deeply sorry for her. For she is chasing shadows, and trying to persuade herself that they are the substance."

"She had an unhappy girlhood," said Maude, unconvinced. "She told me all about it."

"Well, you haven't had that, have you?"

"No—no—but sometimes—lately—I feel as if Father is rather strict about some things."

"Of course you would think so, and being much at Minley Court will make you think so—"

"Now, Miss Arbuthnot, you speak as if you disapprove of Minley Court, and yet you are there yourself in the middle of it all, and you seem almost the centre of it. You laugh and talk with every one and seem quite fond of them. Why should it be good for you to be there and bad for me?"

Maude ended her speech by blushing hotly, afraid that she had been too outspoken, but Rowena smiled upon her reassuringly.

"I dare say I may seem inconsistent to you, but I am there for a purpose—and I want to help Mrs. Burke all I can. I know her better than you do, and know that her empty forlorn time will come, when she will see that this time has been all froth and bubble. I want to be with her then, for she will need help. And I do want you not to make the mistake she did when she was a young girl. She threw away her confidence—she knew she did it—she threw away all her hopes and ideals, for the kind of life she is leading now. You can't have both, Maude dear, and what you throw away is sometimes very difficult to get back again. Don't you do as she did, for those who are with her most, know she isn't a happy woman. And I shall never rest till I see her with her discarded treasures once again."

Maude was visibly impressed. She slipped her hand into Rowena's, and squeezed it.

"You are so good. I oughtn't to have spoken so. I see that people like you, and of course you do them good, just as you do me. I always want to be good after leaving you."

"My dear Maude, don't set me up on a pedestal. Do you know that two years ago I was a godless heathen? and then gradually I began to see beauty in things I had scorned before. I don't know how I did it, but I was gently and surely drawn into quite another environment. It sounds mystical, doesn't it? I came to see what a wonderful creed we have as Christians, and I came to know the Founder of our creed. You have grown up in that atmosphere. Don't try to leave it, I beseech you. Now I'm not going to preach any more, tell me about this sick woman."

After this little talk, Maude's wave of discontent vanished. She did not very often come up to the Court, and when she did, she saw things at a truer value.

The summer wore away. Mrs. Burke's liking for Rowena did not lessen, and she more than once had serious talks with her. If Rowena expressed disapproval of certain things, she was not angry with her, only pursued her way, laughing at her "squeamishness." But occasionally she modified her schemes to Rowena's requirements.

One afternoon in late September, she and Rowena were enjoying their tea together over a good fire in the big drawing-room. The last of her guests had left the house about an hour before, and Mrs. Burke leant back in her comfortable easy-chair with a sense of relief.

"The last of my visitors," she said. "I shall have a quiet week or two, before we move up to town. I hate a winter in the country, but I always come down here for Christmas. It seems the thing to do."

"I am sure that reason does not weigh with you," said Rowena laughing.

"No, perhaps it does not. I hate conventions."

"Will you want me to come up to town with you?"

"Why, of course I do. How should I get on without you?"

"I could stay down here and caretake for you, and do most of your correspondence without you. You leave me such a free and independent hand in your affairs, that I believe I could carry on, with an occasional inquiry by post."

"You are my companion as well as my secretary. Of course I shall want you in town. Don't tell me you would rather vegetate down here, instead of being in the middle of it all."

"Oh, I would much rather stay here," said Rowena frankly; "but of course I shall be ready to accompany you."

"You are an extraordinary creature—a regular hermit; you seem to care for nothing. And as to money! well, it is a good thing you are not wealthy. It would be wasted upon you."

"Oh would it? I don't think so."

Rowena's expressive eyes glowed as she gazed into the fire.

"Wealth can do so much—I have your command laid upon me that I am not to relieve any of the appeals that come to you by post. I know you have your charity list and it is a big one, but you don't know how I ache sometimes to slip a pound note into an envelope and send it off. There are so many private cases of want and misery that never come before the public at all, and therefore never get relieved."

"It's the worst class that begs through the post," said Mrs. Burke indifferently.

"Some are humbugs, of course; but I would have a shot or two. I often think of your early days. They have a strange fascination for me. If I were you, I think I would go round to the country villages and ferret out for myself some of the real deserving cases amongst the poor clergy."

Mrs. Burke looked at her meditatively.

"There might be some sense in that," she said, then added hurriedly, "but you would want a millionaire's income to give away in that style."

"No," said Rowena, still gazing dreamily before her, "you would only have to set apart a few hundreds for the purpose. You could do a lot, say, if you were to spare £500 out of your income for the poor clergy every year; you would never miss it. Think what it would do for them."

"It would be but a drop in the ocean," said Mrs. Burke. "Take up Crockford's, and see the incomes of the married clergy. I always do say it is iniquitous! I know my father was heavily in debt all his life, and though he could not clothe and feed his family in a decent manner, he was supposed to relieve all the bad cases of poverty in his parish, and keep a rotten old dilapidated church in perfect repair. If you have no rich people in your parish, and the Squire is close fisted, all the expenses fall on the poor parson's shoulders. But don't let us talk of such dismal subjects. I did not tell you that I heard from my sister yesterday. I think we have not written to each other for five years. Her husband is ill, and of course wants to be nursed and nourished and sent to a warmer clime the doctors say. It's one of his lungs. She must be pretty low down to turn to me. There was a time when she refused to touch a farthing of my money."

"Poor thing! How awful not to be able to do what is best for him."

"She shouldn't have married a poor curate. I suppose I shall have to send her a cheque. You must see to it for me. I am wondering what she will do, whether she will take him away herself. There is one blessing, all her children are grown-up and doing for themselves I believe. But she seems to have some of her grandchildren dependent on her. Talks of her darling Nester's boy and girls, who are such a comfort to her. I believe Nester was the girl who married a very hard-worked doctor, and he and she both succumbed to some epidemic raging round them. I did hear about it. Send a cheque for a hundred pounds. That will help."

"I will do it to-morrow morning."

"You look as pleased as if you are going to have it for yourself. Don't you think all my charity cheques will go on the credit side of my life's history? I may be frivolous, but I do feed the hungry and clothe the naked—sometimes."

"Yes, you do," said Rowena gravely.

"I know you size me up in your own mind and judge me. Not in the same pharisaical manner as my sister judges me! My heart prompts me to tell her to send along these grandchildren of hers, and I'll look after them whilst she goes away with her husband. But she would only snub me, and say she wouldn't have them contaminated by my society. Do you think I would do them harm? I know you thought I was spoiling little Maude Waring."

"I wish you would let me go and pay them a visit," said Rowena suddenly. "A hundred pounds will not help them much at a time like this. I could find out just how things were, and then we would talk it over together. If your sister will let you help her, you would like to do it I expect."

"She must be quite elderly by this time," said Mrs. Burke musingly; "she is five years older than I am. Oh, I can't spare you at present. Not till we are thoroughly settled down in town."

Rowena said no more. She felt a strange interest in this sister of Mrs. Burke's, and longed that the two sisters should come closer together.

They went up to town, and some very busy crowded weeks followed. From the first Rowena kept out of the incessant round of gaiety. Mrs. Burke turned night into day, and thought nothing of attending three or four reception and supper parties the same night, sometimes cramming in a theatre as well. To these Rowena did not go. She helped Mrs. Burke when she entertained at home; beyond that she begged to be excused. There were charity entertainments, and bazaars in the afternoon, to which she was dragged. People used Mrs. Burke's house like an hotel, but she never complained; and the younger and giddier the company was, the better she enjoyed herself.

The cheque was sent off to her sister, and Mrs. Burke received a letter of grateful thanks; but it was not till a month later that she allowed Rowena to go up north, and see what further help was required.

She came back and gave Mrs. Burke her report. "I was only just in time to see your sister. What a sweet woman she is!"

"She used to be pretty. I suppose she slanged me pretty thoroughly."

"May I be quite frank and tell you her attitude towards you?"

"Oh yes—don't spare my feelings. I have a thick skin and can bear it."

"She said she realized that she had been hard towards you in those early days; but now that you were getting on in years, she felt sure you must be becoming tired of a life of pleasure, and she would like to be friends with you."

"Afraid of losing my money should I die!" snapped Mrs. Burke. "I am much obliged to her. I hope you stood up for me."

Rowena laughed. "I told her how good you were to me and everybody, and then we talked about the grandchildren. She is taking her husband to Bournemouth. It is too late to save his life I am afraid. He has not the strength for a journey abroad even if the means were forthcoming. She has a daughter living at home now. She is a governess, but is out of a situation and has been helping her mother since her father has been so ill. The grandchildren consist of two girls and a boy. The boy is a handsome little fellow of fifteen, the girls are sixteen and twelve. They ought to be all at school. The elder girl teaches the younger one, and the boy goes to the Grammar School. She is leaving them for the present at home with her daughter. I think you would lose your heart to the trio, they are so bright and so good-looking, but are delicate—want of good food I should say."

"Did you suggest they should come to me?"

"No. How could you have them here in London? I said something about the holidays, but you must write to your sister about it."

"We'll have them down for Christmas, and give them a good time. I'll write at once, and if the boy is worth placing at a good school, I'll do it."

"That will be splendid. Oh dear, I do envy you your opportunities!"

"It is you pegging away at me, that makes me seize them." And it was true. Slowly, but surely Mrs. Burke was finding out the delights of sharing some of her wealth with those in need. Before Rowena had come, she made her banker her almoner; now she began to take interest in many individual cases, whom Rowena discovered. Sometimes when her spirits flagged, she would say: "I dare say I shall end my days in some secluded country cottage; I am sure you will gradually get all my wealth from me for your 'deserving poor'!"

And Rowena would reply with a glow in her eyes, "You might do many worse things than that."

CHAPTER IV
AN OLD FRIEND

"And I perceived no touch of change"

"But found him all in all the same."
Tennyson.

"MY dear girl, you must come with me to Lady Graeme's At Home this afternoon."

"Oh, why?" asked Rowena, looking up from her desk with a wrinkle between her brows.

"Well, she made a special point of your accompanying me. She lost her heart to you the other afternoon when she was here. Now I let you off a good many places, but not this one. Will you be ready about half-past four?"

"If you wish."

And so it came to pass that Rowena found herself, on a foggy November afternoon, in a crowded drawing-room in Palace Gate. She knew many of the young people assembled there, for Lady Graeme, like Mrs. Burke, though old herself, loved to surround herself with the young. It was not a very staid gathering. There was a distinctly rowdy element in it. Every one smoked, and voices were loud and voluble. Rowena got as near the door as she could. She hoped she could slip out into an emptier ante-room, but first one and then another detained her. Lady Graeme's second son, Alan by name, was a special crony of hers. He had stayed at Minley Court on several occasions, and was a fresh frank young fellow in the Scots Guards. He now slipped into a seat close to her.

"Thanks be, that you are here, at any rate," he said. "I do loathe the mater's crushes so. I hardly see you anywhere in town. Don't you go about?"

"I'm not a gadder by choice," said Rowena cheerfully.

"You don't look it! Did you ever see such a set of women as are here this afternoon? I'm getting fed up with it. I should like to go off game hunting in Somaliland or in the Rockies."

"Why don't you do it when you get your leave? I agree with you, one does get fed up with all this. So much energy wasted."

"Oh, I know what you think of us. You and I have had some straight talks. Why don't you sober your giddy old friend over there. My word! she might be just eighteen!"

Mrs. Burke was the centre of a noisy group—the other end of the room. One of the men was taking off a well-known parliamentary character, and his audience was convulsed with laughter.

Rowena looked across at her and sighed; then she turned to her young companion and smiled.

"Well, you see what life does to those who grow old in this atmosphere! Get your own soul into fresher and clearer air, and do something before you die. Isn't it Young that says:

"Time wasted is existence—us'd is life."

"You ought to have lived in the mediæval days," laughed young Alan. "How you would have buckled on your man's sword and thrust him forth! Do you seriously think running down a tiger is more soul inspiring than dancing the Tango?"

"Your soul would get a chance of breathing. Life without a pause is so paralysing."

"We always get into metaphysics—you and I! Hulloo, here is Macdonald by all that's wonderful! The mater has beguiled him here under false pretences; he'll never stand this. Take a good look at him. He saved my life out in France—ought to have got a V.C. for it. He's a cousin of ours."

Rowena took one look at the tall figure coming in at the door, and a faint flush rose to her cheeks, a breath of Highland air seemed to accompany him. He looked irreproachable in his London clothes, and yet there was some indescribable stamp about him that set him apart from the men around him.

"Let me introduce him," said her young companion.

"But I know him," said Rowena.

Alan Graeme started forward and shook hands warmly with the General.

"Awfully good of you to come! The mater's just gone into the tea room; here's some one who knows you."

General Macdonald met Rowena's bright friendly eyes, with grave pleasure in his own.

He held out his hand to her.

"It seems a long time since we met," he said. "I have brought Mysie to town for a week or two."

Alan was seized hold of by a young girl in a startling dress of black and white striped velvet, very open at the neck and back; very short in the skirt.

"Oh, you slacker!" she exclaimed, putting her hand on his shoulder. "Don't you know that two lady loves await you in that further corner. They have sent me to fetch you. You promised to sing for one, and—"

They moved off.

General Macdonald's look of disgust made Rowena smile.

"Are you at home in this company?" he asked abruptly; "it somehow does not seem to fit you."

Then before she had time to reply he went on:

"I am told I am old-fashioned and censorious; but a scene like this repels me. Are these the mothers of our future generation? May God help me to keep Mysie out of fashionable society."

"Amen," breathed Rowena.

"Give me news of the Highlands," she said.

He did not respond, but looked at her in puzzled bewilderment.

"Do you often attend these functions? I feel like a fish out of water. Is there nowhere we can get away from this smoke and heat? I came to see my cousin."

"Shall we go into the tea room? I believe she is there." But the tea room was overcrowded, and they stood for a moment in the corridor outside. He told her he had brought Mysie up for a fortnight and they were staying with an old cousin of his in Eton Place. Then he asked her about herself, and Rowena pointed out Mrs. Burke to him.

"I live with her, as a companion-secretary."

General Macdonald looked at Mrs. Burke with her golden wig and rather loud style of dress. He noted the noisy circle in which she was, and he said shortly and sternly, "I am sorry to hear it."

Rowena's eyes first twinkled, then softened:

"I do like you," she said audaciously, "when you act the stern friend."

He did not smile.

"Mysie will be wild to get hold of you. Can you come round and see us?"

"I think I might perhaps to-morrow, darling Mysie! I expect she is grown."

He was silent. Rowena was conscious that she was the subject of his close scrutiny.

"You have been through trouble since we met. I did not know your address or would have written you a line of sympathy. Your brother was a great friend of mine."

"I know. Thank you. My sister-in-law has gone to live with her mother, so I am on my own."

"And you can do no better than this?"

"You are judging me hardly."

Rowena's tone was rather proud, though her heart was beating and her pulses throbbing strangely. She rather resented the effect that this tall grave friend of hers had upon her.

He smiled, and his smile warmed her heart.

"Perhaps I am. You must tell me all about yourself."

At this moment Lady Graeme came up, and whilst she was greeting her cousin, Mrs. Burke seized hold of Rowena.

"I am off. Come along. I have promised to go to the Ford Curries. If you don't want to come with me, you can go home."

So Rowena left the house with her, and when she got home felt strangely dispirited.

"He will never understand. How can I explain? How can I tell him that I am trying to dig out from the mud a treasure which has been lost. It's like the woman in the Bible. But he only sees the racket and the dust: he doesn't know the silver bit is there."

The next day she asked permission from Mrs. Burke for an afternoon to herself, and set off for Eton Place.

She was shown upstairs into a rather gloomy drawing-room, but in a moment Mysie flashed into the room, and in her old impulsive way flung herself upon her.

"Oh, you darling! I can't believe it's you. I yelled when Dad told me, and Cousin Bel asked if I was trying to do the Highland Fling. Cousin Bel has a cold and is in bed, and Dad and I sit downstairs in the smoking-room. There's no fire up here. Come along down."

Rowena found that Mysie was growing into a very handsome girl. She had developed in many ways, and it was pretty to see her with her father; there was absolute confidence and understanding between them.

"He has got younger, and she has got older," was Rowena's conviction. She took Rowena downstairs, and General Macdonald rose to greet her with a bright smile of welcome.

He pulled an easy-chair before the fire for her, and Mysie squatted down on the hearthrug and leant her brown curly head against her knees.

"Isn't this comfy, just us three! Dad and I often wanted you when the days got dark after you left us. And do you know I've got a new name for you. I used to call you the prisoner—now I call you Miss Mignon. I learn French now, so I know a lot of fresh words!"

Rowena laughed.

"Oh, Flora, it is nice to hear you talk again! Tell me all you have been doing."

Mysie was only too delighted to chatter away. She appealed to her father very often, and he sat for the most part listening to his small daughter, but sometimes putting in a word himself.

"Dad says you live with an old lady now. Couldn't you leave her, and come and stay with us for a nice long visit? Dad and I thought you were still in India; we would have come to see you long ago, wouldn't we, Dad, if we had known you were in London."

"I'm sorry to tell you that young Macintosh is leaving us," said General Macdonald. "He has been offered a Church in Edinburgh. That is one of the causes which has brought us to town. We are going to try another governess, but we have decided that she must be quite old; somebody who will be content to sit at home over the schoolroom fire whilst Mysie and I tramp the country together."

"I hope you will find her," said Rowena gaily. "But I am sorry the Macintoshes are leaving. I liked them so much."

Then she turned to General Macdonald.

"Are you more at home now? Perhaps you have finished your work?"

"It finished me unfortunately. I had a breakdown, and was ordered back to my native air. A quiet life is the only thing I'm fit for."

"Oh, I'm sorry, and yet I know Mysie must be glad—and your tenants!"

"That's a fact!" said Mysie, nodding her head.

"And how are the Kelpies and the fairies?" Rowena inquired.

Mysie began to tell her a fresh story she had heard from an old Highland woman of the fairies' existence.

"How is your Highland book?" asked General Macdonald.

"Oh," said Rowena with a little sigh, "I have never got any forrarder. I took it out to India with me, meaning to complete it there; but somehow I couldn't get on with it. The atmosphere was lacking, and then poor Ted died, and I haven't had the heart to touch it since."

"You must finish it."

"Perhaps I will. You have stirred me up afresh."

Presently Mysie slipped away.

"I'm going to hurry up tea," she said importantly. "Dad and I think Cousin Bel's old servants all go to bed in the afternoon. None of them can be found anywhere till tea-time, and sometimes we don't have it till half-past five!"

When she had gone, General Macdonald turned to Rowena. "Why did you not answer that letter of mine?"

"What letter? I remember your saying just before I left Abertarlie, that you would either come over again, or write, but you did neither."

"I most certainly wrote. Did you never receive it?"

He got up from his chair and paced the floor in agitation, and Rowena felt breathless, as if she were on the point of a crisis in her life.

"Never. Letters sometimes go astray, and I am afraid poor Sandy was addicted to the bottle."

"I wrote, and took it for granted from your silence that—"

He broke off suddenly, and looked at her strangely. "Don't think me interfering. I can't beat about the bush. But I cannot bear to think of you with that painted woman and in her noisy set. I know her well by name. My young friend Graeme has talked of her. If you value the things you once did, how can you live with her? I do ask you as a personal favour to leave her."

Rowena was astounded and dismayed by this sudden turn to their talk. She was proud, and she seemed to General Macdonald to stiffen from head to foot.

"I have my reasons for staying with her," she said coldly. "You may doubt and misunderstand my motives, but at present I have no intention of changing my life."

"I am sorry," he said simply, and at this unfortunate juncture Mysie danced back into the room.

"Tea is coming. I coaxed and coaxed old stiff Mary till she said she would bring it at once. And I'm going to pour out, Dad, and we can just imagine we are home in Abertarlie."

But conversation was dead. Mysie chattered away apparently unconscious of the effort it was to her elders to respond to her. And very soon Rowena rose to go. She felt bitterly hurt by General Macdonald's words, and was not inclined to justify herself in his eyes.

As she walked home alone, she said to herself: "Oh what a touchy fool I am! He saw me at that rowdy party, and did not know it was quite an exception, my being there. He thought it was my habit, my life! How can I tell him why I'm not going to leave Mrs. Burke yet! I hardly dare put it into words, but I've prayed so hard, that I will not despair. No, if he misjudges me he must. Oh, how I wish I knew what was in that letter! In any case he is cautious, and canny like a Scot! I hate his cold calculating mood. I almost feel as if I never want to see him again!"

But if Rowena persuaded herself that she did not want to see him again, he most certainly wanted to see her. For the next morning at twelve o'clock he called at the house and asked for her. Mrs. Burke had not left her room yet, but Rowena was hard at work in the library. She gave a little sigh when she heard who was in the drawing-room waiting to see her. She had had a sleepless night, wondering about the contents of the missing letter, regretting the way she had spoken to her old friend, turning over in her own mind if she had been right or wrong in electing to live with Mrs. Burke, and now hardly knowing in what frame of mind to meet him.

But the moment she entered the room, General Macdonald advanced in his most courteous and kindly manner.

"I have come round to apologize for the way I spoke to you yesterday afternoon. I had no right to dictate to you as to your choice in life. May I say in extenuation, it was only my extreme interest in you, my regard for your real welfare that made me so anxious and captious about your present surroundings."

Then Rowena smiled her old sunny smile.

"You treated me as a true friend should. I felt sorry that I had not an explanation I could give you. Perhaps one day I may be able to vindicate myself."

"Meanwhile, whilst we are in town will you give me the benefit of your counsel and advice? My cousin is old. She says, 'Send the child to school.' I tried that, as you know, with disastrous results. Could you—is it too much to ask of you? Could you interview some of these governesses for me? A man is at a disadvantage. I had one afternoon of it last week, and I can tell you I have been in tight corners in my life, and have had to face a good deal, but nothing equal to the horrors of that room behind the registry office, when one undesirable young woman appeared after the other in quick succession, and they all wanted so desperately to come!"

Rowena laughed outright. She pictured the scene.

"You poor man! Of course I will help you if I can. I wish I knew of some one suitable. I wonder—"

She stopped short. The remembrance of her visit to the North came to her.

"It is only a chance, but I do know of a nice woman—a governess. She is a niece of Mrs. Burke's."

"Oh, I hardly think she would suit me," said General Macdonald hastily.

Rowena smiled. "Please don't be so prejudiced. Mrs. Burke's father was a very saintly clergyman. Her sister is a most sweet woman, wife of a hard-worked vicar in Durham, and this woman is her daughter. She has the same sweet face and manners as her mother, but with more character I should say. She is at present looking after her nephew and niece, but she wants a situation as governess. She is certificated."

"Miss Falconer had very sweet manners."

"She is as different to Miss Falconer as chalk is to cheese. She is a real good woman. I know a genuine person when I see her. Couldn't you stop in Durham and interview her, on your return to Scotland? Let me write to her first."

"I wanted to have it all settled up before we leave."

"Well, if you would rather I went to a Registry for you, I will do so."

"Thank you very much. What do you think of Mysie?"

"She has grown and developed wonderfully."

"She is most intelligent—able to talk with me on any subject, and a most interesting companion. But she has a very strong will of her own."

"Like her father," said Rowena mischievously.

"Yes, but women are not required to have as strong wills as men."

"Oh, you old-fashioned person! If a strong will is a good thing why should we not share it? A weak woman very often makes a bad man! Don't try to eradicate the strength in Mysie's character."

"I don't agree with you. The weakness in woman awakens all the chivalry in man's nature. These strong-minded females are abhorrent to me. One of these would-be teachers of my child asked me if I did not believe in the emancipation of the female sex—now what did she mean by that? Mere clap-trap or real immorality!"

Then he checked himself.

"We won't discuss these questions. You and I always slipped into an argument, didn't we, in the old days? I shall be deeply grateful if you can help me. Mysie is to me now a cherished possession and I always consider I have to thank you for bringing me to my senses about her. Now before I go, we propose paying a visit to the Zoo to-morrow afternoon. Could you come with us?"

"I am afraid not," said Rowena regretfully. "It is Mrs. Burke's 'At Home' day to-morrow, and I must be here to help her."

"Mysie will be bitterly disappointed. Where do you go on Sunday?"

Rowena mentioned a certain Church not very far off.

"Canon Villars is a most earnest preacher," she said. "Have you ever heard him?"

"No, I'll bring Mysie round there!"

He got up to go.

"I must not transgress again; but if only you were with one of these philanthropic useful women of the day, how much happier you would be."

"You don't know Mrs. Burke," Rowena said gravely. "You only judge by outer appearances."

He looked at her with a flicker of a smile in his eyes.

"A tree is known by its fruits."

"Good-bye," said Rowena very sweetly. "I will let you have the last word, though it is a woman's prerogative."

At lunch, she told Mrs. Burke about the General's visit, and to her surprise that lady became quite enthusiastic.

"We'll send for Marion at once. I'll pay her fare! She can easily leave those young people for a day or two. It is too great a chance for her to miss. I should like to help her, poor thing, and that handsome General Macdonald must be a nice man to deal with. Let us ask him to dinner; we must get her here first. Nothing like striking whilst the iron is hot. Write directly after lunch, will you, and you had better enclose a cheque for travelling expenses. Don't you think you had better wire?"

"No," said Rowena, laughing, "the poor creature would be thoroughly mystified. You would like it all settled up by this time to-morrow now, wouldn't you?"

"You know how I hate to let the grass grow under my feet."

Rowena wrote the letter. She had been much impressed by Marion's personality and capability, and felt sure that if she agreed to go to Abertarlie, she would not be a failure there. "And oh," she thought with a little grimace of disgust at her own longing for the Highlands, "why did he not offer me the job, instead of wishing to relegate me to these useful philanthropical ladies of his acquaintance!"

CHAPTER V
A SATISFACTORY INTERVIEW

"The character of a generation is moulded by personal character."
Westcott.

ON the following Sunday Rowena met Mysie and her father at the doors of the church which she attended. It was a quiet old-fashioned service, and the congregation was not a fashionable one, but the preacher had an arresting, quickening power of delivery, and he took the Bible alone for his authority.

General Macdonald said when he came out:

"I don't as a rule feel at home in London churches, but that man has the power of raising one from earth altogether."

"Oh, Dad!" expostulated Mysie. "I didn't feel that. I felt I was wedged between the two people I love best in the world, and I longed to hug you both!"

Rowena laughed at Mysie, but replied to the General:

"Yes, Canon Villars always takes me right away with him. He is a wonderful mixture of practical common sense and mysticism."

"And do you never get your—your friend to come and hear him?"

"Once I did."

A shadow came over Rowena's face as she spoke. She had taken Mrs. Burke there soon after they came to town, and the Canon had preached a very scathing sermon on worldliness, and the unprofitableness of it. Mrs. Burke had come away furiously indignant with him, and had refused to set her foot inside the door ever again.

"Didn't she profit by it?"

"I am afraid not. His text was, 'Hear now then, thou that art given to pleasures,' and he was very severe and convincing. But with some people, most I should think, it is absolutely useless to tell them they should give up all that they have; empty their hearts, before they know how to fill them! Love draws, severity drives!"

"I don't quite agree," said General Macdonald. "In these days there is too much laxity and forbearance with sin. But you must remember I have centuries of Scotch training behind me."

"But in vulgar words, the 'proof of the pudding is in the eating.' That sermon has kept Mrs. Burke from going to church ever since she heard it."

"I wish you would leave her," said the General emphatically.

Rowena shook her head and changed the subject.

She began to tell him of Mrs. Burke's niece, and of the letters that had been sent to her, and asked him if he would be willing to interview her, if she would be able to come to town.

"And if Mrs. Burke asks you to dinner to meet her, will you come? I hope you will."

"If I can meet her in a quiet way I shall be glad to do so."

"Now that is nice and friendly of you. I assure you that you will not be shocked in any way."

Then with a little laugh she added:

"We want to see some good people sometimes, you know. They bring a different atmosphere with them."

They took a turn together in the Park before Rowena went home. As they parted he said:

"I hope you have a quiet Sunday. But it seems to be the fashion to receive visitors all the afternoon. Even my old cousin does it."

"You will have to run away as I do if you want to be quiet," said Rowena cheerfully.

She walked home with a little amusement as well as pity at the General's inadaptability to his circumstances. "He is a man in one groove," she said to herself. "I am sure he is much concerned at my atmosphere surroundings; but after all, my business is not his, and he has no right to try to manage my life."

The next day Mrs. Burke heard from her niece. "She is actually coming," she told Rowena, "but only for a couple of nights, as she is in charge whilst her mother is away. My dear, I am frightened of her, and feel I should like to run away and leave her to you. I shall scandalize her every minute of the day, I know; her very letter reeks of righteousness!"

"Oh, don't!" expostulated Rowena in a pained tone. "You really do respect sincerity and goodness in the bottom of your heart. Don't mock at it."

"Well, I respect you. But you're not what I call sanctimonious. Now write off to that good-looking old Scotchie, and ask him to dinner. Who shall we have besides? Some one to frivol with me, I think."

"No, let us be alone for once."

"My dear, I shall be bored to tears. I shall go off to the theatre then, and leave you to entertain them."

"That you can please yourself about. But I don't think it will be very polite."

"Then I shall be as cross as two sticks—unless we can manage to shake a little fun out of our guests. I haven't seen Marion since she was a child in pinafores, but I can imagine she will be a repetition of her mother."

Marion arrived in two days' time. Rowena was glad that Mrs. Burke was dining out, for she had her to herself, and told her all she knew about Mysie and her father.

Marion was a good-looking woman. Her clothes were shabby, but she had a sweet face and a quantity of soft brown hair coiled round a shapely little head. Rowena was satisfied that she would find favour in General Macdonald's sight. They sat over the drawing-room fire and talked, and Marion at last began to ask questions about her aunt.

"I don't feel at home in all this luxury," she said, "and yet I must confess I like it. I cannot understand why my parents were so averse to be helped in any way by Aunt Caroline. You say you are fond of her. She cannot be wholly bad!"

"No," said Rowena, "she is not. She is one of the most kindhearted creatures that I have ever come across, and—remember—she has known what is good and right, and still keeps memories of her young days packed away in her heart. She always tries to appear more empty-headed and frivolous than she really is. And I believe that one day she will search and find again what she has so carelessly thrown away. Bear this in mind when you hear her talking."

Marion was tired with her journey and went early to bed. She did not see her aunt till noon the next day. Her heart sank when she saw Mrs. Burke's smart attire, and noted the powder and rouge on her smiling good-natured face.

"Well, my dear, glad to see you! Rowena has made you welcome, and you will see more of her than you will do of me, for I have a good many engagements in town. Are you ready to go off to this immaculate Highland lair? According to Rowena, the child is a perfect child, and the father everything that an ordinary man is not. He is coming to dinner with us to-night, and I advise you to take stock of him. Now tell me about your father. How is he?"

"Not much better. The doctor says it is now only a question of weeks!"

"Dear me! How sad! But doctors are often mistaken. Now, my dear Marion, have you a decent dinner dress? As my niece I like to see you nicely dressed, and if you don't possess one, I will get Rowena to run you round to the shops. There are wonderful ready-made little gowns at Dalton & Lane's, and I think a nice dark velvet would suit you. Don't trouble about the price. I have an account there and it will be booked to me. And if you do come to terms, and agree to go off to Scotland, you must have a suitable outfit. Rowena will see to it for me, I know."

Marion looked very uncomfortable. She tried to thank her aunt, but Rowena saw that gentle though she was, she possessed a certain amount of pride.

"A governess is always very quietly dressed, Aunt Caroline," she said, "and I have been a resident governess before in quite good families. I shall be able to get what I require."

"Well, I mean to give you a very quiet but handsome gown for dinner parties. Rowena, take her out directly after luncheon."

And so it came to pass that when General Macdonald arrived that evening he was introduced to a very sweet-looking, dignified woman in a brown velvet gown which matched her brown eyes and hair. He came early, and had an interview with her in Mrs. Burke's back drawing-room. There was a light in his eyes, as he joined Rowena just before dinner, and had the opportunity of speaking to her alone. "She'll do," he said. "I like her extremely. A woman with religion and principle. She's willing to come, but not just yet, I'm afraid—says she must wait till her mother returns home. And she does not seem to know when that will be. She has shown me any amount of certificates and references, but I know a good woman when I see her, and I place that first; education comes afterwards."

Dinner was a difficult time. Mrs. Burke was in her usual high spirits, and rattled away in an astonishing fashion it seemed to her niece. General Macdonald was courteous, but rather stiff, and Rowena strove to bridge over awkward pauses and water down some of Mrs. Burke's rash statements.

"I'm sure my niece is one of your sort," she informed the General. "You Scotch people always take life seriously, and she has been brought up in the old-fashioned orthodox style. Her family never has approved of me."

"Why is it old-fashioned to take life seriously?" said General Macdonald gravely. "Isn't life with all of us a very wonderful and mysterious thing?"

"Oh, I have learnt to take things as I find them," said Mrs. Burke, deliberately giving a slow wink to Rowena. "I'm not good at theology, or at any of the other 'ologies. But I remember a maxim of Solomon's—or one of the Bible sages: 'A man hath no better thing under the sun than to eat and to drink and to be merry.' And I practise that every day of my life."

"Oh, Aunt Caroline!" protested her niece.

"We have the story of one who practised that too in the Bible," said General Macdonald, fixing a stern eye upon his hostess. "And his summons to meet his God came like a thunderbolt to him."

"Yes, I think I used to be terrorized by that story when I was a child," said Mrs. Burke with smiling indifference.

Rowena felt so nervous that she almost laughed, a habit which sometimes overcame her against her will.

General Macdonald looked at her in pained surprise.

"I want you to tell Miss Panton about Abertarlie," she said, hurriedly turning to him. "She has never been in Scotland before, and has no idea of the solitude of some parts of the Highlands. Didn't you find an eagle's nest on the crags above your house when you were a boy? Mysie was telling me about it one day."

A smile came to the General's face at the memory of a very bright day in his childhood; he began describing his home to Marion, and Rowena turned to Mrs. Burke and talked nonsense with her for the rest of the meal.

Things did not go much better in the drawing-room afterwards. Mrs. Burke lit up her cigarette, offered the General one, which he declined, and asked him if he would like a game of bridge. Then she told a society scandal, and finally went to the piano and began trying over some topical music-hall songs. Rowena saw that she was determined to show her worst side to her guests, and General Macdonald's stern face had the effect of egging her on.

She sat down by him presently and began talking to him about his child.

"What does a man know about a girl child!" she exclaimed. "Let me give you a piece of sound advice. Give her her head whilst she is young, don't blacken all earth's beauties and pleasures to her. If you tie her up and confine her to one tiny rut, if you make her an obedient follower of all your prejudices and vagrant fancies, she will break away from you when she is older. It's like bottling up steam. Let the young enjoy themselves, nature will have it so. I know what I'm talking about, and I've seen many girls and boys come to utter grief because their parents tried to make them into long-faced canting Puritans."

Then the General had his say:

"Madam, there are two classes in this world. Those who train their children for Heaven, and those who train them for the Prince of this world. I seek to train my child for her heavenly inheritance, and want no advice from anyone but God Himself."

Mrs. Burke had nothing to say. She was strangely subdued for the rest of the evening. She and General Macdonald parted from each other courteously but coldly, and when he had gone she took hold of Rowena and made her come upstairs to her room with her.

"Do you really like that stiff-starched Pharisee, Rowena? Don't tell me that he is your ideal of a gentleman and a father! He's a strong man, I admit. His eyes blazed when he turned upon me. I almost admired him then. But, oh, I wouldn't be Marion for a hundred—a thousand pounds! To be shut away in a lonely Scotch glen with a man of such views would be purgatory to me. How did you stand it when you were ill? But of course I feel he is disgusted and horrified by my ways. And with you he is tenderly sympathetic and protective. My dear, his eyes never left you. He watches for you to speak, and when you do, his eyes glisten and soften as a lover's would do. Has he ever made love to you, eh? I suppose he lives too close to heaven to have anything to do with earthly love. Oh, how I hate your good people! How righteously superior and complacently smug they all are! All except you! And why are you so different? Why have you such love for such poor sinners as I and my friends are? I do believe you have a sneaking love for me even when I am outraging your sense of decency and delicacy, now haven't you? Confess it!"

"I have more than a sneaking love for you," said Rowena warmly. "But you annoy me most dreadfully when you set yourself to disgust and alienate those who would be good friends to you if you would allow them to be. You don't believe or mean half you say. Why do you delight in making yourself out such an utterly worthless and empty-headed woman?"

"Because that is what I am, and no one knows it better than I do myself. I am utterly worthless, Rowena, and one night I shall be summoned to meet my Judge like the man who admonished his soul to eat, drink, and be merry. You see I know all the Bible stories as well as your pious friend does. I wish I didn't remember the Bible so well. We were taught so much of it, and learnt so much of it by rote, that I even now find whole passages and chapters coming into my mind."

"Then you will be comforted by it when you come to the deep waters," said Rowena.

"What do you mean?"

"Why, you surely remember all the lovely promises in it, don't you?"

"They are not for me."

Rowena was silent. Mrs. Burke's face was pathetic, as it sometimes was when a mood of despondency seized her. Rowena bent over and kissed her with one of her warm, sweet kisses.

"I am praying every day for you," she said softly; "now good night, and may you have pleasant dreams."

Mrs. Burke seized hold of Rowena by both hands. "I won't have you pray for me. I forbid it. I won't be made uncomfortable. I want to be left alone in peace. I believe you think you are going to bring me over to your side. I like you, but I hate good people, and I've taken a real dislike to that old General!"

"Good night," repeated Rowena, as she left the room.

Sometimes Mrs. Burke reminded her of a spoilt pettish child. She had to be humoured and left alone.

The next day there was quite a consultation about Marion's future. Mrs. Burke said that she ought to be ready to go to Scotland after the Christmas holidays. "And if your mother has not returned by that time, send me your nephew and nieces. I will look after them, and you can shut the house up, or hand it over to the locum tenens. You can't keep that old tartar waiting. I'm sorry for you to be housed with such a cantankerous saint, but you'll suit him, and he'll suit you. Write and tell him you'll be ready by the middle or end of January."

"Circumstances permitting," put in Rowena.

So Marion meekly did as she was told, writing at the same time to her parents and telling them what she was doing. She left her aunt the next day. Rowena felt she was relieved to go, and Mrs. Burke made no pretence of her feelings.

"Oil and water will not mix. She opens her eyes in fright whenever I begin to speak, and when I smoke she simply turns her head away as if she cannot bear the sight of me. I have done my duty by her, and I get no thanks for it. I hope she will never come here again!"

It was only two weeks afterwards that Mrs. Burke heard from her sister. Her husband had died suddenly, and she was returning home after the funeral.

"And I suppose she is left without a penny," was Mrs. Burke's comment. "Well, it is none of my business. I shall wait and see what she does."

Rowena knew that help would be ready for the poor widow when she would need it.

One afternoon General Macdonald came round to see her. Mrs. Burke was out. Rowena was not very well. She had had a heavy cold, and was only just out of her room. She was sitting over the fire in the drawing-room, and a book was upon her lap.

"I am afraid this is a 'good-bye' visit," said the General. "Mysie will run round to see you to-morrow, but I have business to do in the City, and we leave by the night train to-morrow evening."

"I am sorry you are going," Rowena said frankly; "but you will be glad, I know, for you don't like town."

"I think London is now as frivolous as Paris," said the General gravely. "It is no pleasure to be in it."

"There are many circles," said Rowena thoughtfully. "In every big city there is a certain section who are taking their pleasures madly, but there is a great deal of good going on in a quiet way."

"You see good in every one," said the General with a smile; "even in your giddy old friend with whom you live."

"Now, we won't talk about her. I feel so glad that you are going to have Marion Panton. I am sure she will prove a success. She is devoted to children and wins their love wherever she goes. I have seen letters from some of her old pupils. They were most attached to her."

"Yes, I am grateful to you for the trouble you have taken."

He paused, and Rowena bent forward, a glint of laughter in her bright, soft eyes:

"And don't frighten her too much by giving her your views of a child's training! You sound so very alarming when you talk, and you are so delightfully different when you act! Let yourself go sometimes, and show her that you are human like the rest of us! Am I not impudent in talking like this?"

For a moment the General's eyes held a gleam of corresponding amusement in them, then he stood up, his back to the fire and his whole face full of softened emotion:

"I really came to talk to you about something very important," he said. "Will you give me a hearing?"

CHAPTER VI
THE LAIRD SPEAKS

> "I held her hand, the pledge of bliss,
> Her hand that trembled and withdrew;
> She bent her head before my kiss,
> My heart was sure that hers was true."
> Landor.

ROWENA drew a long breath, then she said very quietly: "Of course I will. I am all attention!"

"I want to refer again to that letter which I sent you before you went to India, and which you never received. In it I asked you if you would write regularly to me as a friend, and I felt then I had no right to ask you if you could link your life to mine, because of my delicate health, and because—I could not offer you the gift you deserve—the offer of a first fresh love! I told you in the letter that if I did not hear from you in response I should conclude you did not want our acquaintance to deepen into warm friendship; and, not hearing, I concluded you felt we must remain merely acquaintances. I have tried to put you out of my thoughts. It is quite impossible. I know I am years older than you, that I am a quiet humdrum sort of creature, who has no attractive qualities for a bright young woman like yourself; but I cannot help that. My child loves you, and I—well, you have been in my heart and life from the first day I ever saw you, and I want your love if you can give it to me. I want to take you away from this life you are leading, back to Abertarlie. Will you give me the right to do it?"

Rowena's eyes were downcast. She did not speak for a moment. The rush of happiness that came to her heart almost overcame her self-control. She had striven for many a long day to put this friend out of her thoughts. She had taken herself to task for thrilling all over when he spoke or looked at her. She had schooled herself to consider that he and she would always remain pleasant friends, but would never get nearer each other. And now he cared—he had always cared!

He waited patiently; and then she looked up. Tears were glistening in her eyes. She stretched out her hands to him.

"Here I am," she said simply; "to belong to you will be bliss, for you have had my love for a long time."

"Really?"

He seemed as if he could not quite believe it. His humble diffidence was most touching. Then he took her in his arms, and no further speech was needed.

"If you had had that letter," he said presently, "you would never have gone to live with Mrs. Burke. Rowena dearest, you must leave her at once. I cannot bear to think of you continuing to live with her."

Rowena looked at him with her old sunny smile.

"Hugh,—you see your name comes quite easily to my lips; I am afraid I have often called you by it in my heart before—if you love me, you must trust me. Look me in the eyes, and tell me if you can."

"Who would not?" was his emphatic response.

"Then don't overpower me with your protecting love and care. I am not a weak young girl. I have had to stand alone, and be a prop to others, and think of their faltering steps before my own. And at present Mrs. Burke is my mission in life. Your love won't shatter that to pieces."

"But you cannot enjoy her society."

"I am fond of her; and I want to help her back to the old paths in which her feet once were. It is slow work, but she is beginning to hanker after them. Her present life satisfies her less and less. You must not tear me away from her just yet."

"I feel I want you at once; and I don't and I can't approve of your home here."

"No; and it is difficult to make you understand. But we won't mar this best hour in my life by talking of disagreeables. Do you know, I am just a wee bit afraid of you? Am I to give up my own individuality and freedom of soul if I link my life to yours? Am I to look-out upon the world only through your eyes, and not through my own?"

"Never!" said the General fervently. "Your individuality is what has drawn me to you. You have always done me good by your wise counsel. I should have lost my child's affection had I not listened to you. No, Rowena, I want you to be your own true dear fearless self always. But—well, we will not discuss it now. You have made me too happy for words. I feel as if I am beginning life again, as if I have been walking under a forest of dark gloomy impenetrable trees, and have just emerged into glorious sunshine!"

"I believe tea is coming in," said Rowena demurely. "It's a pity we still have to eat and drink. Will you stay to tea, General Macdonald?"

The butler was in the room. The General looked as if he wished him farther, but his time alone with Rowena was over. Mrs. Burke returned home, bringing two young men and a girl with her, and General Macdonald promptly took his leave. As his hand touched Rowena's he said:

"When shall we see you? I won't send Mysie round now. May I call to-morrow, after I have done my business, and will you come to lunch with us? I will bring an invitation from my old cousin when I come."

She nodded to him brightly, then turned to help entertain Mrs. Burke's visitors. But she was rather dreamy and silent, and Mrs. Burke's quick eyes perceived it.

When they were alone together later she said:

"What has that old fusty friend of yours been saying to you? Something unpleasant about me I don't doubt."

"No; indeed he has not. We hardly mentioned you."

Rowena felt she could not announce her engagement till she had had some quiet time to herself. She was longing to get away into the solitude of her own room, but Mrs. Burke went on talking. If she had no visitors she liked to chat with Rowena over the fire between tea and dinner. She enjoyed talking over all her doings of the day, and making fresh plans for the morrow.

"I shall be quite glad when that man takes his departure. I think I feel jealous of him. I don't like him hanging round you as he does. Is he going to-morrow?"

"Yes—to-morrow evening."

Rowena stared into the fire as she spoke. Mrs. Burke looked at her sharply; then went on:

"I think we must leave town next week. It is getting near Christmas, and I mean to have a big house-party this year. You will be glad, I know. How you hate town, don't you?"

"It is always such a rush," Rowena said. "You make me breathless. I cannot keep pace with you. And I don't feel so young as you do. I get so tired."

"I'm rather tired myself," Mrs. Burke admitted; "but I'm only tired when I'm doing nothing. Now, to-morrow morning I'm going to drive the Carlton Hughes down to Richmond in a car—we shall lunch there. But I've promised to go to the matinée at Chelsea for the Poor Actors' Fund, so I must be back early. Would you like to come with me?"

"Not unless you really want me."

"I can do without you. I've asked Lady Goring and her brother to dinner, and the Yates, and I think Mr. Wales is coming in afterwards with his violin—I've asked him professionally. Lady Goring is mad on music, and so is her brother. He has just returned from India, rather a nice man. You'll see to the table decorations, won't you? The new parlour maid is such a fool—she's no ideas in the floral line."

"Oh, I'll see to the dinner; and I shall have a quiet day to myself," said Rowena contentedly. "Don't you think we had better write and let Mrs. Gates know we are returning to the Court so soon? She will want to get things ready."

"Yes; write to her to-morrow."

The talk went on. At last the dressing-bell rang, and Rowena was free. She went up to her room and sank into a chair before her fire. She could hardly believe, even now, how her whole future life would become altered by the event of the afternoon.

She realized that responsibilities and cares would mingle with the vista of sunshine and joy that lay before her. She wondered how Mysie would take the news.

"She loves me now; but she is also most devoted to her father. Will she think that I shall step in between them? I hope not. I hope that she will be willing to have me as a stepmother. Perhaps it is a good thing that she is still so young. A few years later, and it would be very difficult with a grown-up daughter. I don't think I should have the courage to go through it! And yet I don't know; with Hugh at my side I feel I would do and dare anything. It is wonderful to have got his love. He has always seemed a little unapproachable. I must make him unbend. I will—I must, for his own sake, get him to be less stern and autocratic. I dare say I shall have a few pitched battles with him. But it is his strength and determination that I love so. I wonder if we shall quarrel over Mrs. Burke? I will not be rushed into a hasty marriage; he must wait my time." Then she remembered that she had not mentioned the invitation to lunch which was coming for her. "I must tell her to-night, and get it over. It is of no use to hide it."

So after dinner Rowena said:

"I forgot to tell you that General Macdonald wants me to go round to lunch with them to-morrow. He may call here himself in the morning."

"Ah! This is your quiet day! Rowena, is there anything between you?"

Rowena sat in her low chair with her hands clasped loosely round her knees. She turned towards Mrs. Burke with a glow upon her cheeks as she said:

"I hope you won't be vexed if I tell you that there is."

"I knew it! It is my fate! Oh, I wish I had never brought you to town, and then you would never have met him! I felt from the first he was determined to take you from me!" Mrs. Burke got up from her chair and paced the floor furiously. "I hate him!" she burst forth. "A narrow-minded bigot! He condemns every one who doesn't think alike with him. He will rule you and keep you under his thumb, and be a despotic tyrant. How can you be such a fool as to marry him? Don't you value your liberty and independence? Is it all settled?"

"We have loved each other for a long time," said Rowena. "You must remember I knew him before I met you."

Mrs. Burke came back to her seat.

"I feel inclined to blubber like a baby. I can't let you go, Rowena. Are you going to leave me at once?"

"No; indeed I am not."

"I believe if you had stayed with me you could have done anything with me," said Mrs. Burke helplessly. "I don't know how it is, but I have said to myself more than once, 'It is no good for you to resist, Rowena means to drag you after her into heaven itself.' And I've been wretched. I confess to you I have. You've never preached to me; but just a word here and a word there—it's been like the dropping of water upon a stone. I've stifled my conscience and gone desperately on; but the honest truth is that I am getting old and tired, and would give worlds to have the peace and rest of soul which you have. Now I don't care! If you leave me I shall plunge along in the old way. I never thought I could get so fond of anyone as I have of you. I feel I could kill that gaunt grey man who has come here making love to you behind my back. I know his sort. He has an iron will, and can make you do anything he chooses. And I beg you to count the cost, and consider calmly while you have your senses in your own possession, whether this contemplated marriage of yours will be a success. I know men better than you do, and I know this Scotchman. I knew him by repute. He did not make his first wife very happy. He ignored and neglected his child, till he was shamed into doing something for her. She was being brought up as a little savage; his cousin, Mrs. Graeme, told me all about it. And he'll crush your spirit and lead you the life of the condemned. Let him marry Marion. She's the sort for him. The kind of woman who would black his boots and lie down for him to tread upon her. But you have character and a will of your own. You will never be happy with him. Do, I beseech you, reconsider it, and tell him you can't marry him!"

Mrs. Burke paused for breath.

Rowena leant towards her and took her hand in hers.

"My dear Mrs. Burke, I can't help being grateful to you for your affection. But you really don't know Hugh Macdonald, as I do, or as my brother did. You must remember he is an old friend of my family's. I won't discuss his character with you. You are doing him great injustice, and he would make any woman happy—of that I am assured."

"Not me!" put in Mrs. Burke emphatically.

Rowena laughed; she could not help it.

"No; I cannot fancy you and him pulling together. But I shall be more than content. Don't let us talk any more of my engagement. I am not leaving you at present. We will go down to Minley and have a nice Christmas together. Don't let us look on too far into the future. You have made me very happy to-night."

"How?" asked Mrs. Burke in a bewildered tone.

"Oh, it was something you said. You are turning round with wistful eyes to the old road on which your feet once travelled. And you will soon be back there again. Now forgive me, but I'm going to quote a prophet's words: 'Stand in the ways, and see and ask for the old paths, where is the good way and walk them, and ye shall find rest for your souls.' You are standing now and seeing. The rest will follow."

"Ridiculous girl!" Mrs. Burke moved restlessly in her seat as she spoke. Then she said: "You have a way of getting confessions out of me, and then you turn and rend me with your Bible verses. People don't believe in the Bible nowadays. It is only a collection of Eastern sages' sayings."

"I used not to believe in it, until I began to read it. You have only to read it, and read it, and read it by itself, without any commentaries or other books which justify its divinity, to be certain that it is inspired. It begins to feed and nourish your soul at once in the most wonderful way. I have proved it."

"And now your sermon is ended," said Mrs. Burke, with a forced laugh, "and we will go to bed edified by it. And to-morrow you will have to hear more of my opinions concerning your Scotch General. I am glad to hear you do not intend leaving me at present. Perhaps the fates will intervene, and he may meet with some accident or illness which will take him to the sphere for which he is fitted. He is certainly not fitted for this one."

Rowena felt it useless to protest. She knew and understood Mrs. Burke too well to be hurt or offended by her words, and she realized that she was talking recklessly to hide her feelings. She kissed her affectionately when she wished her good night, and Mrs. Burke had the grace to be ashamed of herself.

"You will have to go over to your sister-in-law to tell her the news. She will give you the sympathy you ought to have. You can't expect me to like it, if it means that you are going to leave me."

By mutual instinct they both avoided the subject of her engagement the next day. Mrs. Burke went down to Richmond, and about twelve o'clock General Macdonald appeared, his cousin's note in his hand.

Rowena was ready for him. In her dark green cloth coat and skirt, with sable furs, a present from the generous Mrs. Burke, and a green velvet picture hat, she looked very handsome and dignified. But her radiantly happy face as she turned towards him made him exclaim as he greeted her:

"Oh, Rowena, I hope I shall be worthy of you!"

"Now, I must make a stipulation that I have no more speeches of that sort," she said, laughing. "Let us both consider ourselves the best of human beings. It will give us such a nice satisfied, comfortable sort of feeling. Have you told Mysie?"

"In a kind of way."

"How did she take it?"

"She was of course overjoyed at the prospect. You don't think she would object?"

"She might. Stepmothers are not popular with children."

"Oh, I didn't go into details. Have you told your old lady?"

"Yes. She is not very pleased."

"I can understand that. Don't you think you and I could walk into some quiet church here and have the marriage service to ourselves? I don't want to hurry you, but Mysie is expecting you at Abertarlie for Christmas."

A flush came into Rowena's cheeks. That prospect seemed so alluring; but she shook her head.

"I cannot leave Mrs. Burke so soon. I am spending Christmas with her at her country house. We must wait a little longer."

General Macdonald looked disappointed. He called a taxi, and they drove off to Eton Place. Mysie had been watching out for them at the drawing-room window, and came dancing out into the hall. Rowena kissed her very lovingly.

"Oh," the little girl exclaimed as she hugged her tight, "Dad says you're coming to stay with us. What does it mean? Are you going to be my governess? Cousin Bel seems so mysterious about it, and Dad wouldn't tell me properly."

She was taking Rowena up to the drawing-room now, which was empty. For a moment they were alone, as General Macdonald had stopped to take some letters from the old butler.

Rowena put her hand under Mysie's chin and turned her face upwards.

"Now you and I are going to be quite fair and square, Flora. How would you like me to come and live with you and Dad for always?"

Mysie's blue eyes gleamed.

"But why haven't you done it before? I've always been telling Dad that you ought to. And then cousin Bel said the other day that it would not be proper. Such ridic'lous nonsense!"

"I could only do it one way," said Rowena softly, "and that would be by marrying your Dad. He wants me to do it. What do you say?"

Mysie gave a delighted yell.

"Then you'd belong to us for ever and ever! Oh, Mignon, it would be heavenly! And you and I would go and see the fairies' hills; and we'd tell each other stories by the fire when Dad was out; and—oh, I think I could scream for joy at the thought of it! You'd always be there when I wanted you, and you'd help me and love me always. Why didn't Dad tell me the whole of it, not just a little bit? I thought you were only coming for a visit."

Rowena's heart felt as light as a feather. She could say no more, for General Macdonald appeared, leading in his old cousin, Mrs. Peale, who greeted her very warmly.

"Very glad to see you, my dear. Your name is quite familiar to me; and now I have seen you I quite understand why I have heard so much about you. Hugh is to be congratulated."

"And I think I am, too," said Rowena, smiling.

They had a pleasant lunch together. Mysie was in the greatest delight, and chattered incessantly about all that Rowena would have to do and see at Abertarlie. Mrs. Peale checked her at last.

"My dear child, we don't want to hear any more about that wonderful Highland home of yours. I shall advise Miss Arbuthnot to live half the year in London—certainly the greater part of the winter she ought to be here."

"But she loves the Highlands; don't you, Mignon?"

"I adore them, Flora. Sometimes a bit of bracken or the smell of a wood fire will give me a whiff of the sweet Highland air, and then I forget everything and everybody, for my soul flies over there at once, and my body sits with a daft smile, deaf to every one till my soul comes back again."

Mysie clapped her hands.

"Yes, and now you'll belong to us altogether."

When lunch was over Mrs. Peale insisted upon Mysie going upstairs to the drawing-room with her, leaving the General and Rowena alone.

And they had a delightful hour together.

"It will be the first time that I return home regretfully," General Macdonald said; "but if you are leaving town at once, I should not have seen much more of you."

"No; we must just be patient. When the New Year comes perhaps we can make plans. Do you expect to hear from me?"

"Need you ask?"

"I am not very good at writing letters, but I shall write to you in my quiet times."

General Macdonald was standing looking down upon her. How he loved her low mellow voice and her happy laugh. As she raised her glowing mischievous eyes to him now, he just stooped and enclosed her face between his two hands.

"Rowena, I feel as if I cannot part from you. I don't think you know how impatience has seized my soul, and I do want to get you out of Mrs. Burke's clutches. How long are you going to keep me waiting?"

"Until I can provide her with a nice substitute. I want to get a great-niece of hers to come and live with her. If I am successful, I shall not mind leaving her. I promise to write and tell you everything that is going on, even how many At Homes and parties I attend in the week." Then he gently released herself. "I won't tease you," she said. "I assure you I live a very normal life when we are in the country. Very much the sort of life that you do at Abertarlie."

"Oh," he said, drawing a long breath, "what a lot of things we shall have to discuss together when you come down there, and how you will help me in some of my plans for the good of the people round!"

Time slipped away only too soon. Rowena had to return to Mrs. Burke's early, and the General and Mysie both accompanied her to the door. She wished them good-bye there; and after they had left her, she felt a sudden depression of spirit seize her.

"I could have gone to Geraldine for Christmas, got my things ready and married him in the New Year. Why do I cling on to Mrs. Burke so? I shall have to leave her sooner or later. I suppose it is my lack of courage in tackling anything disagreeable. But I do feel awfully sorry for her. She is like a child who has always had her own way."

CHAPTER VII
AN ACCIDENT

> "We cannot well forget the hand that holds
> And pierces us and will not let us go,
> However much we strive from under it.
> The heavy pressure of a constant pain ...
> Is it not God's own very finger-tips
> Laid on thee in a tender steadfastness?"
> Hamilton King.

"MY dear Mrs. Burke, you are never going out this afternoon?"

Rowena looked up from a newspaper which she was reading. She was toasting her feet over a roaring wood fire in Mrs. Burke's pleasant morning-room at Minley Court. It was three o'clock in the afternoon. Outside the house, a storm of wind and rain was raging. For three days the weather had been so bad that they had been confined to the house. The rain was not quite so violent now, but after luncheon Mrs. Burke had told Rowena she was going to lie down in her room, with a novel, till tea-time.

"There is nothing else to do," she had mournfully complained.

Now she burst open the door attired in an old tweed hat and in her fur coat.

"Yes; I'm going out," she said. "I couldn't stand my book, and I couldn't sleep; so I thought I'd go over to Vi and Di. I haven't seen them yet; and I've ordered out the car. And I may go on and look up the Sheringhams. I want the Colonel for my theatricals, on Boxing night."

"I don't expect Vale likes the prospect of driving in this storm," said Rowena, looking at her friend with some dismay in her eyes. "Are you wise in going? You have a slight cold."

"I shall be under cover, so will Vale."

"It will soon be dark, remember."

"What of that? We have lamps."

"I wish I was better at amusing you," said Rowena, with a twinkle of humour. "You are the sort that would appreciate a house fool, like the royalties used to have. He would keep you in the house an afternoon like this, by sitting at your feet and by amusing you with stories and songs and clever wit. I am too dull for you, and that's the fact. If I had only known you were bored with your book, I would have rummaged through Mudie's box and brought you another."

"Oh, you're all right," said Mrs. Burke, patting her shoulder affectionately. "When I come in, I want to look through my gowns for a suitable one for me in the character of Lady Teazle. Your taste is so good that you will help me in that. Don't wait tea for me. I may be late."

Rowena came to the front door to see her off. The wind made a determined onslaught upon them directly the door was opened. The butler helped Mrs. Burke down the steps, holding an umbrella over her to keep off the driving rain. She waved her hand airily to Rowena when she was in the car, and Rowena went back to her comfortable seat by the fire. Her idle time was over; she had an hour's work before her, finishing Mrs. Burke's correspondence for the day. But she was writing letters now of great interest to her. One was to Mrs. Panton, Mrs. Burke's sister, to enclose a Christmas cheque, and to ask her to let her grandchildren come to Minley Court for part of their holidays. Also to suggest to her to come down to the South of England, where schools were cheap, and where she could sometimes be seen by her sister. They were selling their furniture at the Vicarage, and Marion was going to Scotland the last week in January.

When Rowena had finished her work for Mrs. Burke, she began writing letters for herself.

She had seen her sister-in-law before leaving town, and she was, of course, delighted with her engagement. Now she wrote to her telling her she hoped to come to her for a week after the New Year to talk over her coming marriage; and lastly she wrote her letter to General Macdonald. They kept up a brisk correspondence with each other, and his letters revealed more of his real self than did any of his conversation. He possessed the Scotch reserve, in talking, which disappeared in his letters.

Rowena wrote to him with gladness in her eyes and smile.

"MY DEAREST,—"

"Your letter is before me. It arrived in a howling, blustering storm, when outside all was cheerless and grey; and it warmed my heart, as your letters always do, and made me feel as if the sun was shining out upon a gloriously happy world. Dear Hugh! May I prove worthy of such love as yours. Only don't, I beseech you, place me on a high pedestal. I assuredly shall have a tumble if you do; and I want to keep my feet, for Mysie's sake as well as your own. As you are greedy for all details in my daily life I will proceed to describe my day—"

She had only got this far when Dodge, the butler, appeared, ostensibly to close up for the night, as it was getting dark, and to bring in tea; but he moved about so uneasily that at last Rowena looked up.

"The storm seems getting worse again," she remarked.

"It does, ma'am; and I wish the mistress were back. The postman says the bridge across Minley Weir is getting shaky. He thinks it unsafe. The river is terribly high."

"They'll have to go round by Tanbury if they can't pass it," said Rowena.

He said no more; but when her tea was brought in, and she heard the howling wind and the torrents of rain which were falling, she grew anxious. It was a pitch-dark night. Supposing that Vale, the chauffeur, was not told about the unsafe condition of the bridge? She knew he was a fast driver, and Mrs. Burke had more than once remarked that he was not cautious enough. If they dashed over the bridge and it gave way, there would be an awful accident, and the weir was only ten minutes' walk from there.

Rowena shuddered. She began to long that Mrs. Burke was home; then she wished that she had accompanied her. Time went on, an hour passed, then two; and then Rowena expressed her fears to Dodge.

"Couldn't some of the men in the stables go down to the bridge and see if it is all right? I wish we had thought of it before. They could at least have hung up a warning light."

"Webster did go off half an hour ago, ma'am; and he took the two stable lads with him."

"Oh, I am glad. Of course, Mrs. Burke may have stayed with the Miss Dunstans. They have sometimes kept her for the night; but she would have sent a message to us, and we ought to have had it by this time."

There was a slight bustle in the hall. Dodge hastened out, and Rowena followed him. There at the door was Mrs. Burke, streaming wet, the footman and Webster, her coachman, were supporting her in their arms. She was blue with cold, but looked up at Rowena with a glimmer of a smile, though her teeth chattered in her head as she spoke.

"I've had a ducking, and I'm frozen through. Get me to bed."

They did not take very long to do that. Rowena asked no questions, she rolled her up in hot blankets, gave her brandy-and-water, put hot bottles to her feet, and she and her maid rubbed her all over to restore her circulation. Then, when she was thoroughly comfortable, Rowena sat down by her, and Mrs. Burke began to talk.

"Don't stop me, I feel I must speak. People tell me luck is always with me. Why I am not lying drowned under the weir at this moment is the marvel. That fool of a man drove right into the river: part of the bridge had been washed away; and over we went, and the awful part was I couldn't get out. The car plunged its nose downwards, but stuck between some bits of timber, and there I was pinned. I clung to my seat, and the water came in right up to my shoulder, but not over my head. I yelled, but no one came to, my rescue, and it seemed to me I was there hours, and at last I heard footsteps and voices, and I think I must have done a little faint, for I remember nothing more till I was being carried up the steps here. Where is Vale?"

"He is safe," said Rowena. "They say he jumped off, but was lying unconscious on the bank when Webster found him. He struck his head against one of the posts of the bridge, they think."

"He'd better have the doctor."

"Webster will see to him. Lie still. You have had a marvellous escape. We must thank God for it."

But Mrs. Burke would not lie still. She seemed feverish and excited.

"My dear Rowena, I've been in purgatory. I really have. Now I know what it is to be left alone with your sins, and death staring you in the face. It was like a torture trick, to be bottled up in that car, slowly drowning in the dark, and not being able to get out of it. The water was rushing and whirling outside at such a rate that I dare say it was as well I could not get out—I should only have been carried over the weir. Well, you tell me I never give myself time to think; I've had the time to-day; and I was dumb, Rowena, and stupefied. An awful Bible verse came into my mind and stuck there. 'What wilt thou say when He shall punish thee?' What could I say?

Nothing—I had cast away my confidence. And I knew I might be in the other world at any moment. I felt the car being gradually sucked down."

She shivered. Rowena looked a little anxiously at her bright eyes and flushed cheeks.

"Don't think any more about it now, but try to sleep," she said soothingly.

"I can't sleep. Why was I left to hang between life and death for so long?"

Rowena was silent, then she bent over her.

"I am sure you ought to sleep. Let me give you a verse for you to sleep on: I will heal their backsliding, I will love them freely.'"

Mrs. Burke gave a little impatient snort.

Rowena added—

"I am going to send Phillips to watch by you whilst I go and see how Vale is. Do try to sleep, dear. Are you warm now?"

"I have been badly scared and shaken," said Mrs. Burke, trying to speak indifferently; "but I shall be myself to-morrow."

Rowena bent down and kissed her, then slipped out of the room.

She found that Vale was recovering, but she wrote a note to the doctor, for she did not like the look of Mrs. Burke, and she asked him to come over early the next morning.

When the next day arrived, Mrs. Burke was tossing on her bed in agony, and before very long, she was in the throes of rheumatic fever. It was so severe that she had to be wrapped in cotton wool from head to foot, and two nurses were brought in by the doctor to attend to her.

Rowena spent most of her time in the sick-room. All the Christmas festivities had to be postponed. At one time the doctor thought his patient would not pull through. He told Rowena that her heart would not bear the strain of the attack. But she rallied wonderfully, and her constant cry through both her conscious and unconscious times was that Rowena should be close to her.

"Keep death away from me, if you can," she whispered once. "Pray. You will be heard. I sha'n't."

Rowena never left off praying that her life might be spared. On Christmas Day she lay very weak, but perfectly conscious.

"What a Christmas you are having, poor child!" she murmured, looking up into Rowena's face with a flicker of a smile. "Have my sister's young people arrived?"

"No," said Rowena; "I put them off. The doctor said I had better do so."

"That's a pity; but it would be dull for them. Does the doctor think I'm on the mend?"

"Oh, yes—decidedly."

"It's going to be a long business, eh?"

"I am afraid so."

"How is the General? I thought of him when I was in the river. I made sure my summons had come. 'Soul, this night—' You know how it goes on. But it didn't come."

"No," said Rowena softly; "God wanted you here."

"I shall be no good to anyone. I wonder why I was given a fresh lease of life?"

"To live to His glory," said Rowena quickly.

She said no more, for she knew that Mrs. Burke must be kept absolutely quiet and not excited in any way. The sick woman moved her head restlessly on her pillow.

"If He would only put me out of pain. I can't think, when red-hot wires are pulling me in every direction!"

It was long before she was able to leave her bed. Rowena was horrified to see how twisted and swollen her joints were, and she spoke to the doctor about it. He looked grave.

"My dear Miss Arbuthnot, I'm afraid she will never be the same woman again. For a long time she has overtaxed her strength, and lived too fast for health; and now this rheumatism has come to stay, and her heart is much affected by it."

"Yet you have told her she will recover."

"I think she may live many years yet; but she must be content with a quiet invalid's life. She will, I fear, always be crippled."

"Oh, how dreadful! She has been such an active woman. How will she bear it?"

"As many others have borne it. Pluck is not lacking in her composition."

"She is always asking when she will be well again. You must break it to her."

"I would rather leave it to you," said the doctor, with a little rueful smile. "You manage her better than we do."

And so it came to pass that, two or three weeks later, Rowena got her chance; and when Mrs. Burke said impatiently that, if the doctor could not cure her quicker she would go up to town for special treatment, she answered her.

"I wonder if you realize how very, very ill you have been?"

"I should think I do. They say I never do things by halves; and I've never been ill in my life before, so I have done the job pretty thoroughly now!"

"Rheumatic fever generally leaves its effects behind," Rowena went on. "I am afraid you will be no exception to the rule."

"What do you mean?"

Real fright showed itself in Mrs. Burke's eyes.

Rowena leant forward and took one of her poor swollen hands in hers.

"You have never shirked difficulties, or even danger, have you? Can you be brave if I tell you what every doctor would fear in your case?"

"Go on. For goodness' sake don't beat about the bush."

"The fear is that you may never wholly get the use of your limbs again. You are getting better, and you will be able to walk soon, I hope, with the help of a stick; but you must make up your mind to lead a quiet life and be more or less of an invalid."

"Rubbish! I won't make up my mind to it. I will resist with all the power that is in my body against such a verdict. I shall go to Harrogate. I have seen cripples cured there. I shall go abroad to the baths. I will travel all over the world before I'll lie down under such an infamous assertion."

"You see, you cannot do the cures because of the weakness of your heart."

Mrs. Burke laughed scornfully.

"So this old molly of a doctor says. Now make arrangements for the best specialist on rheumatism to come down and see me. I will make him tell me a different tale to that. Write at once, Rowena; don't lose a post."

"But," said Rowena, with a little helpless laugh, "whom can I write to? I must ask Dr. Hole to give me the name of one."

"Telephone to the little wretch at once, then."

Rowena went to the telephone in the hall. She came back presently with the name of a specialist, and as Mrs. Burke happened to know of him, he was summoned at once.

In two days' time he arrived. But he could not give her much hope.

"If you were ten years younger, madam, you would have a better chance. As it is, time may be kind to you, and you may to a great extent get the better of the disease. I should hope for it, if I were you; and you will find that you can still enjoy life quietly and peacefully."

"My good man, I hate quiet and peace! I loathe a quiet life! There, say no more, I never did think much of doctors; and if they can't manage to make a cure of a strong healthy woman like myself, well, they're not of any account at all."

She was so furiously angry that she brought on a heart attack, and lay like a frightened exhausted child an hour later. But when she recovered she said no more on the subject, and for several days was very quiet and subdued.

Then, one sunny afternoon towards the end of February, as she lay on her couch by her bedroom window looking down upon the spring bulbs in the beds below, she called Rowena to her.

"I want to have a real good talk with you. Come and sit down and give me your whole undivided attention. I'm thankful to have got rid of those nurses at last. They were always coming in and interrupting if I happened to get you to myself for a moment or two. And you're rather an elusive sort of creature sometimes, Rowena. You've had such splendid chances of preaching to me on the vanity of life, and the iniquities of my past, and the judgment that has descended upon me, and you've never taken them."

"I'm not good at preaching," said Rowena; "but I have prayed for you hard."

"I know you have. But now I want a thorough good sermon from you. I'm ready and waiting for it. Begin." Rowena smiled.

"What is it you want to be told? You know your Bible as well as I do."

"I want to be told," said Mrs. Burke very slowly and impressively, "how my present life can be made bearable. You tried to take away my zest for the life I loved when you first came to me. Now I want you to give me zest for this changed life of mine. Can you do it?"

"I don't think I can," said Rowena slowly and thoughtfully; "but I can tell you how to get it. Why should your life be emptier now than it has been? On the contrary, you can make it much fuller."

"My dear, when a woman of my age becomes a hopeless, helpless invalid she drops out of everything. Her friends will write letters of condolence. As you know, I have had a good many already, and some of them will come over and see me for a week or two, then they will go their way and forget all about me. Their lives are too much in a rush to remember me. I remember a very young woman. I was very fond of her—struck down by a kind of paralysis. I saw her once after the illness, but never again. It was too painful, and I was too busy. That is how I shall be treated now by my most intimate friends. You see I am looking the thing in the face. Now, what is going to sustain me through this lean time? How can I get through it cheerfully and happily, when everything that I live for has been swept away from me at one fell swoop?"

"You'll never do it. It is an impossibility," said Rowena soberly; "if you still persist in living your life apart from God."

"Ah! now here comes the sermon. Proceed. Do you think I am going to creep to the feet of the Almighty because I am in trouble?"

"It is your proper rightful place," said Rowena firmly. "You used to be happy in His service—you have acknowledged it. You have tried, like the Prodigal, to feed your soul on husks, and you have been brought very low. There is nothing for it but for you to come home with that cry on your lips, 'Father, I have sinned.'"

There was silence in the room, then Mrs. Burke said in a strangely gentle tone for her:

"I told you in town that I was getting old and tired, didn't I? That I envied you the comfort you get out of your religion. Now I lie on my couch here and I think and think and think until I nearly go mad. Do you honestly think, having cast away my confidence, that I can ever get it again? There's an awful verse—I looked it up on the sly this morning when I was alone—it's in Hebrews. It says it's impossible for those who've once had the real thing and have fallen away to come back again—to renew them again unto repentance. What do you say to that?"

"What do you make of the parable of the lost sheep?" Rowena said. "Our Saviour told that Himself, and He gave two other instances in the same chapter. There were the lost sheep, the lost bit of money, and the lost son. Dear Mrs. Burke, if you want to return to your rightful Owner, do you think He will refuse to take you? Don't you remember this verse spoken to the people who had forsaken God for idolatry: 'Return, thou backsliding Israel, saith the Lord, and I will not cause Mine anger to fall upon you: for I am merciful, saith the Lord, and I will not keep anger for ever. Only acknowledge thine iniquity, that thou hast transgressed against the Lord thy God.'"

"How can you remember so much of the Bible?"

"I love it," said Rowena simply. "I am always reading it. If you started to read it, you would find it would tell you all you want to know."

"I suppose I may as well tell you that when I was seeing death so close to me out of the car windows, when we stuck in the river, that I was in such a funk that I vowed a vow—I really did. I promised to alter my life, if it was spared. I suppose I shall have to do it."

"Then if you have made up your mind to do that, you'll end by being a very happy woman," said Rowena. "And you don't want any more sermons from me, for you know what will bring peace to your soul."

They sat very silent then for some time. This was only one of the many serious talks they had together. Rowena marvelled at the gentle childishness which Mrs. Burke showed in these conversations, and then one day she told Rowena that she had begun to pray again.

"I find it much more difficult than I used to do, so many doubts come into my head. But I just go on, and I feel better, after a bit. I want to make my peace with God. If He'll be willing to take just these last failing years of my life, I'm willing to hand myself over to His care."

Rowena at times could hardly believe that this was Mrs. Burke who was speaking. She had never thought the change in her life could come so quietly and gently.

But it was the fact, and before very long Mrs. Burke was able to say, with a happy shining face, that she believed she was forgiven and received back within the fold.

Rowena loved this quiet time of convalescence. She devoted herself to the invalid, and though her thoughts were often in the Highlands, she was content and happy to be where she was.

She knew that the purpose of her stay with Mrs. Burke had now been most wonderfully fulfilled.

CHAPTER VIII
AN ALTERED OUTLOOK

"In any repentance I have joy—such joy
That I could almost sin to seek for it."
Clough.

"WELL, I've come over at last! I heard that Mrs. Burke was receiving visitors."

It was Vi Dunstan who spoke, and Rowena replied: "She has only seen the rector as yet, but I'm sure she will be glad to see you."

"What an awful thing it is! Di and I have been quite upset over her; but we hate sickness in any shape or form, and always keep away from it. We hear the poor thing will never be the same again. Is it true?"

"That is quite true. But you will find her very cheery. Come along. It does her good to see visitors. She will know then that you haven't quite forgotten her!"

"We think it's partly our fault for not keeping her for the night that awful day. It was such a ghastly accident."

Rowena led the way upstairs. It was March now, but Mrs. Burke had not yet left her rooms. A room adjoining her bedroom had been furnished as a sitting-room, and she was carried in there every morning, where she lay on her couch, as she was still unable to walk.

Vi greeted her affectionately, and Rowena left them alone. Mrs. Burke had often wondered that neither of the girls had been over to see her.

"You look better than I expected," Vi said, after she had expressed her sympathy. "I don't believe anything would ever upset your serenity. You look jollier than ever. You must hurry up and get well. Di and I were saying that this part stagnates unless you are down here to stir us up and keep us going!"

"I shan't be able to do that any more," said Mrs. Burke gravely.

"Never say die! Rheumatism is a thing that comes and goes, doesn't it?"

"It won't leave me, I am afraid. I wonder how much you care about me, Vi? I don't expect you'll understand, but an accident like mine makes one think. I've stared death in the face, and it has altered my life. I see now that this world isn't enough. I want another."

Vi gave an embarrassed laugh.

"I can't fancy your taking to Pi jaw! How you've always mocked at such things!"

"And now I'm going to love them and uphold them," said Mrs. Burke with emphasis. "If you give me a wide berth because of it, I shall understand, but I hope you won't. I shan't preach to you; I shall only try to live out my religion. The fact is, Vi, I used to believe in these things once, and then I gave it all up, and it made me extra bitter and reckless against the people who believed in it still. Of course, you'll say I've taken to religion, because I've had to give up all my gaieties. It does seem mean, on the face of it. But I only know that I am twice as happy as I ever was before."

"You look A 1," said Vi.

She seemed slightly uncomfortable at this talk.

"Of course, I know who's talked you over," she said, after a minute's silence. "It's Miss Arbuthnot; she nearly talked me into it once. At least, she didn't talk much, but she suddenly hit the nail on the head fair and square, and left me to think it out. Well, I'm glad you've something to cheer you! We're a pretty dismal house at present. Have you heard the news? Bob is going to be married."

"Oh, my dear, I'm sorry for you!"

"Isn't it rotten? And it's to that Dolly Duccombe of the Gaiety. She's an awful little bounder. Di and I are pretty sick! Out of the house we have to go before next June. I mean to take on old Colonel Sheringham. He's proposed to me five or six times, so I shall still be in the neighbourhood. What Di means to do I don't know."

"Are you really going to marry Tom Sheringham? My congratulations. He's a nice man. I always liked him; but what will the General do?"

"He'll have to go; so that will be another turn out. The house is the Colonel's, not his. It's pretty dreary for us all; and now the hunting is stopping! We're always like bears with sore heads when that's off. When is Miss Arbuthnot going to be married?"

"Oh, don't ask! It's awfully good of her staying on with me. But I know that I shall have to lose her soon."

Vi chatted away for a good half-hour. When she left, she said:

"I'll tell Di to come and see you. And she might be the better for a preach on her iniquities. She's knee-deep in debt, and doesn't know how to pay her bills. Ta, ta!"

Mrs. Burke was relieved when the visit was over. She had rather been dreading it, but her warm heart still went out to the two girls, especially now when they were experiencing, for the first time in their lives, what it was to lose their home.

They were the only ones of her old friends who still stuck to her. The rector and his daughter Maude came round very often. The days were long and monotonous to Mrs. Burke. She had never worked, and got tired of reading. Sometimes Rowena found it hard work to keep her cheerful.

Easter was coming round, and then Mrs. Burke called Rowena to her one morning.

"I mean to have an Easter party. I am well enough to enjoy young people. Will you write to my sister and tell her to bring her grandchildren here? And then, after they are settled in, wouldn't you like to go to your people?"

"I should, very much," said Rowena frankly; "but I can wait."

"And is your Scotch General content to wait? How he must hate me! I'm a selfish woman, Rowena, and the habits of a lifetime can't easily be discarded. I am selfish still. It will be a black day for me when you leave me."

Rowena wrote to Mrs. Panton; she was still in the North, but had been in constant correspondence with her sister; and she gratefully accepted the invitation to stay at Minley Court.

The little party arrived at the close of a bright spring day. Mrs. Burke received them upstairs in her room. There were tears in her sister's eyes as she embraced her. And Mrs. Burke remarked in her cheery way:

"There's nothing left of me to be afraid of. I'm just an old rheumatic cripple, and there will be nothing in my house now to shock or distress you. Now introduce me to my great-nephew and nieces."

George Holt was a handsome boy, slight in make but very upright. The elder girl Bertha was fair, with a sweet, sunny face. The young one, Milly, was a bright little tomboy. Her short curly hair and piquant mischievous face attracted Mrs. Burke at once.

Before very long the young people were chatting to her as if they had known her all her life, and she was, in her genial happy way, promising them all kinds of joys through the holidays—ponies to ride, expeditions to the sea, and boating on the river. Their delight in their new surroundings amused and pleased her.

"We never knew you had such a lovely house," said Milly. "Why it seems like a palace to us! You should just see our lodgings that we have left. Granny was miserable in them—they were so dirty."

"You must all make yourselves at home," Mrs. Burke told them. "Don't ask what you may do, but just do it, if you want to."

It brought much enjoyment to her hearing the young voices about the house. Rowena found her gazing out of the window one day following, with real enjoyment, the antics of George and Milly as they chased each other over and round the flower-beds, a couple of dogs yelling at their heels.

"It keeps me young to have them here, Rowena," she said rather pathetically. "Couldn't I keep them altogether? Must they go away to school?"

"George ought to, of course," said Rowena. "I don't know what your plans are. But you might have a resident governess for the girls and keep them with you, if you would like them."

Mrs. Burke laughed.

"That ridiculous child Bertha tells me she has finished her education. Finished at sixteen! And her French is too awful for words. And her general knowledge hopelessly deficient. But her music is delightful. She has inherited that from her grandmother. Would a governess drive me wild, I wonder?"

"Have over a daily governess from Crossington," suggested Rowena. "It's a big town, and must contain some teachers. She could come in by train, and you would get rid of her between four and five in the afternoon."

"That would be a good idea. I feel inclined to deluge these children with luxuries—they have had to go without so much. And my sister Helen too—she's a mere shadow. I believe the whole batch of them have been at starvation point these last two or three difficult winters. I want to make it up to them now."

"Happy woman!" murmured Rowena, half under her breath, but Mrs. Burke caught the words.

"Well, I am happy," she said; "a good deal happier than I have ever been before. But why do you make that ejaculation at this present moment?"

"Because you have the means and power to give such happiness to others," replied Rowena quickly. "Only don't err on the side of spoiling them. Their grandmother told me she was afraid of it."

"Oh, Helen is a born Spartan; thinks it wrong to have anything comfortable, rejoices in cold baths and open windows all through the winter. But she and I understand one another. I shall make her have a home with me. She has really no money to start one herself."

For a moment Rowena wondered whether the gentle Mrs. Panton would be happy in her sister's house, but later on she had a talk with her. Everybody confided in Rowena, and she found that the sorrowing widow had no desire to start another home.

"It would be no home to me now that he has gone. I am only waiting till I can join him; and if I can be of any use to poor Caroline, I will gladly stay with her. It is very generous of her to offer us all a home. Do you think my noisy young people will be too much for her?"

"I think they will be the greatest comfort and cheer to her. She has always loved the young; and I should let her have her way with them. She won't do them any harm by giving them as much pleasure as she can. You know I must leave her before long. If I can feel you are settled in here, I shall go much more happily."

"She won't let me help her by writing her letters, and you do that for her. Who will do it when you go?"

"I am trying to get her to tackle her correspondence herself. She will have the time now, and it will give her occupation. But I think, when I am gone, that you will find she will be glad of your help."

Rowena had a busy time before she went to her sister-in-law. She managed to find a suitable daily governess who would come over from the nearest town, and teach the two girls. At first gentle Bertha ventured to remonstrate.

"Am I to do lessons with Milly when I have been teaching her for the past year?" she asked her grandmother.

"My dear, accept your aunt's offer gratefully. You are old enough now to realize how little you know. I have not been able to educate you properly. You will not be learning the same things as Milly, and you will be thankful, later on, to have had this chance of improving yourself."

Milly, of course, was delighted. She was a quick, clever child, and had been rather too much for her sister.

"It's so ripping staying on here," she informed Mrs. Burke. "I was so afraid I would be packed off to school. I pinch myself, sometimes, to make sure it is true. Do you think we shall tire you out if we stay on?"

"I don't think so," said Mrs. Burke, with her old jolly laugh. "You'll keep me young, Milly. I've always hated a house full of middle-aged sober people who are past making jokes and playing the fool."

Milly hugged her on the spot.

"You are a delicious great-aunt. George says you might be only twenty, to hear you talk."

And, of course, Mrs. Burke was human enough to be delighted with such a compliment.

The day came when Rowena went down to Sussex to her sister-in-law's home. Geraldine welcomed her warmly, and her gentle old mother received her with old-fashioned sweetness and courtesy. The children were grown almost beyond recognition, but the little boys, Buttons and Bertie, remembered her, and flung themselves into her arms.

"You are looking thin and worn," commented Geraldine. "Mother, we must feed her up, and treat her like an invalid. She must not go to her bridegroom a bag of bones."

Rowena put her hands up to her cheeks, with her happy laugh.

"Spare my blushes; I am not going to be married yet."

"How long are you going to keep him waiting? Now come and sit down and let me talk to you for your good. You have a most unhappy trait of attaching yourself like a vice to any people you meet or places in which you may find yourself. Look at your year in that God-forsaken place, Abertarlie. Who but you would ever stick out a whole winter there?"

Rowena's face grew very soft and grave.

"Not 'God-forsaken,' Geraldine, for I found Him there!"

"My dear, I know; it was the desolation of it drove you to seek consolation in religion. Now you have attached yourself to this old freak Mrs. Burke. I never approved of it from the first. If I had not known she was treating you well, I would have moved heaven and earth to get you away. You have forsaken us for her. You are even making Hugh Macdonald step aside and take the second place. He must be a saint to wait so patiently."

"My dear Geraldine, we have only been engaged four or five months. He is not a young man, nor am I a very young woman. There is no occasion for us to rush into marriage so precipitously."

"The fact that he is not a boy is in favour of a speedy marriage, I consider. You are both quite old enough to be certain of your own minds. He has been too long alone, and that nice child of his wants a woman to look after her."

"She is very happy with her governess."

"Don't go on making excuses for yourself, but tell me if you have fixed the day. The sooner you leave that old woman the better. You are simply a nurse-attendant to her. It isn't good enough. She has her sister now, and doesn't want you."

"I am conceited enough to fear that she will always want me," said Rowena, with a little sigh. "I am really fond of her, Geraldine, and so is she of me."

"Yes, I know all that; I believe if you were shut up with criminals of the deepest dye you would tell me that you were becoming most attached to them, and felt that you could not live with anyone else. It is your fatal adaptability to your environment. There! With that big word, I've finished."

"Well, listen to me then. Hugh wants me to come to him in June. We mean to have no honeymoon, except that perhaps we may stay a few days in Edinburgh on our way down. And you and I must fix the date. Somewhere in the middle of the month."

"That's something; now I see light. And what kind of wedding do you mean to have?"

"A very quiet one. No friends asked at all. Neither of us wishes it. If you will have me here, I would like to walk into your little village church early one morning, with only you in attendance, and he would like it, too."

Geraldine only looked half-satisfied, but Rowena had her way.

She spent a very pleasant fortnight with her sister-in-law, and in that time got a simple trousseau together. Mrs. Burke had given her a most generous cheque for a wedding present, but she displeased her sister-in-law by the modesty of her requirements. In her worldly wisdom Geraldine said:

"My dear Rowena, you must be handsomely dressed as Hugh's wife. He has one of the biggest properties in that part of the Highlands, and you must not shame him, by going to him in gowns that a minister's wife would choose. He will only have to supplement your trousseau afterwards, if you don't go to him with a thoroughly good outfit, and that is most galling to a woman's self-respect, I always think."

"Yes, I see your point," said Rowena humbly, "and I will get all that will be suitable; but as for taking fashionable ball gowns down to Abertarlie, it's ridiculous!"

"Don't you intend to be sociable? For two or three months in the year at least you will be in the habit of meeting your neighbours. Do you know that the Arnold Rashleighs have taken Ted's old lodge?"

"No, I had not heard it. I don't know them. Who are they?"

"She was a McTaggart of Loch Filley. She has two daughters, and a son in the Blues. His mother lives in this part. Quite nice, they are, but not Hugh's sort. Thoroughly up-to-date, and the girls rather strenuous. Think women ought to be in Parliament, and that sort of thing."

"Oh dear, I was looking forward to stealing over there, and having a chat with old Granny Mactavish. But I suppose the lodge is empty most of the year."

"Of course; and I hope you'll bring Hugh to town for the winter. Don't bury yourselves down there all the year round. You've served an apprenticeship with Mrs. Burke in gadding about, so you'll know how to make him sociable. He used to be a very nice fellow before he married. That marriage soured him. I still think he's not quite good enough for you."

Rowena let her sister-in-law ramble on. She and Geraldine were sincerely fond of each other, but held very different views on most subjects, and she did not take the trouble to defend herself from many of the charges that were brought up against her.

She returned to Mrs. Burke when the fortnight was over, and found, to her great delight, that her household was working very smoothly. Mrs. Burke still kept the house-keeping in her own hands, but she was allowing her sister to take over many of Rowena's duties.

George had just been sent to a good public school, and the governess, Miss Cummings by name, had started lessons with the girls. Mrs. Burke herself was getting stronger, and could now hobble up and down the garden paths with the help of two sticks. She was extraordinarily patient and content. Rowena marvelled at it.

"My dear, I never was a discontented woman," Mrs. Burke said to her one day. "I had one phase of it just before my marriage, but that did not last. You know I am one who seizes with both hands all the good that can be got out of life. I have had some years of the world's best, and though I seized as much of it as I could hold, and carried a smiling front to all outside, I was gradually made aware that there was something better still. After you came to me, I saw that I had seized the shadow and lost the substance. And then, as you know, in the most wonderful way I have got hold of the substance again. I have seized it with both hands and, please God, I will never let it go. Of course, I am happy and content; I'm permeated with content now, and don't miss my old life in the least little bit. I'm only-sorry for the shadow-seekers—Vi and Di especially. Di was over when you were away, and she is perfectly miserable at leaving her home. Can see no comfort anywhere. Vi is engaged to her colonel, so is not to be pitied, but Di was badly hit some years ago over a worthless and inconstant lover, and I don't think she will marry. They will be very badly off, I fear, from what they tell me. They have very little, independent of their brother."

"Have her over as much as possible," advised Rowena, "and show her that life is a much grander thing than she has ever thought it yet."

And Mrs. Burke promised to do so.

Time slipped by, and then came the last day of Rowena's stay with her old friend. It was necessarily rather a sad one, and yet, when Rowena looked back and thought of the difference in her friend's outlook when she first knew her, she could not but feel deeply thankful for her present happiness.

"I will write to you," she said, as she was wishing her good-bye; "and you will write to me when your poor hands permit it. And one day you will come and stay at Abertarlie with us, and I will show you the beauties of our glen and lochs."

Mrs. Burke smiled ruefully.

"Well, if your good general bears me no malice for my rude behaviour to him in town, I will come. I think I would really enjoy his conversation now. How different the whole world has become to me!"

As Rowena sat in the express train to town, her soul was full of thankfulness for this bit of her way, and she murmured to herself:

"I always liked her from the first. I knew that sooner or later she would be led back to her old faith, and it has strengthened my own to see her so happy and whole-hearted now. I never, to my dying day, shall regret my time with her."

BOOK III

CHAPTER I
HIS BRIDE

"We in our wedded life shall know no loss,
We shall new-date our years! What went before
Will be the time of promise, shadow, dream,
But this full revelation of great love!
For rivers blent take in a broader heaven,
And we shall blend our souls."
From Cloud of Witness.

"NOW we are together at last."

It was in a tone of deep triumphant content that General Macdonald made this assertion.

He and Rowena were facing each other in a first-class carriage. The Scotch express was taking them up to Scotland, and it was between nine and ten in the evening.

Their wedding-day, and the weather had been perfect: a typical June day, when all the freshness of early summer is at its sweetest and best. They had got their way, and only about half a dozen people were in the quiet little Sussex church when they made their vows together.

Rowena sat back looking radiant. She was dressed in a dark powder-blue coat and skirt with a travelling felt hat of the same hue, which intensified the blue in her eyes. But even now an irrepressible twinkle, of fun shot through them as she said:

"So you think we shall always find our own company sufficient, Hugh?"

"I shall never need anyone but you," he replied quickly.

"Except your little Mysie."

And then the General's grave intense look melted and he smiled.

"Ah—Mysie! I left her in tears because I would not bring her up. I felt it was too sacred a service at which to have a curious child commenting and looking on. How long you have kept me waiting! I can hardly even now realize that the waiting time is over. I thought at one time that the old lady would never let you go."

"Poor Mrs. Burke!" Rowena's eyes grew soft with pity. "You were always hard upon her; but you would not be hard if you could see her now. I used to wonder if she could ever have the necessary strength and pluck to alter her life; but it has all come about so easily."

"Do you think me very hard? You will have to teach me how to look at people leniently when their views clash with my own. I could do with more tolerance and sympathy, I own. But it has always been my way to go straight ahead, and black is never white to me."

Rowena put her hand on his very softly.

"And that is what I always admired in you—you drive straight for your goal. There is no uncertain sound when you sound your trumpet. When I think that my feet and yours will be treading the same path now, that I shall be able to look to you for support when I trip—why, I feel inclined to burst into a song of thanksgiving!" Then she added with a little laugh: "Now, after that rhapsody, may I come down to earth, and ask you if your old housekeeper will give me a pleasant welcome? Do you think she will like having a mistress, after having managed for you all these years?"

"Mrs. Dalziel serves me faithfully," said the General in a contented tone; "and she will, of course, be ready to serve you, too. Long ago she hoped you were coming to us. She actually had the audacity to tell me so. Our Scotch folk are not like anyone else."

"I have never asked you about Marion, yet. Do you really like her?"

"She is a real comfort: keeps in the background, and is never seen unless I send for her. And the child is learning well from her. Rowena, I will not spend these precious first few hours with you in talking about anyone else but ourselves. I want to feel that there is just you and myself here in the world. Let us shut every one else out."

So they talked in the same old way that both young and old lovers always talk, and the journey seemed one golden dream to Rowena. It was so new to her to be waited upon and cared for and protected, that at first she felt inclined to expostulate. Later she learnt to take it as her due.

They spent a few days in Edinburgh, and then turned towards the Highlands. It was a most lovely evening when they at last arrived at Abertarlie. A beautiful car was at the station—a great surprise to Rowena.

"You never told me you had started a car; I expected a shabby trap and horse hired for the occasion."

"I bought this a few months back; I determined that you should be able to get about and see your friends. I realize we are isolated, but I won't have you feel that you are shut up, and stranded away from your fellow-creatures. You are very sociable by nature, I know."

"Am I?" said Rowena, laughing. "I was very happy that year when I was laid upon my back and saw no one. And I have been happy this last year living amongst crowds. They say I can make myself happy anywhere, and I believe I can. Don't you think, you dear foolish man, that your company is good enough for me? But I won't pretend that I don't love a car. You and I can see the beauties of the Highlands in it. You will take me to some of the lochs that I have never seen, won't you?"

General Macdonald was a proud man when, a little later, he drove up to his weather-beaten old house and handed Rowena out of the car. There was a scream and a rush of flying feet, and Mysie was embracing them both. "Oh, you've come at last! At last! Miss Panton and I are simply sick of waiting for you! Oh, Mignon, you darling, stoop down and let me whisper to you. May I really call you 'Mother'? Dad said he would like me to."

"My darling, of course you may. Dad's wishes are mine."

Then up the steps she went, her hand in her husband's arm, and Mysie clinging hold of her at the other side. In the hall was the housekeeper, Mrs. Dalziel, and behind her a little group of servants.

General Macdonald turned to them very simply:

"I have brought my wife home, but she is not a stranger to you, and I am sure you will welcome her."

"Ah, indeed, we will with all our hearts," said Mrs. Dalziel, coming forward.

Rowena shook hands with her warmly.

"That is very sweet of you," she said. "I don't feel a stranger, for I love every inch of ground in the Highlands, and my heart never wanders from it."

Marion Panton was found in the inner hall, where tea was laid. Rowena hardly knew her, she was looking so bright and well. Three long windows that looked into the flower garden were wide open, and the scent of sweetbrier hedges and of wallflowers and narcissi filled the hall. A bowl of daffodils was upon the old oak table that held the tea. The shining silver and platter of Scotch scones and cakes gave a homely touch to the rather gloomy hall with its stone floor and dark oak-panelled walls.

Rowena was led up to the big chair at the table by her husband.

"There!" he said, smiling, as she seated herself. "That is where Mysie and I have been wanting to see you for many a long day."

"And it's strange how thoroughly at home I feel," said Rowena, with her laugh, as she slipped off her gloves and took hold of the massive silver teapot.

Tea was a most cheerful meal. Mysie was in her kilt.

"In honour of you," she informed Rowena. "I couldn't wear it in London. Cousin Bel was quite shocked when I put it on once. She said it was boy's clothes, so Dad said I mustn't offend her eyes. But you love it, don't you? You like me to be thorough Scotch?"

"You can't be too Scotch for me," said Rowena.

When tea was over Miss Panton took Mysie away to the schoolroom, and General Macdonald took his wife all over the house. She had never been over it before, and was surprised at its spaciousness.

"Why, you could lodge fifty people here," she said, when they had finished going in and out of the quaint old rooms, all gloomily and sparsely furnished, except those in use. "We shall never be able to say we have no room for our friends."

Then she returned to the little suite of rooms that had been prepared for her. There was a little boudoir leading out of her bedroom which was now illumined by golden sunshine.

"I love a west room!" she exclaimed. "And oh, Hugh, what an exquisite enchanting view!"

Kneeling on the low window-seat, she leant out of the open window. She faced the loch in the distance, and the blue hills at the farther end of it. The woods in the glen were all in their freshest green, but now they seemed gleaming with gold. The colours and shadows on the silver waters of the loch were indescribably beautiful.

Rowena turned to meet her husband's eyes resting on her in grave content.

"Oh," she said, throwing out her hands, "isn't it easy to be good and happy with such a scene as this before one's eyes! I thought I remembered the beauties of our loch, but it has come to me with fresh force this evening. Hugh, I hope I shall live and die here. I never shall want to leave it."

Her rooms had been freshly papered and painted, and pretty fresh chintzes brightened the old furniture in them. "Miss Panton has helped us get them ready for you," said the General. "She and Mysie made a trip to Glasgow, and were most important and busy over it all. Nothing was too good. Nothing too expensive for you, so Mysie informed me."

"They have given me most charming rooms," said Rowena; then with an impulsive movement she clasped her arms round her husband's. "But what does anything matter, Hugh, as long as we are together? I feel I would be as jolly as a sandboy in an empty attic if you were by my side."

He could only smile at her. Speech was always difficult to him when he felt the deepest.

When they had looked over the house they wandered over the garden and grounds. Here Rowena saw much that could be improved, and longed to set to work at once.

"Do you give me carte blanche, Hugh, to make a lovely garden here? The ground would lend itself to my schemes; and I honestly enjoy having a wealth of flowers round any house."

"You can do as you like, if you can persuade Andrew to carry out your schemes. I think that will be the difficulty."

"I feel afraid of no one," said Rowena lightly. "I know Scotch gardeners are generally very formidable personages; but I will try my powers of persuasion upon Andrew."

They dined later on in the long dining-room, which held on its walls portraits of several generations of Macdonalds, and then Mysie appeared again, and insisted upon taking Rowena out into the garden again to see some of her pet nooks and haunts. She was introduced to the stables and to the dogs; even the poultry-yard had to be visited, and the little girl's bedtime came too soon for her.

"I haven't shown you half. Will you come with me to the Fairies' Knoll up the glen to-morrow? Dad won't believe in them. It's the only place I don't like him to come to with me. If an unbeliever is with you, you never see the little people. You and I will go quite by ourselves, eh?"

"Indeed we will, Flora," was the laughing response; and then she was hugged and kissed.

"Good night, Mother! There, I've said it, and I'll say it a hundred times a day till I get quite accustomed to it. It does seem funny at first, you know. I told Dad there must be no step about it, not one, there's not a single step between us, is there?"

"Not one, I hope," asserted Rowena.

When Mysie had disappeared she turned to her husband, who had been very silent during his child's chatter.

"Hugh, dearest, you and I will have to pray hard that we may be taught to train her aright. She is such a strong character, that she must grow up a noble woman. And don't laugh at her childish fancies. Let us keep her a child as long as we can."

"I have hope for her future now you are here," General Macdonald rejoined. "But a man is quite unfitted to cope with a girl. I have been divided between my love for her and a longing that she should know discipline whilst she is young. I shall hand her training over to you with thankfulness. Make her like yourself, and I shall be happy."

In the days that followed Rowena found that she had plenty of occupation for hands and brain. Mrs. Dalziel was very thorough in her kitchen premises, but the rest of the house sadly needed a lady's supervision. Then there were old friends to be visited, and new ones came to call, and General Macdonald demanded a good deal of his wife's leisure time. He was never so happy as when she was with him. Occasionally he had to go away on business, and then Mysie was to the fore, and often begged for a holiday to go out into the glen with "Mother." One day she and Rowena climbed up the face of a rugged cliff, and explored a cave in which Mysie was pretty sure that Prince Charlie had once hidden.

"Angus says there aren't many caves about here which Prince Charlie didn't know," said Mysie. "It isn't the one that is in the picture when Flora watched by him when he was asleep, but I'm pretty sure he must have found it out. Isn't it a splendid hiding-place? It seems such a pity, there's no one to hide in it. It's quite a waste, isn't it?"

Mysie stood looking round the low-vaulted cave as she spoke with wistfulness in her eyes.

"Only Angus and I know about this," she went on. "It's our secret, but I thought I must tell you. Promise to keep it secret, won't you?"

"Oh, yes," said Rowena, laughing, "indeed I will. And if ever a prince comes by our way, Flora, and wants to be hidden, you and I will hide him here."

"A prince may want our help one day," said Mysie hopefully. "He may be wandering about, trying to get up an army to fight for his throne like David did in the Bible, and then you and I will help him, won't we?"

As Rowena thought of the troubled world in which poor Mysie would be growing up, her face grew grave.

"I hope she won't be a hunter after false visions," she said later on, when talking about her to her father. "She has such a passion for self-sacrifice, and would seal her devotion by death."

"Teach her to fix her devotion upon our Master," said General Macdonald gravely. And Rowena tried to do it, but at present Mysie was not interested in religious talks.

"You're good, and Dad is good, and Miss Panton is good, but you're all grown-up. I shall get like it one day, but not just yet," she would say. Then she would add hastily, "I do pray always when I get into a fix, and God hears me sometimes. But I can't be always thinking about heaven. I do love my dear earth so much; and as for the loch, I adore it, and if heaven has no lochs, I don't think I shall be happy there at all!"

Rowena did not reprove her for such speeches, but she talked to her about having wider views and longer sight, and prayed continually for her.

She heard very often from Mrs. Burke, and then, about a month after her marriage, she received the sad tidings by telegram that her old friend had passed away. The following letter from Mrs. Panton arrived later:

"MY DEAR MRS. MACDONALD,—"

"You will be grieved at the sad news. It was all so sudden, that even now I can hardly believe she has left us. Only last Thursday she was downstairs, wonderfully bright and most interested in the village school-treat which was going to take place in her grounds. On Friday she wrote letters all the morning, and in the afternoon we went for a drive. The girls were with us, and she insisted upon going to the sea and having tea at the little inn there. She seemed rather tired when we returned home, but came down to dinner as usual, and stayed in the drawing-room afterwards till ten o'clock, her usual time for going to bed. She talked to me of you, and, as she often did, lamented her wasted years. I remember her saying:"

"'I am going to try to have some of my old friends down to stay with me. There are just a few who will come, I believe. I want to influence them as Rowena influenced me. I think it was her tremendous sympathy and love that was her power. I felt she never despised me even when I was at my worst. And gradually I came to despise myself and see what empty rubbish filled my life.'"

"She talked of Di Dunstan, who has been over here pretty often lately and is going through a very miserable time. She said of her:"

"'She is being emptied as I was, and I only hope she won't miss the right filling.'"

"I saw her into her room, and her maid was with her till she went to bed. The next morning when her maid went to call her she found she had passed away in her sleep. The doctor says that her heart has been very weak ever since her illness, and that it failed suddenly."

"I can only add that all of us are feeling her loss deeply. She has been so wonderfully good and generous to me and mine."

"Yours most sincerely,"
"M. PANTON."

Rowena felt this blow very much. She and the General both went to England to the funeral.

When Mrs. Burke's will was read, it was found that she had left nearly the whole of her property to her sister. Her great-nephew and nieces came in for a very handsome legacy each, and to Rowena was left the sum of ten thousand pounds.

But what Rowena valued most of all was a little note, "To be delivered after my death," which was as follows:

"MY DEAREST ROWENA,—"

"I have just torn up a will in which I made you my sole legatee, but I see now that my relatives have a claim upon me, especially as they have so little of their own. I never can express my gratitude to you sufficiently. I hope your good husband will not prevent you succouring the worldlings as you go through life. I am convinced this is your mission. I am not good at it, but I commend to your care Di Dunstan, who is wondering if there is another better world than that in which she has been living; she has taken a flat in town. God bless you, dear. My doctor has told me that a long life will not be mine. Happy me to have Eternity in view!"

"Yours always lovingly,"
"C. BURKE."

CHAPTER II
SOME GUESTS

"Be useful where thou livest, that they may
Both want and wish thy pleasing presence still ...
Find out men's wants and will
And meet them there."
Herbert.

"HUGH, we shall have to do entertaining."

General Macdonald gave a little groan.

"I have patiently gone round with you to leave cards when people are out. Then you have dragged me to dinners and lunches and teas, and I hoped now that we might be left in peace. Of course, I expected the neighbours to call, and they have done their duty. Are we to go round and round the treadmill of society as they do in town?"

Rowena laughed lightly. She was a three-months-old bride now, and was quite able to manage this husband of hers.

"My dear, we have our duties as well as they. And we are told to be 'given to hospitality.' We cannot accept invitations and never give any in return. Shall we have a simple garden-party? An 'At Home' in about a fortnight from now? The strawberries and peaches will be ripe, and we can have tea under the cedars on the lawn."

"I believe you love crowds. Personally, I loathe them." General Macdonald's tone was sharp. He added more gently:

"We have not been very long married, Rowena, and we had no proper honeymoon. You must forgive me if I still wish to keep you to myself."

"We must not be selfish, dear. You wrong me when you think I love gaiety. But I do love my fellow-creatures; and this one afternoon in their society will not hurt us. I want to get it over before Mysie's holidays begin. Now, please, put on your pleasantest expression, for I am going to ask another favour. Don't you think Mysie would like some companions sometimes? It would be so good for her as she does not go to school. I thought we might ask George Holt and his sisters up here and give them a good time; and Marion would be able to have a nice quiet holiday with her mother. Will you let me invite them here for a month of their holidays? Oh, do!"

She had drawn nearer him, and General Macdonald put his arm round her.

"I will do anything you like, Rowena, when you look at me like that!"

She laughed again gaily.

"What a confession of weakness!" she said. "Now I know how I can get my way with you."

And so the garden-party was given, and Rowena moved about amongst her guests and captivated them all by her charming words and smiles. Mysie, in a soft muslin frock and large shady straw hat, was such a transformation from the little kilted tomboy that some who had seen her scrambling about in the glen before hardly recognized her now. The General was drawn out of his shell. He even found points of interest with Colonel Arnold Rashleigh, who had taken the lodge where Rowena had spent her year of convalescence.

The Miss Arnold Rashleighs spent most of their time on the tennis-courts, but one of them, Dora by name, attached herself to Rowena during the latter part of the afternoon, and they made friends over Shags, who had been with old Mrs. Mactavish when she was caretaker of the lodge, and who now had been adopted by the Arnold Rashleighs.

"I was very fond of him," Rowena admitted; "but when I came here, I heard that you had taken him, and my husband has six dogs already, so I felt I had better not add to the number. Shags is very human. As you may have heard, I spent a lonely year at the lodge, and he was my constant companion."

"How could you have stood it? Three months are all we can put in. Joyce and I are much too energetic to waste our time over these wilds."

"But you are young and strong. I had to follow doctor's orders, or I dare say I should have been on my back still. And I found during that year at the lodge that life was much fuller and richer than I had ever imagined before. I was introduced into a perfectly new environment."

"How interesting! Tell me."

"How can I tell you in a few words? I found that a part of me had never been cultivated or enjoyed life at all, it was sleeping—almost dead. It began to wake up, and every day or so I saw fresh things."

"Oh, I suppose you set to work to study Nature with microscopes, and that kind of thing?"

"I must tell you about it another day," said Rowena, smiling down upon the puzzled face of the girl. "Anyhow, I learnt some of the secret joys of solitude; and when I was frivolously inclined, Shags whiled away my time with his tricks and gambols. I wish you loved the loch and glen as I do. Now tell me about your life in town."

"Oh, I'm not quite so ambitious as Joyce. She means to go into Parliament, but I'm not keen on politics. I work a good deal for women's industries. We aren't idlers, I can assure you. We mean to take our proper place in the world now."

"It's splendid having work like that," said Rowena enthusiastically. "Are you an idealist, I wonder? What is your goal?"

"Oh, I suppose it is to do something worth living for before one dies," said Dora. "We can dispense with men, you know; they're very good for recreation and amusement, but as for settling down with one in these wilds, as you have done, I couldn't, to save my life!"

"You think it waste of time."

"You're right. Utter waste!"

Rowena shook her head, with her sunny smile.

"No," she said; "I hope and trust I'm not wasting my life. I have my own scheme of work, and I can pursue it even here. I would like to press you into it as a recruit, but we must know each other better first before I can venture to give you a full explanation of it."

"You sound most mysterious. May I come over one day when you're alone and have a talk with you?"

This was just what Rowena wanted. She felt that her party had not been waste of time when she parted from Dora Rashleigh. The girl had taken to her and wanted to know her better.

In talking over the afternoon with her husband afterwards, Rowena said:

"There are so many kinds that make up a world, Hugh. And so many of these modern girls have such high ideals of work, and of benefiting one's fellow-creatures, that I long to save them from the mistakes they are bound to make if they are building without a foundation. You showed me what a full life could be lived in empty circumstances; I want to show them that the fullest life cannot be full unless they have the 'One thing needful.'"

The three young Holts arrived soon after this. Mysie and Milly became firm friends at once, and though at first Mysie stood a little in awe of George's superior age and inches, yet when she realized he was up to any mad escapade she quickly made friends with him. Bertha was more staid, and loved nothing better than wandering about the garden, book in hand; when she could get Rowena to herself she was supremely happy, for she adored her, but, as a rule, General Macdonald absorbed all his wife's leisure time.

Then one morning Rowena received the following letter from Di Dunstan:

"MY DEAR ROWENA,—"

"I'm taking you at your word, for I know you're the real good sort and mean what you say. Will you have me on a visit now? I have to put in a fortnight with some cousins in Perthshire at the end of the month, and I'm fed up with town. I don't believe I shall ever stick a flat all the year round. It isn't good enough! I'm bored stiff with the pack of humanity round me. I want light and air and breathing space; and, oh, for a horse and a gallop through the fresh untainted air on the heath or moor! Does your good man keep horses? Or is he all for those smelly cars? Rowena, I must come. I think I shall go mad if I don't get out of town pretty soon. So send me a wire on receipt of this, and I'll leave my slang and most of my cigarettes behind, and will be on my best behaviour lest I shock your high-principled husband. Poor Mrs. Burke used to rail against him! In her jolly days, I mean. Poor dear, she wasn't much fun latterly, though she was wonderfully plucky in bearing her lot! I don't see much of Vi—one is at a disadvantage in a married sister's house. She does the high and mighty with me, as if I'm on a lower plane to her. And I can't cotton to Gregory—I never could—and he's too selfish to make a good husband—was a bachelor too long. So long."

"Yours,"

"DI."

Rowena consulted her husband. With a wry face he agreed to send a wire.

"I'm trying to be sociable," he said, "and you must have your friends. I know her sort, and trust that you will not leave me to entertain her."

"Indeed, indeed, I won't!" laughed Rowena. "But, Hugh dear, if you let her ride your cob, she'll want nothing better. Di off a horse is only half herself. And I'm truly sorry for her. She has lost such a lot, and seems to have no object in life."

The wire was sent, and the next evening Di arrived. She was a handsome girl still, but she looked worn and weary, and Rowena saw that she was in a restless unhappy state of mind.

She talked recklessly at dinner and showed her worst side to the General, who was wonderfully forbearing and courteous in his manner towards her.

Bertha Holt looked at her in amazement; never had she in the course of her quiet life come across this type of woman. Di's horsey slang, her astounding statements, and her perfect indifference to the impression she was making upon those around her, startled and puzzled the young girl. When dinner was over the young people disappeared into the garden. Rowena walked her guest along the terrace and down a grassy path which led to a low wall overlooking the loch.

Di promptly lit up her cigarette.

"At last I've got you to myself," she said. "It's no go, Rowena, I can't put on pretty manners to charm your out of date husband. I've come down here hoping you can tip me a wrinkle or two. I've run to earth, and unless I can find a way out I shall come to a bad end like the villain in the story book. I cannot live on my income, and it's no good talking about it. I hate cadging on my friends, but there seems nothing else to do. I know a woman who has any amount of houses open to her the whole year round; but she's one of these adaptable pussycats who settle down by any fireside, and do errands for the hostess, and make up an even number at bridge or dinner, or chaperon a schoolgirl when the mother is too busy or bored to go round with her. I'm not that sort, and in the hunting season I expect my host to mount me well, or I'm off him! I demand too much, and that's the fact, and people aren't keen on having me. To stay in a London flat the whole year round is unthinkable. If Bob would only hand out a little of his superfluous cash, I would try my fortunes at Monte Carlo. I must get money somehow, but I can't rise to the ticket out there!"

"I hoped you had made a fresh start as far as your debts were concerned," said Rowena slowly and thoughtfully.

"Oh, you knew that transaction between Mrs. Burke and myself? She was a trump. But she's gone now, and I haven't a friend in the world. Town life makes money go like water. There's nothing for me but a wealthy marriage. I know one man who would have me to-morrow, but he's nearer seventy than sixty, and is rotund, and gouty and jocular. I shudder at the thought of my spending my years with him. Fate is against me. I never ought to have been born. You'll hear one day of the suicide of a society spinster. I shall be driven to it."

"Now, Di, listen to me. It's wicked and foolish for a girl of your intelligence and gifts to talk so. You're just drifting down the stream with all the garbage and useless rubbish that is being washed away. Do, for goodness' sake, pull yourself together and have a better outlook. Is there any real reason for your always living neck-deep in debt? Couldn't you with determined effort cut your coat according to your cloth?"

Di shook her head gloomily.

"What's the use? I've no purpose or interest in life. The only thing I did care for was hunting, and it has been taken from me. Go on, pitch into me. It does me good, but I'm almost past feeling it."

"You're not past feeling. You would never have come to stay with us if you were. You know you're reaching out towards something that will lift you out of your sordid life. There's no other word for it. You're an earth grub, that's what you are. The life you're leading—spending money because other people do it, treating those who take your generosity as a matter of course, and living in mortal dread of every post because it brings you bills and duns which you cannot pay—why, it is a hell on earth!"

"Say on! Hammer me down!"

Rowena laughed a little unsteadily.

"Di, dear. I've always liked you, partly because Mrs. Burke was so fond of you, partly for your own sake. Do use your mental powers. There are many circles in the world, all different, but all moving round their own centres. Change your centre. If one circle fails you—or one centre I'll say—

for goodness' sake don't go on tramping it for ever, but leave it and try another."

"Now this is what I like. My brain is just clever enough to understand it!"

"You may laugh and mock at me, but I'm in dead earnest. I feel like Alice through the looking-glass, as if I should like to shake the red queen into a kitten. I would like to shake and shake you till your foundation tumbled down, and you were shaken into a new kind of creature altogether, with fresh joy in life, and fresh springs in your heart, and fresh hopes and ideals in front of you."

"Don't mix your metaphors. Keep to the circles. I won't be shaken into a kitten."

"There's only one circle I want you in."

"Of course, I know which one that is—the one you're in yourself, the one into which you dragged Mrs. Burke. I'll allow it made her happy; but she always was a happy creature, and always would be in any circumstances."

"Do you think she would have been when everything that she cared for was taken from her?"

"Perhaps not; but that was where you and your circle came in. Just in the nick of time you moved her out of the one that was destroyed and planted her in another. Now, I haven't come to the end of mine."

"I thought you had."

"No; I'm not crippled and confined to bed. I can move, and have all the faculties for still enjoying life, but want of money and position prevents me from using them."

"Do you think it's a good thing to wait till utter ruin comes to you?"

"How comforting you are! I honestly want worldly wisdom from you, not pious talk."

"I'm not worldly wise, but I'll try to be. Live within your income, and make the best of your circumstances. Take up some other hobby that will take the place of the one in which you now cannot indulge."

"What dull and impossible counsel. As well tell a fish to live out of water and cultivate the air for his home."

"Exactly," said Rowena. "You've hit the nail on the head."

There was a little silence between them, then Di threw away the last bit of her cigarette, and stared gloomily down from the wall to the waters of the loch below.

"The centre of my circle is, of course, myself. I see that," she said. "Whom else should I revolve round but my dear precious self? It is so very disappointing if you revolve round another. I did that once, but never again."

Rowena knew she was alluding to her unfortunate love affair some years previously.

"I think we're a great disappointment to ourselves," said Rowena. "I see my husband coming. Cheer up, Di. I believe you're going to see light soon. We'll have another talk later."

Di turned to the General with her most charming smile.

"Here is your treasure! I make no apology for having purloined her from your side for a bit. Have you discovered any faults in her yet General?"

"Yes," said General Macdonald promptly. "She has too big a heart."

"You mean that you can't keep every hole and corner in it for yourself! Isn't that a man all over? And you've brought her away into your lonely stronghold, where you mean to keep her under lock and key. Oh, you are all alike! A woman's heart must be satisfied with her house, and man, he can roam the whole world over, and open his heart to all the treasures in it."

General Macdonald was about to reply when Di said:

"Rowena and I have been talking ourselves dry. I want to see your stables; may I?"

He led the way without a word, and when she saw a beautiful brown cob which had been a noted hunter, and was offered the use of him for the time of her stay, she was quite elated.

"I'm going to make hay while the sun shines," she said to Rowena, when they were wishing each other good night, later on, "so you'll get no more grave talks out of me for the present."

She took George out with her for a ride over the moor the next morning, and they were away for most of the day. George, of course, was very flattered at being chosen as her cavalier. He was not so critical as his sister Bertha, and thought this new acquaintance most amusing and entertaining.

Two days later, General Macdonald went to Inverness on business. He had to stay away the night, and when he returned home the following afternoon, Rowena saw at once that he had something on his mind.

He called her into his study.

"Have I ever mentioned my cousin Hector Ross to you?" he asked.

"Never," said Rowena.

"He and I were brought up together as boys, and went to the same school, but he went abroad when he was quite a young man, and we have drifted apart. He was rather wild, and got through a lot of money. Then settled down on a South American ranch. I tumbled across him in Inverness yesterday. He has come home, and is thinking of buying back his father's old place in Fifeshire. I told you I have an old cousin living in Inverness. He is her nephew, and I met him at her house."

A smile flitted across his face. "It was like seeing a bull in a china shop! His aunt lives in a tiny terrace house, and everything as orderly and neat as an old maid could have it. He's a big, broad, happy-go-lucky fellow still, but he's made his money, and seems to have steadied down. He came across to the war; I never knew it, and he never told any of his people. I think his experience at the Front altered him, and made him determine to come home and look up his relatives. He wants to come to us."

"Of course he must."

Rowena laughed; she was standing by the open window as her husband talked. Now she turned and gave him a swift little kiss on his forehead.

"You dear old hermit! Has the thought of another visitor brought these aged wrinkles to your brow? We have plenty of room, and I personally shall be delighted to welcome him."

"He's not our sort," General Macdonald said. "And the fact is, Rowena, I am always longing to have you to myself. We have the house full enough now; every additional visitor absorbs more of your time. It sounds selfish—but it's a fact. I want a quiet life."

"My dear Hugh, think of the coming winter. In another month or so all our neighbours will have departed, and you and I will have our fireside to ourselves. I am looking forward to a winter with you alone. And we shall enjoy it all the more for not having the house to ourselves now. When does Mr. Ross want to come?"

"In a few days. Next Saturday—he mentioned. Of course, I could not refuse him; and I know you'll make him welcome. But I only hope he won't hang round me and want me to do the entertaining."

"Is he married?"

"No, he says not."

"I think he'll manage to amuse himself without worrying you; and if you were boys together, you must have some interests in common. It will do you good to have a man to talk to, Hugh. We females are so much in the majority."

Rowena had been so accustomed to a constant relay of visitors at Mrs. Burke's, that she could not understand her husband's dislike to them. And she felt that unless she got him to shake off his solitary habits now she would never succeed in doing it later on.

Beyond preparing a room for this fresh guest she gave little thought to his coming. When she mentioned it to Diana, that young woman shrugged her shoulders:

"What a bore! If he's like your husband, Rowena, I shall elude him all I can. We'll shut them up in the sacred study with their pipes, and leave them to themselves."

Rowena shook her head.

"No, my husband won't have that. But if this glorious weather lasts, there will be no need to amuse him. The beauties of the loch and glen are enough for any man; and there's shooting and fishing for him. I must speak to Donald about that—or Hugh will. He has not preserved his coverts this year. But there's always plenty of rough shooting here they say."

CHAPTER III
HECTOR ROSS

"A man of integrity, sincerity and good nature can never be concealed, for his character is wrought into his countenance."
Marcus Aurelius.

ROWENA and Di were on the lawn in front of the house when Hector Ross arrived.

The children were all out on the loch with Donald. It was a very hot afternoon; Rowena was sewing, and Di was lazily reclining in a hammock under the old cedar tree. The car had gone to the station to meet an earlier train, but he had not come by that. Now he walked up to the house, and came striding across the lawn directly he saw the white-gowned figures under the old cedars.

Rowena rose to meet him in her usual happy way.

"My husband had to attend a quarterly parish meeting this afternoon," she said, "or he would be here to welcome you. You must accept my welcome instead."

She introduced him to Di, who was rather taken aback by his youthful figure and brisk alertness of his speech and manner.

Hector Ross was a good-looking man, with blue eyes and fair hair. His face was tanned and rather weather-beaten. One could see he had had an open-air life for many years. As Rowena looked at him, the determination of his mouth and chin, the resolute look in his eyes, and the quick short way in which he clipped his words, showed her that, whatever else he might be, he was very wide awake.

"Couldn't wait to be driven," he said, "so I left my baggage to follow. I'm not a stranger in these parts, you know."

Then he turned to Di.

"Can you be Hugh's daughter?"

Di laughed frankly and freely.

"My good man, his daughter is still in the submissive stage. Her years demand it. Can you see me as the General's daughter, Rowena? What high jinks I would lead him! I'm just a stray visitor, Mr. Ross; and your cousin will be more relieved than otherwise when I've gone!"

Then she swung herself lightly out of the hammock and, leaning against the tree, took out her silver cigarette case and began to smoke.

"Have one?" she said, offering her case to the newcomer.

He shook his head with a smile.

"I go in for a pipe."

He looked at her reflectively, then at Rowena.

"I'm taking stock of you both," he said pleasantly. "Mrs. Macdonald is the old order of woman, and you are the new. I've come across plenty of the modern girls, but the old-fashioned ones are rare."

"I suppose I am old-fashioned," said Rowena laughing, "but it gives me rather a shock to hear you say it. I used not to be considered so a few years back."

"It's good manners does it," said Hector tersely.

"Complimentary to me," laughed Di.

In a few minutes he was talking to them as if he had known them all his life. Incidentally he touched upon his ranch life.

"Why have you given it up?" Di asked. "If you were making your pile, and having a jolly free life out, there, why on earth didn't you keep on a few years longer?"

"I sold up when I went over to France—or, rather, when I went over to Canada to train. I went out with the Canadians, and had a stiff two years at the Front. Then I went back, for I'd a few things to settle up; and I came over here three months ago. I meant to look up Hugh when my aunt had had enough of me. I'm going to my people's old place. It came into the market the beginning of this year, and I was able to buy it in the nick of time."

"And you're going to settle down as a laird, I suppose?" said Di. "Everybody is a laird over here. I've seen some funny specimens."

"And here's another," he returned. "My good aunt told me solemnly, when I left her, that she had never seen my like before. I was a complete bewilderment to her—I believe that was the word she used. I'm going to take her in my pocket when I go back to Kestowknockan; she'll keep house for me and look after my morals and manners."

Rowena looked at him with fresh interest.

"You'd better get a wife to keep house for you," said Di carelessly. "Aunts are out of fashion."

"Same as parents, I suppose," he said, with a slight curl coming to his lips. "I came over with some flappers all intent upon a high old time in London. I asked them if they were orphans. You should have heard them yell."

"Oh, the world is out of gear," said Rowena, "but the pendulum will swing back again. And here, amongst our lochs and glens, we do not see much to puzzle or alarm us. Here come the children! Now you will see Hugh's little daughter. And shall we go indoors to tea? We are having it in the hall to-day. It is cooler than out here."

They moved towards the house. The children met them on the way. Mysie looked up frankly into Hector's face when she was introduced to him.

"Did you know Dad when he was a boy? He says you did. What was he like? Always good, or did he sometimes get into scrapes?"

"Ah! Ask him to tell you about Adolph and the cave, or the night he was left alone, and his parents were in town."

"What cave?" gasped Mysie. "Mine? Oh, do you, know the caves about here? Do tell me all about them."

She seized hold of him, and during tea he enlivened them all by tales of boyish pranks in the holidays.

Towards the close of it General Macdonald came in, and the younger members of the household slipped out into the garden again.

Before the evening was over Hector was a universal favourite, and his hearty laugh and cheery talk caused Di to say to Rowena—

"Make him stay on, do; I like him, and he wakes the General up!"

But she and he had some pitched battles about the present generation. Di was for progress and liberty of speech, and action for all women; he was by way of relegating them to the back shelf. Sometimes he amused himself by rousing her ire, and would be dogmatic in denouncing modern habits with which he was really in sympathy.

Rowena listened to the two, and smiled to herself. It did not hurt Di to hear a man of the world's impression of the present race of girls. She had had very few who had hitherto dared to criticize and contradict her. One bond they had in common was their love for horses. Hector said he meant to breed them when he took possession of his place.

"I'm having proper stables built before I get in," he said. "I'm sick of these cars. Give me a horse, and I want nothing more."

"Hear! Hear!" said Di, and the next morning she and he rode off together. Hector was very sociably inclined—a marked contrast to the General. In a few days' time, he was friends with the Arnold Rashleighs, and with several of the other neighbours round. He had invitations to shoot and fish and to dine and sleep, and sometimes his host did not see him for three or four days.

But on Sundays he invariably turned up at the morning service in the little church of Abertarlie.

Di laughed at him for it one day.

"You are going back to the training of your youth," she said. "Church-going is not the fashion now."

"Neither is heaven or hell," he retorted; "but I'm not a man of fashion—never was."

She looked at him meditatively.

They were smoking together on the terrace. It was Sunday afternoon, and there was a peculiar stillness in the air and scene. Rowena always had Mysie for an hour after lunch in her boudoir upstairs. She had told her frankly that she was going to try to teach her to love her Bible. Milly and Bertha had asked to come too, so the hour's Bible reading was now quite an institution. Sometimes George joined them, but upon this occasion he had gone for a walk with the General. Hector raised his eyes, and when they met Di's, he smiled.

"Well, what's the verdict?"

She shook her head.

"You're too complex for me!"

"I'll give you a chink of light to help you on. I was three years in the war. As you say, religion is now not the fashion, and it isn't good form to talk about it; but in the trenches we did a good bit of talking, and we didn't care a hang if a chap started a yarn about life and death and hereafter, for we were all interested in it. Of course we were. We were shot out of this world into the next all day long. We all had our theories; but in my section at one time there was a parson who knew his job, and did it; and he was a jolly good fellow all round. He made us believe in him, and then he got us to believe in the things he believed. And my belief has stuck ever since; see?"

There was for a second a wistful gleam in Di's eye. Then she said coolly:

"Oh, yes, I see. And Rowena is doing the same with me as your parson did with you. But I'm as hard as nails, and she has a tough job."

"They say," said Hector, as he leant over the stone balustrade, and puffed away at his pipe, "that we all drift back in time to our starting-point. I was an irreligious little beggar when I was a boy, but every Scotchman is brought up in the way in which he should go. I had the head knowledge, and then I chucked it and ran amok for a few years. I found that didn't pay, and settled down to be steady. But it was at the Front I found my early Faith was the only one worth having. And our parson taught us how to live as well as how to die. I never shall be a shining light as, for instance, my cousin Hugh is; but I've got the comfort of settled and rooted convictions. And they make life a bigger and a more understandable thing!"

Di was mute. If a bolt from the blue had tumbled down at her feet she couldn't have been more amazed. She began to wonder if she was always going to be beset with people who would worry her with their religious convictions. To her great relief Hector did not pursue the subject, and she listened with interest to an account he gave her of a journey of his across the Rocky Mountains, when he was shooting bears. But the following Sunday she accompanied the others to church, and never missed a service from that time forward.

Hector only stayed a fortnight with them. He and Di had a long ride together the afternoon before he went, and when they were returning, he said:

"You'll have to come and see my horses one day, when I'm settled in. I shall give a house-warming about Christmas time. Will you come?"

"Is this a bona fide invitation?"

"Rather!"

"Then I accept, with thanks. I'm wondering what kind of a house you'll run. You'll be a bit of a despot I know."

"I jolly well will. I mean to be master in my house, I can tell you."

"Don't try to take to yourself a wife; disaster will follow if you do."

"Why?"

"Because now no woman will lie down for a man to walk over her."

"That's a bit of clap-trap."

"No; it's real fact. You want a wife who will meekly do her lord's will, and that kind of women are out of date. They don't exist."

"I'll wait till they come into fashion again. I'm in no hurry."

"You're so cocksure of yourself!"

"I'm not going to make a mess of my life now," he responded with emphasis. "Look through the daily papers and see the result of these modern wives and husbands. They both want to rule, they both want their own ways, and they go them, and then the fat is in the fire, there is a flare up, and divorce follows."

"But it's all wrong," said Di with sudden heat. "Why should men be selfish brutes? Why should they make life impossible for their wives unless they are their slaves and tools? Women will never again be subjugated by men, never! And I hope you'll never marry; I hope you'll never get a girl whom you are able to crush and mould according to your liking."

He looked at her with a gleam of mischief in his eyes. "Women really like to meet their masters," he said. "I've knocked about the world a good bit, and I assure you they do. There's still the instinct of the ages left in most of them, that they're really made to be loved and protected. You've only to read some of the present-day novels written by your sex to see that the strong man always prevails."

"I shan't argue with you any more," said Di a little huffily. "But you'll meet with your deserts one day, I hope." She parted with him later in the most friendly fashion, and when he had gone told Rowena she felt quite flat.

"He kept us alive; and though I hate some of his principles, he's good company," she said.

She was the next to go. She had been with Rowena much longer than she had intended.

Rowena came into her bedroom the last evening of her stay.

"I'm sorry to lose you," she said; "but you must come again, if you don't find we are too quiet for you."

Di squeezed her hand.

"You're a trump. I wish I could tell you that all your talks have had the effect you want, but I'm too old to change my ways. And I don't want to, if I could. You have made me believe that I'm living on a lower level than you. You're in touch with Unseen Things, and I'm not. And you've made me see I'm a useless cumberer of the earth, and I'm not fulfilling the purpose of my creation. But I've no ability to alter my line, or any desire in that direction. I think you've left me a little more hopeless than when you found me."

"Oh, how dreadful!" exclaimed Rowena. "What can I do to remedy that? After all, dear Di, it's only a question of your will. You know Who will help you to adjust your life differently. You have only to ask, and it will be done."

"I know! I know! And you're a dear old thing to care a snap about me. No one else does." Then, with a change of tone, she said, "I mean to spend next Christmas with Hector Ross. He's a rum sort, isn't he? My word, how he'll bully that little aunt of his! He wants some one to stand up to him. I wish he'd give me carte blanche to bring a few girls to add to his house-party. I know some who would make him sit up. But I don't care for girls myself, as you know. Give me men, even if they're rotten. And he's hardly that, is he? I rather fancy he'll turn into a man like your good husband if left to develop his own line. These Scotchmen are like blocks of granite. You only hammer yourself if you try to hammer them."

Di left and Rowena thought about her much.

Then the young Holts went back to their grandmother. She was living in Mrs. Burke's country house which had been left to her, and meant to stay there. Marion had returned, and took up lessons again, and the house settled down to a very quiet life, much to the General's satisfaction.

Rowena had a long talk with Marion upon the first evening of her return.

"I feel now that your mother is in such comfortable circumstances that you ought not to be out teaching," she said. "Doesn't she want to have you with her?"

"She has Bertha and Milly. She does not need me. I shall never forget your goodness in getting me this work. Why should I give it up? I've never been so happy in my life as I am with you. And I love Mysie, and she is a real pleasure to teach. If you are satisfied with my teaching, don't try to send me away."

"My dear Marion, I'm only too delighted to keep you. We will say no more about it."

"It is so delicious to see mother living in ease and comfort at last," Marion went on. "Of course she's sad still, and sometimes I think grudges herself the little luxuries she can have, because of the thought of my father and of all that he had to be denied. But she is taking increasing interest in the children, and she loves helping the poor in the village and continuing Aunt Caroline's village charities. I often thank God that you were led to live with my aunt. If you had not gone, how different things would have been with us I don't believe she would have left any money to mother at all, because she was so angry that she refused to be helped for so many years."

"I think it was rather quixotic of her," said Rowena.

"Perhaps it was; but she felt my aunt's marriage was everything that was sinful, and she would have nothing to do with it. I think she and my father were rather too strict in their judgments. You lived with her, and loved her, before she changed her life so."

"Yes," said Rowena thoughtfully. "I do not regret it, though, perhaps, I would not advise others to do the same. The life we lived was very deadening to the soul. I do not know what it was, but the very first day I saw your aunt, there was something peculiarly childish and appealing in her face. I felt she was one who wanted a real friend. And then I soon discovered that underneath all her gaiety and love of fun she was really an unhappy woman. I determined to help her if I could; and that determination helped me in many a bad time when I felt inclined to run away and leave it all."

"You were wonderful!" exclaimed Marion.

"Not at all. I undertook a job, and I stuck to it, just as you are sticking to your job now."

The conversation ended, and Marion took up the lessons happily. She was, as she said, only too happy in the present life to wish to change it, and Mysie adored her.

CHAPTER IV
WINTER IN THE GLEN

Oh Winter ruler of the inverted year ...
... Thou hold'st the sun
A prisoner in the yet undawning East,
Short'ning his journey between morn and noon,
And hurrying him impatient of his stay
Down to the rosy West; but kindly still
Compensating his loss with added hours
Of social converse and instructive ease,
And gathering at short notice in one group
The family dispersed, and fixing thought
Not less dispersed by daylight and its cares.
Cowper.

IF Rowena had been asked if her married life now had fulfilled all her desires, she would have answered emphatically in the affirmative. Her husband adored her, and so did his child. She had full scope for her social activities all the summer; she had time, as she said, to find her soul and brain during the silent winter. For they did not move up to town as her sister-in-law wished. Neither of them had any desire to leave their Highland home.

Rowena tramped round the snowy moors with her husband, sometimes skating on part of the frozen loch, and sledging when the frost held the roads in its iron grip. Then when dusk came, she would sit sewing by the blazing log fires and the General would read aloud to her. He loved the solitude of their life and always protested if there was talk of having any visitors. One afternoon Rowena had taken Mysie with her and they had wandered into some fir woods, cracking the dry leaves and twigs underfoot with keen enjoyment of the aromatic scent of the pines, and of the fresh green moss and moist earth around them.

They were listening to some owls hooting just before turning towards home, when a cooee-ee rang out, and the next moment Dora Arnold Rashleigh came crashing through some undergrowth with her dogs.

"Why, Dora, what are you doing here!" asked Rowena. "I thought the Lodge was shut up and you were all back in town."

"So we were till two days ago, but Joyce suddenly developed scarlet fever, and I hate illness, so I came off out of it, and I remembered how happy you had been at the Lodge by yourself one winter so thought I'd try a month or so. Fact is, the Glen has got hold of me—it's a way some of these Scotch places have! And I arrived yesterday morning with a maid, and Granny Mactavish is delighted to do for me, but she quotes you on every occasion. We've been trespassing in your woods, haven't we?"

Rowena was astonished. She had not seen as much of Dora as she had hoped to do. Di and she had not got on together. They were both too masterful, and Dora had kept away from Rowena in consequence.

"How ripping to be in the Lodge quite by yourself!" said Mysie. "Do ask mother and me to tea one day; it will make me think of the days I went over to tea with her. It was a jolly old time!"

"I invite you to tea to-morrow," said Dora gaily. Rowena looked a little perturbed.

"My dear girl, you can't stay in the empty house by yourself. Surely your parents won't like it. You had better come to us."

Dora shook her head.

"You forget that women can do anything nowadays. I'll come over to you whenever I feel dull. I'm going to have a couple of friends down next week. They're overworked and want a rest."

Then, as Mysie danced along in front, calling the dogs after her, Dora turned to Rowena with an intent look upon her face.

"I want a talk with you. I've been longing for it. I want to have the highest goal. I've discovered mine is pretty low down, and I want to right it."

"Oh, Dora dear, I'm so glad."

As they walked homewards, their talk was a serious one, and when they parted, Dora said:

"Come to-morrow, and we'll make Mysie happy with the dogs somewhere whilst we have another talk. I really came back here to see more of you. Things you said to me have stuck."

Rowena went home with a light in her eyes and a glow in her heart. Di had disappointed her with her irresponsiveness, and all the time another was standing by who was longing to be helped and guided.

The next day she and Mysie went to tea at the Lodge as arranged, and when Mysie, in her old fashion, had gone out to see Granny in the kitchen, Rowena and Dora had a long talk together.

"You see," said Dora after a time, "I don't want to alter my life or give up my work. That's all right. But I want to put something in it that I haven't got. And when we are working away at these women, and getting them into Clubs and Guilds and all that sort of thing, we are continually knocking up against cases embittered by their circumstances and soured by trouble, and then one feels rather helpless. To tell them to go to church makes them smile. I think they feel they want something more. You have a living Power in your life. I can see it. I want to have that too, and I want to tell others how they can get it. You can't cure a vicious minded woman by giving her a dancing club, or comfort a broken-hearted one by teaching her how to make baskets! If one's work is to be a success, you must give of your best; and my best is not worth having. You quoted a verse to me one day in the summer: 'Except the Lord build the house they labour in vain that build it.' And of course I've been thinking we, and every one of these women we try to help, are made or built by God in the first instance, and if we come to grief, there's no one can rebuild us properly except our Maker. I want to put myself in His Hands; tell me how to do it."

It was not difficult for Rowena to help the girl. She was anxious and willing and quite convinced that a life without God was a failure.

Before many days were past, the light came to her. She was very happy in the empty Lodge, spent most of her days with Rowena, and sat chatting in the kitchen with old Granny after her simple dinner was over. But in three weeks' time she went back to town.

"I shall lodge with a friend till our house is disinfected," she told Rowena. "Joyce is nearly well, they tell me. I must be getting on with my work, and now I have got what I came for, there is nothing to keep me. I wish we had a few more of your sort in town, Mrs. Macdonald. You are so very definite. I find people so very vague when you start talking religion. If I get into a fog, I shall write to you. I have made you my father—no—mother-confessor!"

And when she said good-bye to General Macdonald, she said to him with a little laugh:

"I consider Mrs. Macdonald is wasting her life down here. You ought to come to town oftener. Of course, if the mountain won't come to Mahomet, Mahomet must come to the mountain, and that's what I've done, but there are lots of others who couldn't afford the time or money to do it. Think of your fellow-creatures sometimes, General, and bring your wife to town. We want her there badly."

When she had gone Rowena told her husband about her. As a rule she did not betray the confidence of any who confided in her. She had learnt the wisdom of that in her life with Mrs. Burke. And her husband did not understand even yet, the gift that she had for drawing out the best in people, and winning their confidence and love.

"Well," he said, "I'm glad you were able to help her, dear. I must confess these loud-voiced, self-sufficient girls, do not appeal to me. The Miss Rashleighs were ardent suffragettes a few years back. I suppose they may do good in their own set; it is an age for strenuous exertion and work, but I can no more understand Dora Rashleigh than I can Miss Di Dunstan. I suppose Miss Dunstan is the more selfish of the two, as she never seems to think of anything but amusing and taking care of herself."

"I'm afraid you don't care for girls," said Rowena, looking at him rather ruefully. "And yet you have a little daughter of your own!"

"She is more than enough for me," said General Macdonald with a smile. "You say her will ought not to be broken, but I will not have her grow up into one of these modern young women."

"I cannot think why you ever took the smallest interest in me," said Rowena with her laugh. "I was an ordinary young woman—not an old-fashioned one by any means."

"You? Oh, you stand by yourself. You were perfectly adorable from the first moment I set eyes on you! I don't wonder you are so popular with these girls. I wish I could be more sociable and sympathetic. I am just an old bear who likes to remain in his den, and have his family with him."

"Then my dear Bruin," was Rowena's laughing retort; "it will be one of my endeavours to make you dance to our music sometimes. We are not meant to shut ourselves away from our neighbours. How can we help them if we do; how can we bear each other's burdens, as we are told to do? I consider that my time with dear Mrs. Burke was given me to show me how many of the people we consider frivolous and empty-headed, are really needing help and comfort and counsel. Don't think I set myself upon a pedestal above them. I don't. I'm just as foolish and ignorant in many ways as they are, but by coming together and being friendly with a number of them, I have discovered that we all have the same cravings, and needs, and that what has helped me will help them."

General Macdonald was silent, but when a few days later an invitation came from Hector Ross for them to spend Christmas with him, he did not cavil at it, as was his custom.

After talking it over, Rowena and he agreed that they wanted to be in their own home for Christmas; but Rowena wrote, suggesting that they should pay him a visit in the new year, and this was finally settled.

And then came an invitation for Mysie to spend part of her holidays with the young Holts and their Grandmother. Marion said she was not particularly anxious to be at home at Christmas, and would willingly wait, and take Mysie with her later.

At first Rowena had difficulty in getting her husband to consent to this arrangement.

"What does the child want to go away from home for!"

Mysie was enchanted with the invitation. She had never been away alone before, and Milly Holt was her "bosom friend." So she informed her father.

"It does her good to get away from us, sometimes," said Rowena. "Yes, I really mean it. We are too old and staid for her. I would not send her anywhere, but she can get nothing but good where she is going."

"I should have thought it would be better for her to have a change from her governess rather than from us," said her father.

"I agree with you, but as it happens, Marion is not going to stay at home. She has promised to visit some old friends of hers in the North. And Mysie will have her company on the journey there and back, which is necessary, and as we are going to Kestowknockan it will all fit in beautifully."

So General Macdonald gave in to his wife, which he generally did, after making his protest.

Sometimes Rowena wondered if he would ever lose his old bachelor ways and ideas.

Christmas came and the weather was bright and frosty. They had a very quiet time, but a happy one, and Mysie's high spirits never flagged.

She received a gold watch and chain from her father as a Christmas gift, and a most beautiful edition of the Life of Flora Macdonald, with coloured illustrations, from Rowena. It would be hard to say which present she prized most. She was allowed to dine late on Christmas day, and in the midst of the meal she put down her knife and fork and leaned her elbows on the table, looking across at her father very earnestly.

"Dad dear, do you remember Christmas last year when you and me sat here alone together, and it was raining and squalling, and you kept sighing, and then we talked of mother, and you said she might possibly be here another year; and then I sat on your knee by the fire afterwards, and you read me bits of her letter to you, and about the poor ill lady she was with! Doesn't it seem years ago! And we've got her now for ever. Isn't it lovely?"

"Haven't you got tired of me yet, Flora?" Rowena said laughingly; but a shadow crossed her face as she, too, cast her mind back to a year ago, when she was nursing Mrs. Burke through that terrible attack of rheumatic fever.

"Tired of you! Oh, mother, what an awful thing to say! Mrs. Dalziel said to Angus the other day that you'd let all the light and sunshine into the dark corners of this old house, and it does seem quite, quite different; doesn't it, Dad?"

"We'll drink Mother's health presently," said General Macdonald, and Rowena declared that they would make her feel quite self-conscious and shy.

Later on, they sat round the fire, in which reposed a huge Yule, and Mysie roasted chestnuts and persuaded her father to tell her some stories about his youth. When she finally went off to bed, Rowena asked her husband if he would come out on the terrace for a moment or two.

He got her fur cloak, and insisted on wrapping it round her. Then, together, they stood for a few moments looking down through the vista of pines and bare trees to the silver Loch in the distance. It was a brilliant starlit night; here and there on the hills and moor in the distance, a faint light from some shepherd's cot or farm shone out. Owls were hooting in the neighbouring wood, but otherwise there was a great stillness.

And Rowena said with a half-caught breath:

"I expect it was just a night like this when the earth was hushed and still to hear the angel's voices. The whole world waiting till the Saviour of the earth was born!"

Something in her voice made General Macdonald draw her very closely and tenderly to him.

"Why, dearest, what is the matter? Tears on Christmas night!"

Rowena smiled through misty eyes.

"I only thought I'd like to tell you to-night, that before another Christmas comes round, I may be a mother. I seem to feel the Manger-throne so close to me to-night."

General Macdonald bent his head and kissed her. For once his composure was shaken.

"My darling," he said, "what a wonderful joy to give me to-night."

"Are you pleased?" she whispered. "I did not know if you would be."

Her husband tightened his hold on her; then he looked up into the starry sky.

"If God sees fit to give us a son," he said in a husky tone, "to carry on the old name and family, I-I think my cup will overflow."

"We will ask Him to do so," said Rowena, smiling up at him.

And then they went back to the fire, and talked together in low happy tones of the future, with all its golden possibilities.

CHAPTER V
ROWENA'S POWER

You are endowed with Faculties which bear
Annexed to them as 'twere a dispensation
To summon meaner spirits to do their will
And gather round them at their need; inspiring
Such with a love themselves can never feel.
Browning.

"HERE you are! It's good to see you both. Now come and be introduced to my little aunt."

Rowena and her husband were in the big hall of Kestowknockan, and Hector was welcoming them both in his cheerful, hearty manner.

There was a group of his guests round the big fire, and tea was just beginning. Miss Ross rose from her chair behind the silver urn, and shook hands with Rowena. She was a little grey-haired woman with happy smiling eyes, but she appeared a little flustered. Something in Rowena's face made her say in a low tone to her:

"Come and sit by me, Mrs. Macdonald. I have heard all about you from my cousin Hugh. You will help me. Three utter strangers have arrived to-day. Hector knows them, but I don't."

Rowena took a seat by her, but Di Dunstan seized hold of her.

"Here I am! The bad half-penny back again! I came this morning, and Allan Graeme joined me at Euston, so we've been fellow companions all the way. Also Hawtry Norris; do you know him? I've only met him once at the Graemes'—but it seems that he and Mr. Ross ran a ranch together once."

Di was looking very handsome in a dark blue cloth costume with fur trimming. Her fair hair and fresh complexion were set off by the sombreness of her gown. Captain Graeme was delighted to see Rowena again:

"We owe your husband a grudge for carrying you off to these lonely wilds," he said. "Several have been asking 'Where is that bright, jolly girl with the Saxon name, that used to be about town so much with Mrs. Burke?' And I've answered sadly, 'Married and done for.'"

"Do I look done for?" Rowena demanded; then Hector came up and introduced Mr. Norris to her and a Sir William and Lady Bampford. Sir William had been the English Minister at Panama. He was a thin, wiry little man, a great talker; his wife was a silent, stately woman, who seemed rather out of her element in Hector's free and easy household. The only other guest was a young widow, a Scotch cousin of the Rosses, a Mrs. McClintock.

They were all in very good spirits, and Hector was standing a good deal of chaff about his "ancestral halls."

"I own it isn't up to much at present," he said, looking round his rather empty hall with a grimace of disgust. "The last tenant took away everything with him, and my aunt and I have just got a few things together from Glasgow for the time being. I'll furnish it in good style later on."

"What style do you call good?" asked Mrs. McClintock.

"My own, of course. And I shall go in for simplicity and comfort and not have Birmingham suits of armour, and sham tapestry, and faked bronzes. If I haven't the real article—and I haven't—I shan't counterfeit them."

"You've got a few bearskins of your own," said Mr. Norris. "I should have them stuffed and placed about the hall. Try a few natural attitudes. They would keep away burglars, perhaps."

Through this talk Miss Ross was dispensing tea and talking to Rowena.

"Do help me," she said. "I have never visited country houses and I don't know how to entertain. Hector laughs at me if I ask him who is to take who in to dinner. 'Let them sort themselves out,' he says, 'I'm not going to run the place like the fashionable johnnies! It's to be Liberty Hall.' But if you have guests, you must treat them with courtesy and consideration; and I'm too old to be ignorant. I don't like it."

"I think we all enjoy unconventionality sometimes," said Rowena. "If I can help you, I will; but every one seems very happy at present."

Hector's house was like himself, simple and unpretending. There was an absence of soft couches and cushions, and of all the little knick-knacks that women gather round them. Miss Ross sighed for her comfortable little Terrace home, when she encountered the blasts of air through the long draughty passages and big windows that flanked every room. She had never lived in this house; for Hector's father had taken possession of it when she and her sister were living in London; and he had kept it, till his many debts had forced him to sell it. But she valiantly tried to do her best, and she was so anxious and deferential in her efforts to please her nephew's guests, that they could not but respond to her nervous and timid advances.

That evening Di asked Rowena to come into her bedroom the last thing at night. When she did so Di planted her in an easy-chair before the fire and began to talk.

"Isn't it queer that I should be down here so soon again? Why did he ask me, I wonder? What an odd fish he is! Did you hear his butler come to him for orders for to-morrow morning. 'How many for church, sir?' he asked. 'Will the wagonette be sufficient?' And then he looked round the hall and counted us all. 'Ten,' he said, and the widow looked up sharply: 'How do you know we all mean to go?' she said. And he laughed and thrust his hands in his pockets in his Colonial way: 'Oh, everybody goes to church in my house,' he said. 'And I give notice to you all that there'll be no billiards and bridge going to-morrow. I'm going to keep Sunday as it used to be kept when I was a kid.'"

"'Of course, in Scotland, we do things still that we don't do in England,'" I put in, and then he rounded on me:

"'Why should Scotland march into heaven first? Can't you English keep to your old traditions and Faith?' I enjoy watching the faces of his guests as he talks."

"And how is it with you?" Rowena asked affectionately. "Are you happier?"

Di shrugged her shoulders.

"I hate town more and more, and have left my flat already. I won't go back there. I'm going to Vi for a little hunting. For the sake of that I'm going to endure a course of snubs from her; and then I don't know what I shall do. Try to be good like you, perhaps, and see how it pays."

"Oh, Di dear!"

"Well, don't you want another convert? You made Mrs. Burke very happy. Will you make me?"

"I have no power to do it; and you know I haven't."

Di laughed.

"I don't want a sermon to-night; but we'll have some jaws together before I leave. What do you think of Mrs. McClintock? She's very sweet on

Mr. Ross. Can hear nobody speak in the room but him; she watches him and listens for his every word. I know her sort well."

"I felt sorry for her," said Rowena frankly. "She lost her husband just this time last year. She told me she had come up here to get it off her mind. It is her first Christmas without him, and she dreaded being alone in her empty house."

"Oh, she'll soon solace herself with another husband," said Di, with a scornful smile. "Lady Bampford is the one I am sorry for. I should think her life is an hourly martyrdom with that foolish chatterbox of a husband. She turns from him so wearily sometimes. I should feel inclined to choke him if he belonged to me. Dear Rowena, I'm so glad you don't look shocked! Now tell me your opinion of Mr. Norris?"

"I have only said half a dozen words to him. He's very Colonial; but he's really fond of Hector. He said very pathetically to me 'I should like to have a home of my own—one that belonged to my family, but we've only owned town jerry-built villas for generations.' He told me he had a superstition against buying an old house from anyone else. 'I know I should see strange spooks in it,' he said. 'One wouldn't mind spooks belonging to one's own people, but strange spooks might be up to any jinks!'"

Di laughed.

"We shall be a scratch pack in church to-morrow. I'm wondering whether Mr. Ross will be able to whip us all in!"

But Di need not have wondered. Hector had a way of getting people to do as he wanted, and the next day there was not one absent guest in the little church, five miles away in the hills.

"You're a splendid whipper-in," Di said to him at the church door.

He nodded to her, and from that time the nickname stuck to him.

There were shooting parties in the following week, and Di was out-of-doors all day. General Macdonald took his wife home at the end of the week, but the other guests remained on. Rowena had had several long talks with Di, and parted from her with real regret. Di promised to correspond with her.

"I'm a tough subject," she said to her, laughing; "much tougher than our old friend, Mrs. Burke; but your words stick, and I'll have plenty of time to think them over when I get back to town."

Husband and wife reached home one wild, stormy evening. The warmth and cosiness of their house when they came into it made Rowena look up at her husband and say:

"Isn't it true that one's own fireside is always best? I was sorry for poor little Miss Ross going about that big house wrapped in her voluminous shawls. Hector ought to have central heating."

"He is going to. At present his place is like a barn, but my house was very like his before you came into it. You women have a wonderful gift for making a true home atmosphere."

He drew her to him for a moment and gave her a kiss, then held her out at arm's length from him, and said with smiling eyes:

"I am criticizing my wife. Wondering about this particular glamour in her composition. Do you know, madam, that Miss Dunstan actually held a long conversation with me in the smoking-room this morning? It was when you were completing our packing, and she told me things that have been simmering in my brain ever since."

"Tell me about them."

Rowena moved towards the library fire as she spoke, and seated herself on an old carved log-box in the wide chimney-corner. Her husband followed her.

"She was talking about you; asked me if I knew what was your power over your fellow-creatures. She made me realize, as I never have before, that you have a distinct gift in reaching out and winning people's confidence. She told me that Lady Bampford poured out her soul to you 'on the sly.' Her words, of course. Is this true?"

"Partly, I suppose. Poor thing! She has so longed for children, and her only little girl died of cholera in India at the age of two. She doesn't like England, and has a twin sister married in South America. She wants to go back there, but her husband's appointment is up. I'm afraid he wasn't quite a success out there. He has not much reticence or dignity, has he?"

"The woman appeared to be an iceberg to me. Miss Dunstan said you had thawed her, and would never leave go of her once you had taken hold. Is that true?"

"Di is so ridiculous; she only heard Lady Bampford beg me to write to her, and I have a confession to make: I asked her to pay us a visit some time next summer." Rowena looked up anxiously into her husband's face as she spoke. But he did not frown; only smiled.

"I guessed as much; and the little widow is to come too, is she not?"

"Mrs. McClintock? Oh, Hugh, my heart ached for her. Do you know that her husband was a really good man? She used to laugh at him for his religion, she told me; but now she's just longing to be like him, so that she may join him again. She has been drawn into these spiritualistic circles in town, and has been rather disillusioned. Says her husband did appear one day, or his form did, but his words were so unlike him that she believed some other spirit must have personated him. I would love to see more of her."

"Of course, that's what Miss Dunstan said, and Graeme has always been your devoted pupil, and even Norris argued for a good hour with you on the Divinity of the Bible. How is it that you attract them all so? I repel them. Miss Dunstan says I ought to open my house every summer to worn out disillusioned worldlings. She says you would make a cure of them all. She calls you 'The Society Shepherdess.' I begin to see that I have been a stumbling block in your path. And so, Rowena my darling, I am going to give you carte blanche to have as many visitors as you like, for short or long visits, in winter or in summer, or all the year round. And I'll help you and back you up as much as I can, for I see now that this is the work that has been given to you to do, and which very few others can do."

Rowena hid her face in her hands, and then she looked up, her blue-grey eyes misty with tears.

"We'll work together," she said, taking her husband's hands in hers. "I feel, as I have told you before, that my time amongst Mrs. Burke's friends showed me their need, as I should never have seen it otherwise; and one can't help loving them all. I can't. I long to draw them into the golden sunlight of Christ's Kingdom on Earth. We'll use our home for that purpose, Hugh. You have made me very happy."

Only a few weeks afterwards Rowena was made happier still.

She had a long letter from Di Dunstan.

> "DEAREST ROWENA,—"
>
> "You shall be the first to receive my news. For I owe my happiness to you entirely. And looking back I bless the day when you first came into my life. I think of it now—Vi and I were curious to see you; Mrs. Burke had told us that she had seen a charming girl who 'viewed life with half-hidden laughter in her eyes.' I remember how we roared over that

description of you, and then you came to lunch, and your friendly confiding mischievous eyes—how well I remember them!—they rested on me as if you liked me from the first minute you set eyes on me. And you weren't a bit shocked by our talk and slang. Well, reminiscences are rather fetching, aren't they? Now for my news: Hector Ross has actually proposed to me, and I have accepted him. Now honour bright, did you think that he was taken by your humble servant when we were at Kestowknockan? I thought if he was smitten by anyone it was by the young widow. But after you left, he and I got very pally. And somehow he has your faculty for expecting the best out of one, and knowing how to extract it, too. Not that I have any best, but one day when I said that horses satisfied every part of my soul and body he took me up in his quick way:"

"'Don't pretend your soul is as small as that, for I know it isn't.' Another day he asked me if I'd come with him to see a keeper who was very ill. 'But I'm not a sick-bed visitor,' I said. 'I run away from sickness always.'"

"'You aren't going to run away from it now,' he answered, 'for you've a warm heart and a woman's pity. I've seen you nurse a sick dog in my stable, and a man is worth more than a dog. You'll come along with me now, and we'll try between us if we can't give the old fellow a word of cheer, before he gets into the Dark Valley.' I was terrified, but off I went with him, and he told me how he'd been left guarding an empty trench one night with two dying men close to him, and how he'd repeated to them like a parrot, a speech he'd heard from a chaplain the day before. Can I tell you about that shepherd's hut? I'll try. Picture a dark little smoke-filled, smoke-dried hole and a low trestle bed by a peat fire, and a dog lying by it, and then an old blue-grey bony face looking up at us through the folds of a ragged plaid. Quite alone he was. A neighbour came across to him two or three times a day. And then, when I was just going to turn tail and run, what did the Whipper-in do but say in his clear, cheerful voice—'This lady has come to see you, McFarlane, and she'll read you a verse or two to comfort you.' With that he stuffed a little Testament into my hand which he produced out of his coat pocket. 'That's what the Padres always do,' he said."

"Imagine me, Rowena. I nearly went into hysterics, and then I thought to myself that I always was considered good at acting any part, and I would do the same now. And I opened the Testament and read the first words I came across. They actually seemed to interest him, but I was in such a state of bewilderment that I can't remember now what they were, and the old chap looked up in my face and thanked me quite gratefully, as if I'd given him a tenner! And then the Whipper-in sat down and talked to him like a father. He made me gasp—the things he said. He told me afterwards he had seen many a life flicker out in France, when there was nobody near to have a word with them, and then he said quite humbly, like a boy, 'And if I can't tell them all the orthodox doctrines of our Creed, I can just tell them to catch hold of the Hand that was pierced for them, and that wants to hold them safely.' I tell you, Rowena, he almost made me choke—the way he said it."

"Well, we were good friends till I came away, and I thought I had seen the last of him. And then a week ago he turned up in town and I happened to run across him in the open street. I was staying with the Clarkes—one of the girls was being married. He asked me with beaming eyes whether I would help him choose a few carpets for his house. Said he had meant to come down and see me at Vi's—for that was the only address I'd given him—and he told me his little aunt was ill of bronchitis, and she had only rugs on a polished floor in her bedroom and he wanted to carpet her room from corner to corner and with carpet 'three inches thick.' It was no good laughing at him. He was in dead earnest, and we went off together, and he ordered me about as if I were a two-year-old, and stood me lunch at the 'Carlton.' And then we chose his carpets, and the shopman, of course, alluded to me as his 'lady.' When we came out, we walked in the Park, and he said he wanted me as his 'lady' for life! I was quite bowled over. I am no young girl, and, as you know, I've had my disillusion, but there's something about him I can't resist. You feel he has been everywhere and done everything and knows the world as the majority of us don't know it, and yet he has come back as simple and fresh and believing as any boy. The War taught him, he says, some of the best lessons in life, and he is going to pass on his lessons to me. And I tested myself, Rowena, when he had gone. I said to myself, 'If he lost all his money to-morrow, and his horses, would you be happy married to him?' And I told myself that I would follow him round the world with only a crust between us! So I have no qualms or misgivings. Of course, Vi is enchanted. She's seen him and likes him and the wedding is coming off next June."

"So now my heart thumps madly when I realize that I shall be a close neighbour of yours. Only thirty or forty miles between us, isn't it? And his dear little aunt can stay with us, unless she would rather go back to her doll's house. The Whipper-in thinks she would like that best. Do you think I shall make him a good wife, Rowena? He is determined to make me a good woman. And I've come to the conclusion that the truly good people in this world must of necessity be the happiest, for they have the assurance and hope of a perfect life beyond the grave, and a very comforting one in this."

"So, so—well, you raked my soul fore and aft when you talked to me, so in simple words I tell you that I've taken hold of the Pierced Hand, and believe It will hold me safe through all Eternity."

"My love for always, my dear Shepherdess,"

"One of your grateful flock,"
"Di."

Rowena read this to her husband.

"I know she would not mind. It will show you that she is not so hard as we have thought her."

"I will never think anyone hard again," said General Macdonald gravely, when his wife had finished reading.

And then his eyes rested on her with peculiar satisfaction and trust.

"At least," he added, "I shall never think anyone too shallow, too frivolous, too worldly-minded, to be influenced for good by you, Rowena. I humbly hope I may catch some of your love and tolerance for your fellow-creatures as we journey on together."

Rowena was not fond of hearing her praises sung, but she turned to him with one of her sweet smiles.

"And may I catch some of your single-heartedness and just uprightness. There now, aren't we a model couple! After all, Hugh, we may be seed-throwers, but the real vital work is not done by us at all. Thank God He takes it out of our hands and does it all Himself!"